AGE BEFORE BEAUTY

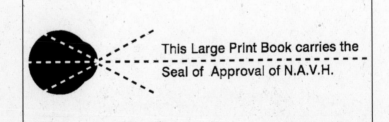

This Large Print Book carries the
Seal of Approval of N.A.V.H.

SISTER-TO-SISTER #2

AGE BEFORE BEAUTY

VIRGINIA SMITH

THORNDIKE PRESS

A part of Gale, Cengage Learning

GALE
CENGAGE Learning·

Detroit • New York • San Francisco • New Haven, Conn • Waterville, Maine • London

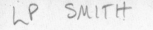

GALE
CENGAGE Learning

Copyright © 2009 by Virginia Smith.
Sister-to-Sister Series #2.
Scripture is from the HOLY BIBLE, NEW INTERNATIONAL VERSION®.
NIV®. Copyright © 1973, 1978, 1984 by International Bible Society.
Used by permission of Zondervan. All rights reserved.
Thorndike Press, a part of Gale, Cengage Learning.

LIBRARY OF CONGRESS CATALOGING-IN-PUBLICATION DATA

Smith, Virginia, 1960–
    Age before beauty / by Virginia Smith.
        p. cm. — (Thorndike Press large print Christian fiction)
    (Sister-to-sister ; bk. 2)
    ISBN-13: 978-1-4104-2747-2
    ISBN-10: 1-4104-2747-1
    1. Motherhood—Fiction. 2. Sisters—Fiction. 3.
Kentucky—Fiction. 4. Large type books. I. Title.
PS3619.M5956A73 2010
813'.6—dc22   2010015357

Published in 2010 by arrangement with Revell Books, a division of
Baker Publishing Group.

Printed in Mexico
1 2 3 4 5 6 7 14 13 12 11 10

This book is dedicated with much love
to

Christy Delliskave, Betsy Banks, and
Maggie Tirey —
the oldest sisters in my family's next
generation

1

The mirror had to be warped. That was the only explanation for the image staring back at Allie from its treacherous surface. Her thighs couldn't be *that* wide, her belly *that* flabby. Could glass warp? Of course not. But the weather so far this fall had been wetter than normal, following a horribly humid Kentucky summer. All that dampness wreaked havoc on the wooden front door at Gram's house. And this mirror had a wood frame. That had to be it.

But the warping seemed only to be in the middle, like one of those fun-house mirrors. She squinted down at her pink toenails. Her feet looked normal. Her face looked okay. Pretty good, even. This was the first time she'd put on makeup in weeks, and a little color worked wonders. She could use a haircut, though the dark blonde layers falling in waves to rest on her shoulders managed to hold the extra length well.

She blew her bangs out of her eyes. Actually, the long hair made her face look fuller, and that offset some of the width of her hips. Which needed the help, especially now that she got a good look at them wearing only a nursing bra and panties. If she cut some of the volume out of her hair, she'd look like one of those toys she and Joan and Tori played with as kids. What were they called? Weebles. She'd look like Mother Weeble.

She swayed from side to side, eyeing her oversized bottom half as she sang the toy's jingle. "Weebles wobble but they don't fall down."

"Did you say something?"

Allie whirled to find Eric standing in the bedroom doorway, a grin twitching at his mouth. She felt a blush creep up her neck. Though he was the world's most awesome husband and devoted new daddy, she still felt awkward parading her postmaternity body around in front of him. A flabby belly covered in stretch marks was *soooo* sexy.

"How long have you been standing there?"

His voice dropped an octave as his smile deepened. "Long enough to admire my beautiful wife."

No mistaking that husky tone. She snatched her jeans off the bed. "Don't get frisky, lover boy. My sister will be here any minute."

Eric's lips twisted. "Story of my life lately."

Allie crossed the room and placed a tender kiss on his cheek. "I'm sorry my family is here so often. They just don't want to miss a day with the baby. She's growing so fast."

"I know, I know." He grinned. "But tonight I get Joanie all to myself. Our first father-daughter date."

Allie sat on the edge of the bed and slipped her feet into the jeans, avoiding Eric's eyes. He had been looking forward to this evening for a full week, ever since Joan invited her to go to a stupid party where some fanatical woman would try to force her to buy something she didn't want and for which she had no use. If only Joan hadn't asked in front of Eric, she would have turned the invitation down without a second thought. But he had insisted it was time she took her first outing without the baby.

Pulling the waistband up around her knees, she gave Eric a worried look. "Are you sure you'll be okay? She's only taken a bottle a few times, you know. She might cry."

"I'll deal with it."

"But —"

He held up a finger. "No buts. She's five weeks old. In three weeks she'll be taking a bottle at the daycare center when you go back to work. She needs to get used to it."

Tears stung Allie's eyes, and she looked away so Eric wouldn't see. "I guess you're right."

"Of course I am. Now finish getting dressed while I go wind the baby swing again."

He left, and Allie sat staring at the hand-woven rug in front of their bed. Three weeks. Then she'd have to leave her precious little Joanie in the hands of a total stranger.

If only . . .

She jerked the shirt over her head. No. One of the things she and Eric had talked about before they got married was how they'd handle life after they started having children. She'd insisted on laying it all out, because Eric's mother had been a stay-at-home mom, and Allie wanted to make absolutely sure he didn't have the same expectations. Her toenail caught the edge of her sock as she tugged it up, and she hissed with pain. No way would she become one of those women relegated to a dull life of child rearing. She was a career woman — the second sock followed the first — with a college degree and plans for her professional future. She *liked* her job, liked the independence it gave her. Besides, they agreed on having two incomes so they could afford things like nice clothes and good cars and vacations at the beach.

But that was before she'd had a baby.

If only there was some way she could pursue her career *and* keep her daughter at home. She had quietly investigated every work-from-home scheme she could find lately, but all of them sounded more like scams than jobs.

Banishing the tears, she stood. No sense crying about it. She had no option. In three weeks she'd return to her job as a team leader at the social services office. She might even be able to recapture some of the excitement and ambition she'd felt before she got pregnant. At the moment, though, it sounded like a life sentence with no chance of parole.

She pulled her jeans up over her knees. This was the first pair of zippered pants she'd tried to wear since Joanie's birth, having lived in sweats and oversized T-shirts once she put away the maternity clothes. Wiggling her hips back and forth, she inched them upward. Come on, come on, they had to fit. They were her biggest jeans, stretchy and so loose that she'd worn them all the way up to her fifth month of pregnancy. Just a little farther . . .

Ugh. She panted from the effort. But at least she'd managed to get them pulled all the way up.

Now the zipper. Suck that gut in. Pull hard. Harder. She hopped up and down, tugging at the waistband. Okay, if the zipper wouldn't go all the way to the top, it didn't matter. She'd just wear her shirttail out. Everybody did these days. As long as she could get the button fastened.

There! They fit! She was wearing pre-baby Levis! Well, sort of.

She stepped up to the mirror and bit back a gasp.

The stupid thing had to be warped.

"Hey, look at you all dressed up." Joan stood on the doorstep, car keys clutched in one hand. "You look great."

Allie scowled and tried not to think of the jeans she could *almost* wear shoved in the back of her bottom drawer. "These are maternity pants. Nothing else fits."

"Oh." Joan's smile drooped a fraction, then brightened again. "But that's not a maternity shirt. And turquoise is totally your color."

Her eyes shifted to a point inside the room, then she practically bowled Allie over as she rushed toward the swing to snatch up the baby. Sighing, Allie closed the door. So much for Joanie's nap.

Allie tried to ignore a wave of insecurity as she admired her sister's slim frame, the way her jeans fit without a single bulge. Straight dark hair fell forward to tickle the baby's face as Joan cooed at her slumbering namesake while she unfastened the safety strap. Soft baby noises answered as little Joanie's eyelids fluttered open. Allie clasped her hands together to keep from taking the infant from her middle sister's arms. She was so sweet when she first woke. Tiny fists rose above her head and she kicked her legs out to their full length and arched her back to stretch.

"Look at her! I swear she's grown an inch since the last time I saw her."

Allie answered dryly. "I doubt that, since you came over yesterday." She held her hands out. "Here, let me change her."

Joan clutched the baby closer. "I'll do it."

With a sigh, Allie followed her sister into the nursery. Bright pink daisies on fields of green bordered the white walls and also decorated lacy curtains and crib bedding. Joan laid Joanie on a daisy-covered pad atop the changing table. While she unsnapped the pink onesie, Allie took a diaper from the stacker and popped open the plastic cap on the wipes. The sweet smell of baby powder was quickly replaced with a less pleasant odor when Joan peeled the tape off the dirty diaper.

Eric stuck his head through the doorway as Allie pulled out a wipe and handed it to Joan. "Whew, I'm glad you girls got that out of the way before you left. Of course, the way this little piggie eats, I probably have at least one unpleasant surprise in store tonight."

"Don't worry." Allie dropped the soiled bundle into the Diaper Genie and twisted the knob. "We won't be gone very long. I'm sure we'll be back for the next dirty diaper."

"I'm kidding, Allie. You know I don't mind taking care of my girl." He leaned over and buried a kiss in Joanie's chubby neck, eliciting a gurgle and an excited waving of arms and legs.

Joan snapped the onesie back in place over the fresh diaper and picked up the squirming infant. Allie stepped forward to take her, but instead Joan thrust her into Eric's arms.

"It's time to go. I don't want to be late." With a meaningful glance in Allie's direction, she marched out of the room, Eric right behind her with Joanie hugged tightly to his chest.

Left alone in the nursery, Allie fought a wave of panic that caused her throat to tighten with unshed tears. Cheerful daisies mocked her. She knew this feeling, had sensed the edges of it creeping toward her all day. The moment had come. After five weeks of constantly being in Joanie's presence, she was about to leave her in someone else's care.

Don't be ridiculous. She scrubbed at her eyes with the back of her hand. Joanie wasn't staying with a stranger. She was staying with her daddy! He'd watched her many times while Allie enjoyed a long bath or a nap.

But what if she cries? What if she misses me?

She started toward the living room, and then stopped short as an even more distressing thought struck her. *What if she doesn't even notice I'm gone?*

"Allie, are you coming?"

Joan's voice propelled her feet into motion. She would *not* think about that.

"I'm ready."

One step took her from the hallway into their tiny living room, where Eric had deposited Joanie on the mat beneath her baby gym. Allie fought to suppress a wave of regret when chubby infant hands waved with erratic enthusiasm at the dangling toys, and happy coos filled the room. It had only been in the past few days that she'd started noticing the toys. She was growing so fast, changing every day. What if she did something really cool for the first time tonight, while Allie wasn't here to see it? She dropped to her knees and showered Joanie's face with goodbye kisses.

"There are a couple of bottles all ready to go in the fridge," she told Eric. "Run hot water over them to warm them. Don't use the microwave."

Eric stood and pulled her up with him. "I won't." He planted a kiss on her cheek.

"She ate two hours ago, so she'll probably be hungry around eight. If she gets fussy before —"

Joan grabbed her arm and steered her forcefully toward the front door. "Come along, Mother. It's time to go."

Thoughts of all the terrible things that could happen pummeled her mind like giant hailstones. She pulled away and whirled toward Eric. "Don't give her a bath until I get home. You know how slippery she is when she's soapy."

He put his hands on her shoulders and

turned her to face the door. "Stop worrying. We'll be fine. Now go have a good time." A gentle shove pushed her forward.

From the porch, Joan seized her and jerked her through the doorway. Allie shook her off and spun around to remind Eric to put the baby's sweater on because the house would cool when the sun went down, but the front door slammed shut in her face. Tears welled in her eyes.

"You're pathetic." Joan folded her arms across her chest and leveled an unsympathetic look on her.

Allie sniffled. "It's the first time we've been apart in five weeks."

"Then it's about time you gave the poor kid some breathing room." She shook her head. "You're becoming one of those hovering mothers. I can totally see you stalking her on the kindergarten playground during recess."

Actually, Allie didn't see a problem with dropping by to check on your kids during the day, but in the face of Joan's sardonic expression, she didn't dare mention it. Instead she lifted a chin. "I will not be a hovering mother."

A snort blasted from her sister's nose. "I know my big sister. You'll hover like a helicopter."

Her head held high, Allie marched past Joan toward the driveway. "I thought you didn't want to be late."

She rubbed her hands on her arms. It was a chilly fifty degrees, and the orange October sun was rapidly dropping toward the horizon. They'd shoved her out the door without a jacket, but she didn't dare go back inside now or she'd never hear the end of it. Serve them both right if she caught pneumonia and died.

2

Joan pointed her remote control at the car and a soft *click* came from inside. Allie slid into the passenger seat, relishing the warmth left over from Joan's drive across town. An air freshener stick, tucked discreetly into the heater vent, filled the interior with the scent of freshly sliced lemons. She breathed deeply, willing the sharp citrusy odor to banish the tears that hovered behind her eyes as Joan rounded the front of the car. If her sister caught her sniffling with separation anxiety, she'd harp on it all night.

"How did you get roped into this thing tonight, anyway?" Allie asked when Joan slid into the driver's seat.

Joan started the engine and turned to look through the back window as the car rolled down the driveway. "A friend from church invited me. She said she was sort of pressured into having this party, and since Eve is part of our mission trip group, I didn't feel like I could refuse."

Joan was totally into the whole church thing ever since she started dating Ken Fletcher. Her church group was planning a trip to Mexico in January to build houses for poor people, and it seemed like every weekend they had some sort of fund-raiser going on.

"Well, don't expect me to buy anything," Allie warned. "I hate pushy makeup sales-women."

Joan turned a corner and the sun, a fiery orange sphere half concealed by the horizon ahead of them, stung Allie's eyes. She put a hand up to block the rays.

"Apparently it's more than makeup," Joan told her, squinting to see through the glare. "Eve said they sell all sorts of stuff."

"What's it called, anyway?"

"Uh, Varie Cose, or something like that."

"Very cozy? Is it some kind of treatment for varicose veins?" Allie slapped her thigh, whooping at her own joke.

"You're a riot." Joan lifted a shoulder, eyes fixed on the road. "I think it's Italian."

Still chuckling, Allie adjusted the heater vent to direct warm air toward her arms. "I hope your friend is serving snacks. If I'm going to suffer through a sales pitch, the least she can do is feed me."

Joan executed a few turns, the volume on the radio tuned so low Allie could barely make out the strains of an unfamiliar song. Joan hummed along, though, as they turned into an apartment complex and parked. As Allie opened the car door, she glanced at her watch. 7:04. Joanie wouldn't be ready to eat for another —

Jerking upright in the seat, she realized that she hadn't thought of her baby in a whole five minutes! She started to brag to Joan, but then decided she'd probably be accused of obsessing.

Joan bounded up a set of stairs, and Allie followed. Eight steps, turn a corner, eight more steps. She lost sight of her sister, who had trotted on ahead of her and disappeared around the next corner, but she followed Joan's progress through the sound of her footsteps as she skipped upward. Going up and down these stairs every day would kill her.

By the time Allie reached the third floor, she was hauling herself up on the handrail, huffing with effort. "For cryin' out loud, why don't they put elevators in these buildings?"

Joan waited for her on the top landing. "Stairs are good for you. They'll get your heart pounding and your blood circulating."

"Yeah, well, it's pounding alright." She collapsed against the wall to pant. "I think I'm going to have a stroke."

"You'll be fine."

No sympathy from her little sister, not that Allie expected any. Miss Fitness Freak turned her nose up at french fries and ran a gazillion miles every morning before work.

At Joan's knock, the door opened. A cute young woman with dark, curly hair and deep dimples in her cheeks said, "Hey! Come in," and threw the door wide.

Joan hugged her briefly on her way into the apartment, waving a hand in Allie's direction. "Eve, I don't think you've met my sister, have you?"

Allie stepped forward and shook the girl's hand. "Allie Harrod. Nice to meet you."

"I'm so glad you could come. And congratulations on your new baby. Joan has told us all about her at church. Her pictures are adorable."

Allie instantly warmed to the girl. "I have some new ones." She patted her purse, which contained photos she'd printed on her inkjet just that morning.

"I can't wait to see them."

As she stepped into the room, Allie whiffed a sweet vanilla-scented aroma, the promise of freshly baked snacks later. She glanced around as Eve closed the door. A half-dozen women crowded a living room smaller than hers at home, three on a blue floral print sofa, one in the matching chair, and another on a wooden dining room chair in front of a sliding glass door. Joan was shaking the hand of a sixth woman who stood in front of a small television stand. The woman's face wore the wide, unmistakable smile of one who is accustomed to being the center of attention. Ah, the saleswoman. Her dark lipstick and perfectly penciled eyebrows marked her instantly. As did the heavy scent of perfume that cloyed at Allie's nose as the woman approached.

She extended a slim hand with manicured nails the exact shade of her lips. "I'm Sally Jo Campbell, the Varie Cose consultant."

She pronounced it *VAH-ree-yah CO-see,* but any European glamour she might have hoped to portray with her assumed Italian accent was destroyed by a heavy southern drawl that doubled the regular number of syllables in her name. Allie glanced at Joan, then quickly away when she saw her sister's lips twitch.

Allie shook the hand, wondering why in the world people bleached their teeth. Didn't they know that blazing white looked unnatural? "Nice to meet you. I'm Allie

Harrod."

"If you'll just take a seat, honey, I think it's about time to start."

Joan sat in a wooden chair and patted the empty one beside her. Allie settled there as Eve dragged the last chair from the dinette set to the opposite end of the semicircle. In the corner nearest Allie, a white sheet covered a pile of something-or-other on top of a spindly legged card table. Ah. The stuff they were going to be pressured into buying.

Sally Jo's dazzling smile swept the room. "First off, I want to thank y'all for coming tonight. And special thanks to Eve, our hostess for the evening." She inclined her head toward Eve, whose dimples deepened.

Sally Jo continued. "To start out, I'd like to ask y'all a question. Have any of you ever heard of Varie Cose before?"

Allie glanced at the others as she shook her head. A thin woman on the sofa raised a tentative hand. "I have."

"Of course, Mrs. Tankersley." Sally Jo nodded, and then announced to everyone else, "Eve's mama hosted a party last month. She earned a lovely gift when her guests bought more than *four hundred dollars* of Varie Cose products!"

Her lacquered lips formed an *O* of aston-

24

ishment, and her slim fingers tapped gently against the palm of her other hand as she nodded around the room for everyone to join in the applause. Allie clapped her hands a few times without enthusiasm. That's how these people suckered you in. They made you feel like a heel if you didn't spend enough money for your hostess to win a "lovely gift."

"Varie Cose got its start in Italy two decades ago when an orphaned woman named Fiorenza Hyppolito fell in love. Her beloved was from an old Italian family that put a lot of store in tradition. She learned that her beau's mother was gossiping about her around the small town where they lived. She didn't want her son to marry Fiorenza because she was poor and didn't even have a proper dowry." She shook her head sadly, tsking over the travesty of an inadequate dowry.

Allie leaned toward Joan and whispered, "That's what bridal showers are for."

Sally Jo flashed an irritated look in her direction before continuing. "So Fiorenza decided to create her own dowry. She scoured the Italian countryside for bargains. Within a year she had assembled everything she needed to set up a proper Italian household." A pained expression flooded Sally

Jo's features, and she placed a hand lightly at her collarbone. "But alas, Fiorenza was so exhausted by her efforts that she fell ill. While she was recovering, her beau visited her in the sanitarium and fell in love with her nurse."

Gasps around the room drew Allie's attention from the story. A vaguely familiar blonde in jeans and a lime green blouse wore an outraged expression. "That's terrible! The poor girl."

Oh, come on. Surely they weren't falling for this story. No doubt it had a few grains of truth, but it had to have been embellished. Allie caught Joan's gaze and lifted her eyes toward the ceiling. Joan nudged her foot and stared pointedly at the saleswoman.

"I know." Sally Jo nodded toward the blonde. "But actually, it turned out for the best. Fiorenza couldn't stand the sight of the dowry she'd gathered, so she sold it piece by piece." A flash of white teeth blinded them. "And she made money, lots of it. Many people wanted to buy the items she'd found, but nobody wanted to roam the countryside to seek them out. When she'd sold everything, she started over. Before she knew it, word had spread, and she had customers calling from other towns, and then other countries. Varie Cose was born."

"What does Varie Cose mean?" asked a heavy brunette with gigantic hoops dangling from her ears.

"It means *various things.*" Sally Jo's ready smile burst forth again. "Which is just perfect, of course, since that's what the product line includes. Everything you'll ever need to run your household. It's all delivered right to your door by your Varie Cose consultant. Once you become a Varie Cose customer, the only time you'll ever need to shop in a store again is for groceries."

"Boy, Tori would hate that," Allie mumbled.

Joan's lips twitched. Their baby sister was an enthusiastic shopaholic.

A knock sounded on the door, and Eve jumped up to answer it. Sally Jo paused as the room's attention was diverted toward the new arrival.

"I'm so sorry I'm late," a girl's voice said from outside. "I started packing up the car an hour ago, but then he woke up and I had to feed him, and then he messed up his outfit so I had to change him. Here."

An arm with a diaper bag hanging from it thrust through the door, followed quickly by a young woman whose other hand clutched the handle of a blue bundle. As Eve took the bag, Allie sucked in an outraged breath. That girl was carrying a baby seat! A blue receiving blanket formed a tent over the handle to cover it completely, presumably protecting a baby inside.

She whirled in her chair to glare at Joan. "I didn't know we could bring our babies."

Sally Jo coughed politely. "Of course we welcome babies, but we hope a Varie Cose party will be a relaxing time away from the responsibilities of motherhood. You know," she tilted her head toward the new arrival, "a girl's night out."

Allie would have bristled at the insinuation in her tone, but the young mom didn't take offense. She laughed as she set the baby carrier beside the chair Eve had vacated. "I haven't had one of those in so long I wouldn't know what to do." Her smile swept the room. "Hi, everybody. I'm Darcy."

A chorus of greetings welcomed Darcy as she sat. She peeled the blue blanket back with exaggerated care to peer inside. Allie wanted to jump up and see the baby, but Sally Jo took control once again.

"You're just in time for the fun part. The demonstration!"

She turned toward the corner and removed the white sheet from the card table

28

with a flourish. Allie craned her neck to see the array of products piled on the table's surface. There sure was a bunch of stuff.

Sally Jo pulled a stack of catalogs out of a bulging leather satchel and handed them to Allie. "Take one and pass them around, honey." She spoke to the group. "When you get your catalog, turn to page four and you can read all about the first fun product I'm gonna demonstrate." She snatched an item from among the jumble on the table and, beaming, held it aloft like a precious jewel. "The laundry pen!"

As she handed the stack to Joan, Allie whispered, "Oh, joy. A laundry pen."

Eric jiggled the bottle up and down in the kitchen sink, hot water showering over its side from the faucet. Clutched in the curve of his left arm, Joanie cut off her shriek long enough to draw a quick breath and start again.

He bounced the baby in rhythm with the bottle bobbing up and down in the hot water. "Just a minute. I'm warming it as fast as I can."

When he shook the bottle to test the temperature, the milk still felt cold. This was taking way too long. He glanced toward the microwave. Surely a few seconds wouldn't hurt.

No. If Allie found out — and she would, because she had a sixth sense that surfaced whenever he tried to keep something from her — she would do him bodily harm. He wasn't sure he bought her argument that the microwave changed the chemical makeup of the milk, but she certainly did. He thrust the bottle beneath the water and continued jiggling, wincing as Joanie roared her impatience.

"Shhh, shhh, it's coming. I promise. Food is minutes away."

Her face a deep purple, the baby gasped another lungful of air and then launched into a series of short shrieks, her body rigid. Just like his nerves. Allie had told him about the occasional fit Joanie threw if her demand for milk wasn't instantly satisfied, but he'd only half believed her. How could such a tiny set of lungs produce such volume?

There. Surely that was warm enough. It was still a little cool, but at least he'd knocked the chill off. He shoved the nipple into the gaping mouth, and the noise cut off mid-screech as Joanie latched on and sucked like she hadn't eaten in days. Better not tell Allie how easily she accepted the bottle.

Eric headed for the living room and

settled onto a couch cushion. Feet propped on the coffee table, he tucked the bottle into his neck, held it in place with his chin, and punched the remote control On button. As he surfed through the channels, his taut nerves began to relax. They'd enjoyed some quality daddy-daughter time for the first thirty minutes after Allie left. Then Joanie lost interest in the toys dangling from her baby gym and started to fuss. She couldn't be hungry, he'd reasoned. She'd nursed at five o'clock and wasn't due for another meal until eight. Besides, it would be good for her to fuss a bit, build up an appetite. Learn to wait for the things she wanted. That's how character developed.

His resolve lasted a whole five minutes — until the shrieking started.

He gazed down into her red face. "You really are a little fiend when you're hungry, aren't you? Your mama said you could be, but I had no idea." Eyes scrunched tight, her greedy sucking filled the room with piggy noises. "I guess I've lucked out so far, since she has a ready supply of milk."

A sitcom rerun caught his attention as he flipped through the channels. When the show first aired, he'd thought it ridiculous, another of those kid shows starring a cherub-faced blonde with a too-cute-to-be-

believed lisp. But the little girl's dimpled grin and bouncy curls as she grinned up at her on-screen daddy snagged his eye, and he let his finger hover over the channel button for a moment. In a few years, Joanie might look like that kid. Already her downy blonde hair pressed against her skull in damp waves when she finished her bath. Maybe when it was longer, it would curl like that. And her eyes, though still infant dark blue, would probably get lighter as she grew, maybe greenish like Allie's.

He pressed a finger into his daughter's fist. "You're gonna be a knockout like your mom, kid," he told her.

At the rate she was growing, she'd be crawling before they knew it, and then walking, and then skipping on a jump rope or whatever little girls did.

An image flashed into his mind, the picture of a pretty four-year-old who'd gone missing from her babysitter's yard over in Lexington a few years back. Dozens of those photos decorated the bulletin boards in the hallways at Eastern Kentucky University where he'd attended the dispatcher training program. Kids who got snatched came in all shapes and sizes, but cute little blonde girls seemed to be special targets for the sickos of the world.

He gripped Joanie tighter to combat the fear that accompanied the thought. "Not you, though," he vowed, his voice a whisper. "Not on my watch."

Surprising how quickly he fell into the role of Protector of the Family. The depth of his protective instincts for his kid still astonished him because they'd come on so quickly. Allie, of course, changed personalities like the wind changed directions. He'd watched her go from sexy college student to eager wife to expectant mama to a maternal force to be reckoned with, all in the space of a few years. The way she threw herself into each part, embracing it with gusto, was nothing short of amazing to him. He, on the other hand, remained basically the same guy as the one who flirted with the gorgeous blonde at the campus pizza restaurant a few years back.

Until the baby came along. He set the remote control on the cushion and traced a finger lightly over the soft skin of Joanie's cheek. From the moment that squalling bundle drew her first breath, something like awe settled on him, and it hadn't left yet.

The doorbell chimed, followed by an impatient *rap, rap, rap* on the metal frame of the storm door.

He wasn't expecting anyone. Probably

Carla, Allie's mom, stopping by to see how he was doing with his first babysitting job. Good thing he liked his in-laws. He saw a lot of them lately. He heaved himself to his feet as carefully as he could, trying not to jostle Joanie as she ate. Not that it mattered. The little piggie sucked with vigor, gulping loudly.

The doorbell sounded again.

"Hang on a sec," he shouted. Bottle propped beneath his chin, Eric twisted the door handle and pulled it open. When he saw who stood on the front porch, his jaw went slack. The bottle dropped to the floor, and Joanie let out a shriek.

Stunned, Eric could only stare.

3

Allie sipped from her glass of diet soda, a paper plate covered in cake crumbs balanced on her knees. Sally Jo had interrupted her product demonstrations long enough to allow them to fill a plate, grab a drink, and return to their seats to view the next batch of stuff-no-home-should-be-without.

Joan leaned sideways. "If you see anything you like, let me know. I still haven't gotten you a birthday present."

Allie awarded her a withering glance. "If you buy me a laundry pen for my birthday, I'll never speak to you again."

Joan laughed as Sally Jo selected an item from the table and made a show of holding it behind her back. She flashed a grin with the manner of one who is about to show them a map to the fountain of youth. "And now we move into my favorite product line. Can anyone guess what that is?"

Allie turned her head so Joan could read

her lips. *Tooth care?* she mouthed. Beyond Joan, the girl named Brittany noticed and hid a laugh behind her glass.

"Makeup!" Sally Jo announced, beaming as she whipped out a tube of lipstick and held it before her like a kid taking a turn at show-and-tell. "But actually, it's so much more than makeup. Varie Cose offers an entire line of skin care products far superior to anything else I've ever tried. And believe me, ladies, I've tried a lot of them."

Judging by the amount of makeup layered on her face, Allie figured she must have tried them all tonight, one on top of the other.

"Skin care is by far our most popular product line, with the cleaning products coming in a close second. Why, sixty percent of my sales each week are makeup items."

"Sixty percent?" Allie glanced at the table in the corner, at all the stuff piled on top of it. "You must sell a lot of makeup."

"Trust me," Sally Jo said, her smile secretive. "I really do."

Allie's ears perked up. How much money did the woman make selling this stuff? Enough to support herself?

As Sally Jo drew breath to launch into a description of the lipstick she held, Allie interrupted. "Do you have a job, Sally Jo, or do you do this full-time?"

Around the room, the ladies stopped flipping through the pages of their catalogs to listen to Sally Jo's answer.

"Varie Cose *is* my job, though I only work part-time. In fact . . ." She paused and let a conspiratorial smile sweep the room. "I've been so successful, I got my car only four months after I signed on as a consultant, and I moved up three levels in just a year. You may have seen my Lexus in the parking lot."

Allie looked closer at the woman. Nice clothes. Expensive shoes. Lexus. The Varie Cose business must be pretty lucrative.

She sat back in her chair as Sally Jo launched into a detailed description of the amazing staying power of Varie Cose's lipsticks. Just how lucrative, though? Enough to match her paycheck as a state employee? If she worked part-time as a Varie Cose consultant, she wouldn't have to take Joanie to daycare at all. Most of the parties would be held in the evening, like this one. Now that Eric was on first shift, he would be at home in the evenings. All the business stuff, the ordering and paperwork and all that, could be done during the day while Joanie napped or played.

Could Varie Cose be the solution to her

problem?

She set her empty plate on the floor and leaned forward in her chair, ready to pay closer attention to Sally Jo's demonstration.

"Listen, honey, why don't I give you a call tomorrow and we'll talk more. What's your number?" Sally Jo held her pen poised above her notepad, an eager glint in her eye as though she had fresh meat in her sights.

Around the room, partygoers stood in clusters of two or three, comparing their order forms and discussing items in the catalog. Judging from the amount of writing on some of those forms, Allie figured Sally Jo would make a bundle tonight. And Eve would definitely earn her "lovely hostess gift."

Allie recited her phone number, aware that beside her, Joan's eyeballs looked like they were about to explode out of her head. As the consultant moved on to the next group with a satisfied smile on her shiny red lips, Joan shoved her face into Allie's.

"What are you doing?" She glanced behind her and lowered her voice. "Rule number one is *never give them your phone number.* You should have taken her card and offered to call her. That way when you wake up in the morning and realize you were suffering from temporary insanity tonight, you can forget about it. Now she's going to bug you to death."

"But I want her to call." Allie kept her gaze fixed on Sally Jo's back where she stood talking to Eve and her mother, and spoke in a whisper. "If she's selling enough to earn a Lexus, just imagine how much money she's making. And if she can do it, I'm sure I can too."

Joan tilted her head sideways. "I didn't know you wanted a Lexus."

Allie rolled her eyes. "I don't want a Lexus. I want a job where I can stay home with my daughter."

Joan's mouth dropped open. "You do? I thought you liked your job at the state."

"I like it okay. It's not that." Allie let her gaze slide away from her sister, toward the baby carrier sitting safely in a corner, its sweet little occupant snoozing away, totally oblivious to the chattering women in the room. "But I'm having a little trouble at the thought of leaving Joanie with someone else."

"What does Eric say?"

Allie shook her head. "We haven't talked about it."

Joan's eyelids narrowed. "Don't you think you should let your husband know you're considering a career change? Communication is vital in a healthy relationship, you know."

Allie aimed a breath at her bangs. Now that Joan was finally enjoying a serious relationship with a guy, she turned into Dear Abby. "If I want marital advice from my *single* sister," Allie told her, "I'll ask for it."

Joan threw her hands up, palms facing Allie. "Okay, okay. I'm just saying you should talk to him before you jump into something."

From the corner came a whimper. Every woman's face turned toward the infant carrier. Two little fists waved in the air as the baby stirred.

"Ooh, he's waking up!" Eve's mother turned a wide, baby-hungry smile in the infant's direction. "Can I hold him?"

Darcy, seated on the sofa and leaning over her order form on the coffee table, nodded. "Sure, but let me change him first."

Allie itched with Empty Arms Syndrome. What time was it, anyway? She glanced at her watch. 8:47. She'd been away from her baby for almost two full hours. Her body, conditioned to supply Joanie's milk needs, stirred as Darcy's baby let out a loud cry. If she didn't leave soon, she'd look like Elsie the Cow had sprung a leak.

"Hurry up with that form," she ordered Joan. "I need to get home."

When they turned onto Allie's street, she saw a strange car parked in her driveway.

"Who drives a white Camry?" Joan asked as she glided to a stop at the curb in front of the house.

"I have no idea. A friend of Eric's maybe?" A flash of irritation tightened Allie's lips. What happened to father-daughter time? How could he give Joanie the attention she needed if he had a friend over?

"Well, I won't come in since you have company. Thanks for going with me tonight. I hope you didn't see what I got you for your birthday."

"I didn't," Allie told her as she reached for her purse in the backseat. "But I hope it was that salad slicer thingy. Something like that could save me a fortune in Band Aids."

Joan grinned. "You'll just have to wait. It's only two days, though. Gram's planning to fix your favorite dinner — fried chicken and mashed potatoes with gravy."

Though Gram lived in an assisted living facility, she came to the family home and cooked every Sunday and on special occasions. A family celebration wouldn't be the

41

same without Gram's home cooking, and especially her homemade yeast rolls.

"I can hardly wait." Allie opened the door. "You coming over tomorrow?"

"Probably not. It's Wednesday. You want to come with me?"

Joan attended a Bible study at some church in Lexington on Wednesday nights. She really had embraced the religion stuff in the past couple of months. But at least she wasn't pushy about it.

"No, thanks." Allie got out of the car and leaned over to look back inside. "See you Thursday."

"Bye."

She slammed the door and stood watching as Joan's car pulled away from the curb. With a final goodbye wave, she headed toward the house. Eric had better not be ignoring Joanie to talk with his buddy. And whoever-it-was had better take the hint that it was time to leave. It was past nine o'clock. Their nighttime bath ritual was overdue.

She opened the storm door and swung the wooden one inward. The living room was empty. And what was that smell? Like cheap perfume.

"Eric? Where are you?"

"Allie!" Eric stepped into the room from the kitchen, Joanie tucked into the curve of his elbow. "You're home early. I didn't expect you until ten or so."

He tossed a glance over his shoulder. Why was he acting nervous? Sick fear made her stomach flop. Did he have a woman in there?

Allie stepped forward, her arms outstretched to take Joanie. She struggled to keep her tone even. "Whose car is in the driveway?"

He handed the sleeping infant to her, then shoved his hands into the pockets of his jeans. "Uh, car?"

Allie looked sharply at him. She'd definitely caught him at something. A buzzing started in her ears as her face heated. "Unless you bought a new Camry while I was gone, someone must be here."

He grabbed her arm and drew her toward the center of the living room, away from the kitchen, then leaned forward and placed his mouth next to her ear. "Don't get upset, okay? We'll work it out."

She jerked away, and Joanie whimpered in her arms. If he thought another woman wearing cheap perfume was something to "work out," he'd better think again. "Work what out?"

"Hello, Allie."

Allie whirled, shock coursing up her spine,

her mouth hanging open. Then her grip on Joanie tightened. This was no girlfriend, no affair. It was much worse. Staring at her from just inside her kitchen stood the only person in the entire world who hated her guts. And the feeling was definitely mutual.

Her mother-in-law.

4

Seated on the bed, Eric leaned against the headboard and watched his wife stomp back and forth from the bedside table to the closet. At the rate she was going, they'd have to replace the carpet. "You're acting like this is my fault, like I did something on purpose just to upset you."

Allie's eyes shot blue-green darts across the room. "You can't expect me to believe she showed up on our doorstep, suitcase in hand, with no warning whatsoever. Nobody is that rude, not even your mother."

He clamped his jaw shut. Actually, that's exactly what had happened, but to admit it would be agreeing that his mother was rude. Maybe she was, but Allie wasn't exactly exuding generosity and charm at the moment.

"Honest, Allie, I'm just as shocked as you are." He allowed a hint of steel to seep into his voice. "But insulting my mother won't help. She's having some problems, and she needs some time to work things out. Try to show a little compassion."

"Compassion?" Allie clutched Joanie so tightly Eric was surprised the baby didn't wail in protest. "She came into the bridal room on my wedding day and called me names in front of all my bridesmaids. She said I was self-centered and she didn't think our marriage would last a year. And I'm supposed to welcome her into my home with open arms when she shows up unannounced?"

Eric had heard the incident recounted a dozen times in the five years of their marriage. After a few months he grew tired of trying to come up with excuses for his mother's behavior, and usually just ignored Allie when she brought up the ill-mannered comments on their wedding day. But after the conversation with his mother in the kitchen before Allie got home, he felt like he needed to defend her tonight.

He folded his arms across his chest and glowered. "Your mother shows up unannounced almost every day, and I welcome her into *my* home."

Allie whirled on him. "That's different. She stays an hour and leaves. Your mother lives in Detroit, so I assume she's planning to be here for a few days. And what do you mean, she's having problems?"

He couldn't hold her gaze and let his slide downward toward his feet. He needed to tell her the whole story, but she wasn't going to like it.

"Actually, that's what we were talking about when you came home. Mother doesn't have any plans at the moment. She . . ." He cleared his throat. "She left Dad. Moved out."

He risked a glance at Allie. If her mouth were open any wider, somebody could toss a basketball into it.

"I know this is a shock," he went on in a rush. "Trust me, I'm still reeling. I never in a million years thought Mother would leave Dad."

Allie sank onto the edge of the bed, looking dazed. "Did she tell you why?"

"No." Eric shook his head. "I was trying to get something out of her when you came home, but all she'd say was 'I need a change.' "

She lowered the sleeping baby to the center of the mattress and arranged a fuzzy pink blanket over her, then turned a stern look on him. "She can change all she wants somewhere else. Your mother is *not* moving in with us, Eric."

He heaved a sigh. "I know. But what was I supposed to do, slam the door in her face?"

"You could have offered to drive her to a hotel." Her eyes narrowed. "There are a couple of nice ones just a few miles away."

Eric leaned forward and covered her hand with his. "I can't do that. She *is* my mother."

"And I'm your wife."

Allie locked gazes with him, and he had to force himself not to look away from the intense depths of her eyes. "I know that. You are the most important woman in my life."

Okay, blatant flattery, but if that's what it took to restore peace, he'd resort to sweet talk. Besides, it was true. Hopefully Allie sensed his sincerity.

She must have, for she said, "Well . . ." and gave a sniff. "She can't stay here indefinitely. I'll lose my mind if I have to deal with her for more than a few days."

Eric didn't heave a sigh of relief, but his breath came a bit easier. Hopefully a few days would be all it took for Mother to come to her senses and go back home. Besides, he'd never admit it to Allie, but it was actually kind of good to see her. He'd been trying not to feel offended that neither of his parents had made the trip down from Detroit to see their first grandchild, while

Allie's family was here so often they might as well pitch tents in the yard. He looked forward to the opportunity to show his daughter off to his mother.

He tightened his hand around Allie's and pulled her toward him. She lost all resistance then and snuggled in his lap. He held her close, breathing deeply to catch the unique scent of her hair, a faint mixture of soap and flowers that always —

The door opened abruptly, and Mother stuck her head into the bedroom. Allie jerked away from him and leaped off the bed.

"I hope I'm not intruding." Mother gave a tight-lipped smile. "I just wondered if you have some clean bed linens. These don't seem very fresh."

A deep flush stained Allie's face as her eyes grew round.

"I'm sure they're clean, Mother," Eric hurried to say before Allie could respond. "Nobody has slept in that bed since we moved into the house."

Mother's expression did not change. "So that means you haven't changed the sheets in how many years?"

Allie's arms hung at her sides, both hands tightening into fists. Her gaze was fixed on the floor in front of her, but Eric knew his wife well enough to know that she was struggling to control her temper. And judging by the blotches that were starting to appear on her neck, she was about to lose the struggle.

Eric leaped off the bed. "I'll show you where the linen closet is. I'm sure we have some more sheets to fit that bed."

With a single nod, Mother turned away and disappeared from view. Avoiding his wife's eyes, Eric sidled past her toward the doorway. She grabbed his arm, fingernails biting into his skin, and pulled him roughly toward her.

"I want a lock on that door *tonight*," she hissed.

In the face of Allie's fury, Eric judged the wisest course of action was to do whatever it took to pacify his wife.

"Yes, dear."

A solitary trip to Wal-Mart to buy a locking door handle sounded like an excellent idea.

Allie settled Joanie gently into the crib and flipped on the baby monitor. These predawn feedings were killer. She backed toward the door, staring at the precious little face nestled inside the pink bundle. That crib was so big, and Joanie was so tiny. She would have preferred to keep the baby in the bassinette a few more weeks, but all the books said to let her get used to sleeping in her own bed as soon as possible. Though she didn't admit it to Eric, she'd slept better herself without straining all night to hear every breath her daughter drew. And with the receiver on her nightstand turned all the way up, she could still hear the softest baby sigh. She tiptoed backward through the doorway and closed the door with a soft *click*.

Turning, she came nose to nose with her mother-in-law and nearly jumped out of her skin.

"Betty, you scared me." Allie put a hand over her heart and heaved a steadying breath. "I didn't know you were up."

A single row of pink plastic curlers formed a ring around the base of her mother-in-law's skull, and a tight curl of dark, steel-colored hair was held in place by criss-crossed bobby pins in front of each ear. She looked a lot older this morning, her eyes heavily hooded and the skin at each side of her jaw sagging to form droopy jowls. She must be, what? Sixty-two or -three? A lot older than Allie's mom, anyway. Right now she looked every day of it.

Her wide mouth tightened, deepening the

lines at each corner into twin crevasses as she gave a little sniff. "It's five thirty. I'm always up at this time, making Don's breakfast and packing his lunch." She glanced across the living room at the closed master bedroom door. "What time does Eric leave for work?"

"Not until seven thirty." Allie edged a step away, toward the safety of her bedroom with its newly installed locking doorknob. "His alarm clock will go off in another hour. But if you're bored, I'm sure he'd love it if you pack him a lunch. It'd save him some time."

The lines between Betty's eyes deepened with disapproval. "You mean you don't make his lunch for him?"

Allie hid a sarcastic response behind a tight smile. "No, he makes a mean ham sandwich. In fact, before I went on maternity leave, he sometimes made my lunch at the same time he did his own." She gave in to a wide yawn. "I'm not much of a morning person."

The older woman's dark eyes, a nondescript gray-brown color, seemed to gather sadness as the lids drooped even farther. "I suppose he's grown accustomed to taking care of himself. Marriage must have been such an adjustment for him."

Allie's jaw clenched at the thinly veiled

insult. Actually, when she first met Eric he had been a rowdy college boy, living in a pigsty with three other guys and doing his best to prove that the human body could thrive on beer, leftover pizza, and powdered sugar donuts. He'd been completely resistant to any "taking care of" she'd tried to perform. Wouldn't even let her do his laundry when she offered to take it home with hers, and they almost broke up over her attempts to wash a sinkful of disgustingly filthy dishes in his kitchen. One of the things that attracted her to him in the first place had been his independence.

Allie forced a smile. "Marriage is always an adjustment, isn't it? For both parties."

"But wives are called on to sacrifice more than husbands." Her chin inched upward. "Our role in the family is to be the homemakers, to take care of our husband and children. That's our job."

Allie stiffened. In another minute Betty would be telling her she needed to *submit* or something, and then Allie would totally lose it.

"Well, that works for some people." She turned before Betty could respond and stomped across the living room. When her hand touched the knob, she said without looking back, "Make yourself at home in the kitchen. I'm sure Eric would love to have his breakfast waiting when he gets up. Just like the good old days."

With the door safely closed behind her, Allie leaned against it, fuming. She refused to be lectured about her wifely duties in her own home. What kind of Stone Age thinking was that, anyway? Men were perfectly capable of taking care of themselves, and some, like Eric, resented a woman trying to mother them. Betty had been living in some sort of time warp for the past forty years, dressing in checkered aprons and scrubbing the floors on her hands and knees, or something equally ridiculous. That was exactly what Allie *didn't* want, the reason she couldn't quit work and become a stay-at-home mom. She and Eric had a modern marriage. They shared everything, right down the middle, from the household duties to the responsibility for paying the bills.

That last thought flushed away Allie's irritation with her mother-in-law as it ushered in a new set of worries. She crossed the bedroom floor on tiptoe, careful not to disturb the blanket-covered figure in the bed. The Varie Cose catalog lay on top of her dresser, and she fingered its glossy cover. Could she really sell enough of this stuff to cover her part of the bills? Sally Jo's success proved it could be done. But Allie didn't know the first thing about sales.

On the other hand, Allie knew people. Her favorite classes in college were the behavioral psych courses. She loved figuring out what made people tick, what made them act certain ways, like certain things. Surely that kind of analytical look at behavior could help her in a sales career. Maybe if she approached selling with that idea, she could make a go of it.

Behind her, Eric murmured something and rolled over. She left the catalog where it lay and slipped beneath the blanket to wrap her cool arms around his sleep-warmed body. He snuggled closer and, with a soft sound very much like his infant daughter's, settled once again into a deep slumber. Allie lay with her cheek pressed against his chest, her mind busy with plans. She'd talk to Sally Jo today, find out the details of becoming a Varie Cose representative, and then present her plan to Eric tonight. They'd probably have to lock themselves in the bedroom to have some privacy, though. She heaved a breath that sounded like the snort of an irritated bull.

He was just going to have to do something about his mother.

5

Allie whipped her car into a parking space in front of the restaurant where Sally Jo agreed to meet her. From the backseat, Joanie's screams echoed off the windows and stretched Allie's nerves to the breaking point.

"I know, I know." Allie winced as the sound of her voice caused the volume to increase. About a week ago Joanie had decided she hated the car seat, and every trip they took with the infant became a nightmare.

Allie leaped out of the car, glancing at her watch as she jerked the back door open. Ten minutes late. Terrific.

"Calm down, sweetie." She pitched her voice in a low, soothing tone as she pulled the umbrella stroller out and unfolded it, but Joanie refused to be consoled. She wanted out, and she wanted out now.

"Mama's here," Allie soothed as she

pushed the release button and slipped the little seat belt straps off the baby's shoulders.

She scooped Joanie out, and her screams began to quiet almost immediately. Hugging her tight against her chest, Allie bounced up and down until the infant's cries softened to shuddering breaths. She eyed the stroller. Better not take a chance on that right now. She slammed the car door, dropped her purse into the stroller seat, and headed for the front door of the restaurant.

Inside, the smell of hot yeast dough and cinnamon stopped her in her tracks. She inhaled deeply, her gaze sliding over the yummy pastry items in the display case. A waving hand with shiny red nail polish from the booths lining the rear windows caught her eye. She guided the stroller in that direction, nodding at the smiles Joanie collected as she threaded her way through the tables.

"Oh, look at the tiny baby," Sally Jo cooed. "Why, isn't she just the cutest thing? How old is she?"

Joanie's face was still bright red from her tantrum and her little forehead puckered with fury. A downy blonde spike stood straight up on the top of her head like a baby mohawk. Allie arranged her headband

57

so the pink organza bow was positioned to one side of her damp head.

"Five weeks." Allie slid into the booth. "Sorry I'm late. I'm still trying to get used to packing the entire nursery into the diaper bag whenever we go somewhere."

"Actually, I would have preferred to meet at your house." Sally Jo's shiny lips formed a pretty pout. "It would be so much easier to do business there."

Rocking the baby with a slight movement, Allie shook her head. "Trust me, it wouldn't." She scowled. "My mother-in-law is visiting."

"Ah." Sally Jo nodded. "Well, in that case, we might as well start."

A tired-looking woman in a brown server's uniform approached the table and placed a menu in front of Allie. "What are you drinking, sweetie?"

Allie noted the lipstick-stained coffee cup in front of Sally Jo. "I'll have a decaf coffee with cream." She paused, the smell of hot cinnamon doing battle with her resolve to lose weight. Resolve lost. "And one of those iced cinnamon rolls. And some water, please." She slid the menu back across the table.

When the server disappeared toward the kitchen, Sally Jo opened up the huge leather satchel sitting on the seat beside her and extracted a thick three-ring binder. "I'll start out by telling you about our company, Varie Cose International." She angled the binder so it faced Allie and flipped open the cover. The first sheet, encased in plastic, showed a modern stone office building with dozens of rows of windows shining in bright sunlight. A huge flag hung suspended above an arched glass entryway depicting the Varie Cose logo, a multicolored fan held in an elegantly sketched feminine hand.

"As I said last night, Varie Cose started in a small Italian village. But in the twenty years since, it has grown into a multibillion-dollar corporation that operates in more than twenty-five countries. This building is our main headquarters in Milan, Italy, but we have offices all over the world, including New York, San Francisco, and Chicago."

Allie watched as she flipped through the first few pages, each depicting a different building but all flying the colorful Varie Cose banner. Then came several pie charts and line graphs, and Sally Jo launched into an animated discussion of worldwide retail sales volumes and market shares. Allie clenched her jaws shut against a yawn and tried not to look at the thickness of the stack of pages still to come in that binder. Hopefully Sally Jo would get around to something interesting before she nodded off from boredom.

The server brought her coffee and pastry. Allie smiled her thanks as the Varie Cose representative kept right on talking.

"And when the company hit the million-dollar sales mark in the early nineties, they decided to launch the cosmetics line." A satisfied smile curled the corners of Sally Jo's mouth. "That's when the business really took off. Since then we've steadily increased our market share of worldwide sales in the cosmetic, housewares, and cleaning product lines, and our clothing line has held steady." She leaned across the table toward Allie, excitement dancing in her eyes. "At the division conference in Atlanta last month, they discussed some exciting new ideas that I'm not at liberty to share. But trust me, honey, Varie Cose is a company to watch." She leaned back, nodding, and picked up her coffee cup.

Joanie, finally lulled to sleep, barely stirred when Allie transferred her to the stroller and fastened the straps around her.

"So how does it work?" Allie asked when she had the baby settled. "Do I get a paycheck from the company, or do I just collect money from my customers? And do I have to pay anything to sign up?"

Sally Jo gave a small smile that made Allie squirm in her seat. She felt like a large-mouthed bass who'd just been hooked.

"Well, no," Sally Jo said, "you don't *have* to pay anything. But you won't be able to do much of a demonstration if you don't have any product to show, will you?" She sipped her coffee and set the cup down. "We're getting ahead of ourselves. Let me keep going with my presentation."

Allie tore a chunk of warm cinnamon roll with two fingers and popped it into her mouth. She barely tasted the soft, sweet bread as she forced herself to focus on the charts Sally Jo showed her.

"Eric, I'd like to talk to you about something." Allie placed the last supper dish in the top rack of the dishwasher and closed the door before turning to catch his eye and mouth a silent addition to her request. *Privately.*

He winced as he nodded, which sent a wave of guilt coursing through her. No doubt he thought she was going to harangue him about his mother again. She shifted her gaze toward Betty, who was just giving a final swipe with the dishrag to the kitchen table. Actually, the pot roast she cooked for dinner had tasted delicious, and Allie had to admit her whipped potatoes were as good as anything Gram made at home. The woman knew how to cook, and judging by the way she'd taken control of the kitchen this afternoon, she enjoyed it. That was fine. Cooking was not Allie's forte. She was more than willing to give over control of the kitchen for the duration of her mother-in-law's short stay.

"Okay." Eric set the broom inside the pantry. "Mother, would you mind keeping an eye on Joanie for a while?"

Allie opened her mouth to protest, but when she caught sight of the eager look on Betty's face, she closed it again. Why, she had barely even looked at the baby all day! In fact, she had confined herself to the kitchen or the bedroom since Allie returned from her meeting, and didn't say a dozen words until Eric got home. She hadn't once tried to touch her granddaughter, which was the total opposite of Allie's family. Allie had begun to wonder if perhaps she was uncomfortable around babies.

But now, a Mona Lisa smile tugged at the corners of Betty's mouth as she glanced at her sleeping granddaughter nestled in her infant seat.

Maybe it's not Joanie who makes her un-

comfortable.

She cleared her throat and forced herself to smile when the woman's gaze shifted toward her. "Um, thank you for cooking supper, Betty. It was really good."

The older woman's lips flashed upward in a tight smile. "I'm sure we all appreciate a home-cooked meal every now and again."

She turned away to hang the dishrag across the sink, leaving Allie to stare in growing disbelief at her back. Did that woman just insult her in her own home? Was she insinuating that Eric never got a home-cooked meal, that his wife wasn't capable of feeding him properly?

Moving quickly, Eric grabbed her by the arm and propelled her toward the doorway. "Holler if you need anything, Mother."

Allie allowed herself to be guided through the living room and into the bedroom. When Eric closed the door behind him, she jerked out of his grip and pushed the lock button, then whirled on him.

"Did you hear that? She just —"

Eric shut her up by pulling her toward him and covering her lips with his. Almost unwillingly, she felt the tension ease out of her body as she succumbed to his blatant ploy to calm her down. Poor Eric. His mother really had put him in a tough position. It wasn't his fault she went out of her way to insult his wife. She slipped her arms around his neck and yielded to the kiss.

Then she stiffened. She needed to talk to him about Varie Cose. They didn't have much time before Joanie woke and demanded her fifth meal of the day.

She pulled away and smiled with regret up into his face. "Later, lover boy. Right now I need to talk to you about something important."

Disappointment flooded his eyes, but he gave her a crooked grin. "Story of my life lately." He took a reluctant step backward. "Okay, I'm all ears."

"Uh, have a seat." Allie pointed at the chair in the corner, and then perched on the edge of the bed as he settled himself. "As you know, I'm supposed to go back to work in a few weeks."

"November eighth."

She nodded. "Well, I've been thinking. What if I took this opportunity to change careers?"

His stare was completely blank.

"It's great timing, actually," she rushed on. "I mean, they've had five weeks to get used to doing things without me at the office. I talked to Gina the other day, and she said the girl who's been covering my desk is really on top of things. I'm sure they barely miss me anymore." In fact, her boss had called to confirm the exact date of Allie's return to work, but she *had* mentioned that things were going well at the office.

"I thought you liked your job."

"I do. But really, there's only so far I can move up in state government. If I'm ever going to make a change to private industry, I'm just saying this might be a good time."

He nodded slowly. "Okay, I see that. So what did you have in mind?"

"I was thinking of a career in . . . in sales."

His eyebrows arched. "Sales? You?"

"Why do you say it like that? You don't think I could be successful as a sales-woman?"

"Well, no, I — I mean yes, but —" He shook his head as though trying to clear his thoughts. "I guess I just never thought about it."

"I'd like you to think about it now." She leaped off the bed and snatched the Varie Cose catalog off the dresser. "I want to sell this."

His eyebrows rose even farther. "You want to be a makeup saleswoman?"

"Oh, it's more than just makeup. Varie Cose offers a full range of housewares, cleaning supplies, even clothes. See for yourself." She thrust the catalog into his unresisting hands. "The lady who conducted the demonstration I went to the other night started with the company just three years ago, and she's already a regional director. She drives a *Lexus,* Eric!"

He paused in the middle of leafing through the catalog to look up at her. "No kidding?"

Allie sat back down on the corner of the bed, watching him carefully. "There is a small start-up fee, of course. Like there would be in any business."

His eyes narrowed. "How much?"

"Five hundred dollars." He gave a low whistle, and she rushed on. "That buys me a complete demonstration kit. I'm sure I could make it back in a couple of weeks. Besides, we'll save more than that in daycare costs in a month."

He looked up, piercing her with a direct gaze. "Daycare costs? Does that mean you wouldn't put Joanie in daycare?"

"No, that's the best part. Most of my demonstrations would be done at night and on weekends, so I could be at home during the day. Now that you're working first shift, you could keep her on the evenings when I have to work. I'm sure my mom and sisters would love to watch her if you have to work

66

late or something."

He was studying her with a look that seemed to go directly inside her brain. "Be honest with me. Have you changed your mind about being a stay-at-home mother? Because if this is just a scheme you've cooked up so you don't have to take Joanie to daycare, we need to talk about that."

"Of course not." Allie couldn't meet his gaze. "Well, maybe I have revised my opinion about working moms a little bit."

Eric leaned forward, arms on his knees, a flicker of excitement in his eyes. "Allie, I'm okay with that. Remember, I was raised by a stay-at-home mom. I would love to be able to provide that kind of atmosphere for our kids."

Stunned, she stared at him. Was he saying he wanted her to be like his mother? Like that mild-mannered, passive-aggressive woman currently residing in their guest room? Surely not. Not her Eric.

"But . . . but . . ." She swallowed, trying desperately to gather her thoughts into something sensible. "We can't afford to lose my paycheck."

"It would be tough, and we'd have to tighten our belts, but I think we could swing it."

Her mouth completely dry, Allie simply

stared at him. What had possessed this man she thought she knew so well to suggest such an outrageous idea? Did he really think she could stay home and do . . . what did stay-at-home moms do with their time, anyway? Make cupcakes? Run the vacuum cleaner?

Cook pot roasts?

Her voice sounded tight in her own ears as she spoke through a constricted throat. "I don't want to just *swing it,* Eric. I intend to keep working, paying my half of the bills. I just want to refocus my efforts in another direction, that's all."

He studied her a moment, his expression guarded. Then he gave a single, slow nod. "Alright, Allie. If you really want to do this, I'm with you."

A weight lifted from her chest at his words. "You mean it?" She jumped up and flew across the two steps between them to throw herself into his lap. "You don't mind the five hundred dollars?"

His arms wrapped around her as she snuggled into his embrace. "Like you say, it's a start-up cost."

"Uh, I might need a little more than that. I'll probably need some new clothes so I look professional."

"What's wrong with the closetful of

clothes you have now?"

She squirmed, glad her face was pressed against his neck so she didn't have to look him in the eye. "They don't fit so well since the baby was born." The cinnamon roll weighed heavily on her conscience.

"I'm sure we can afford a few new clothes. I've been wondering what I could get you for your birthday."

She stiffened. "Eric! My birthday is tomorrow and you haven't gotten me anything yet?"

His arms tightened around her. "I've been looking for the perfect gift for my beautiful wife."

"You still think I'm beautiful? Even if I'm fat and my clothes don't fit anymore?" She pressed her lips against the soft skin behind his ear.

"Are you kidding? You'd have men lining up around you if I wasn't here to fight them off."

She pulled away slightly so she could look into his eyes. "I love you, you know that?"

The smile that curled his lips was too good to resist. She covered it with hers.

6

Allie's eyes flew open. Red numbers on the clock told her the time was 6:15. Why hadn't the baby cried? She always woke up at five for her early morning feeding.

A terrible fear tried to take root in Allie's mind as she threw off the comforter and raced from the room. Heavy silence nestled throughout the house. In passing, she noted a line of light beneath the guest room door, meaning Betty was awake. How could she stay in there, while right next door in the nursery her granddaughter might be —

Allie pushed the horrible thought away before it could take hold. She choked back a sob as she burst into the nursery and raced to the crib.

Joanie lay sleeping, her little chest rising and falling beneath a white receiving blanket. Tiny veins lined the fine skin of her eyelids, the blonde lashes fluttering as though in response to the pulse pounding like a drum in Allie's ears. Joanie was okay. Not dead, not suffocated. She was just sleeping.

Limp with relief, Allie leaned over to rest her cheek against the crib railing as her heartbeat returned to normal. Joanie's last feeding had been at one thirty, which meant she'd gone almost five hours without eating — a record. Next thing they knew, she'd be sleeping through the night.

Something on the baby's face caught Allie's eye. Squinting in the dim glow of the Winnie-the-Pooh nightlight, she tried to make out what looked like a small discoloration to the right of her dainty nose. Allie ran across the room and flipped the light switch, then returned to peer anxiously into her daughter's face. There. She wasn't imagining it. A small red mark marred the soft infant skin. In fact, there were a couple on the other side of her nose as well. Allie licked her finger and rubbed one. The splotch didn't come off and it felt rough, like a welt. Red welts, on her baby's face!

She snatched Joanie out of the crib and ran toward her bedroom.

"Eric! Eric, wake up."

Eric mumbled in his sleep.

"I said, wake up!"

She flipped on the lamp beside the bed,

and Eric, moaning in protest, pulled the comforter over his head.

Allie jerked it down. "There's something wrong with the baby. Look at her!"

"Huh?" Squinting, Eric cupped a hand over his eyes to shield them from the bright light. "S'rong 'th 'er?"

Joanie began to wake. She raised little arms above her head and stretched. Allie gripped her tighter.

"I don't know what's wrong with her." Tears clogged her throat, making her voice come out in a squeak. "She's got a terrible rash. Look!"

Eric struggled up on one elbow, peering at the baby through sleep-heavy eyes. "Where? I don't see anything."

"On her face. Right there, and there."

He studied the tiny face for a moment, then shook his head. "That's not a rash. It's just a few red marks."

"What do you think a rash is? It's red marks! This is probably the beginning of something terrible. It'll probably spread. What if —" She sucked in a breath, horror creeping over her. "Eric, what if it's measles? Babies this young can die from measles, can't they?"

"It's not measles." He lay back on his pillow. "Measles are practically nonexistent these days. They wiped it out with vaccinations."

"Then it's something else. Maybe she has an allergy." Allie wracked her brain. What had Joanie encountered that was new? "Maybe she's allergic to something in your mother's pot roast and I passed it along to her in my milk."

"First of all, neither of us have al—"

"Or wait! Maybe it's your mother."

Eric's stare became hard. "You think my daughter is allergic to my mother?"

The sound of his voice and the sudden set of his jaw told Allie she was edging up close to a line she didn't want to cross this morning. "Not your mother, but maybe her perfume or something. After all, she held the baby last night for the first time."

His lips tightened for a moment before he spoke. "Allie, this is ridiculous. That is not a rash. You're overreacting."

Outrage stiffened Allie's spine. "Overreacting? Our daughter's life could be threatened, and your advice would be . . . what? Ignore it?" She took a step backward, clutching Joanie to her chest. "I'm going to call the doctor."

Eric ran a hand through his already-rumpled hair. "For crying out loud, it's not even six thirty in the morning. Don't bother

73

the doctor."

"I'm not bothering him. It's his job."

With a resigned sigh, Eric sat up in bed and reached toward the nightstand to turn off the alarm clock before it buzzed. "Why are you being bullheaded about this? It's almost as if you want something to be wrong with her."

She gave him a resentful look. "That's a terrible thing to say. Of course I don't want anything to be wrong."

"Then relax. The baby is fine."

A touch of doubt crept in as Allie looked down at the tiny face. Joanie whimpered and turned an open mouth toward her, searching for breakfast. The red splotches didn't look as angry as they had a moment before, but what in the world had caused them to appear? A thought made her breath catch in her throat. What if there were more? Why hadn't she stripped off Joanie's clothes immediately and checked her over?

She whirled toward the door. "I'm going to go change and feed her now," she said over her shoulder.

"Hey, wait a minute."

She paused in the doorway and looked back. Eric smiled sleepily. "Happy birthday."

"Hey, Mother, could you come in here a

minute?" Eric called from the nursery door.

Seated in the rocking chair with the baby, Allie's head jerked up as she gave him an angry look. Mother came from the kitchen immediately, drying her hands on a towel. She'd obviously been up for a while, long enough to dress, fix her hair, and cook a stack of pancakes for breakfast. His stomach bulged uncomfortably beneath his belt buckle. He wasn't used to eating more than a bowl of Wheaties in the morning. If Mother stayed much longer, he was going to have to tell her to stop cooking such big meals.

Of course, if she stayed much longer, he might find himself minus one wife.

Maybe he could force an alliance by emphasizing a common bond — Joanie. He took his mother by the arm. "Could you take a look at these spots on Joanie's face? Allie's worried she might have an allergy or something."

Reluctance flooded Mother's features, and he practically had to pull her across the room toward the rocker. Allie stopped rocking and visibly clutched the baby closer, a stubborn set to her jaw. He bit back a sigh. What was it with these two? You'd need a chain saw to cut the tension between them.

He gave Allie a stern look. She slowly

loosened her grip on the baby enough that they could examine the sleeping face.

Mother peered, and then shook her head. "That's not an allergic reaction. It looks to me as though she scratched herself."

"What?" Disconcerted, Allie looked down at Joanie.

Eric smiled. "I'll bet that's it."

Mother reached down to pull one little hand from beneath the blanket. She splayed Joanie's fingers, and then turned a look of disapproval on Allie. "Look at those nails. When was the last time you trimmed them?"

Allie stiffened, and Eric winced at the accusation in his mother's voice.

"Uh, I don't know," Allie replied defensively. "Maybe two weeks ago."

Mother sniffed. "She drinks nothing but milk. That makes her nails grow. You need to check them often. She relies on you to keep her safe, you know."

Eric grimaced. Even to him it sounded like Mother had just accused Allie of being incompetent.

"Mother," he said in a voice full of warning, "Joanie is perfectly safe. Allie is a terrific mom."

One of the small, cold smiles he remembered so well took her lips. "I'm sure she is."

She left the room, and Eric reluctantly met Allie's furious gaze.

"I won't take that from her, Eric." Her whisper came out in a hiss. "I don't care if she *is* your mother."

His heart in the pit of his stomach, he leaned over and planted a kiss on the top of his wife's head. "I know. I'm sorry. I'll speak to her tonight when I get home from work."

Eric pulled his pickup into a space between the two vehicles already parked in the small 911 Dispatch Center lot. He paused at the door, watching the traffic drive past on Fourth Street. Motorists were behaving themselves today, no doubt due to the presence of a police car parked conspicuously midway down the hill from the Dispatch Center. Probably Officer Lewis. That was one of his favorite stakeout locations when it came his turn to use the radar gun.

"Good morning." The other daytime dispatcher, Molly Green, called a greeting from the control room when he stepped inside.

"Hey, how's it going?" He went into the small kitchen and stowed his lunch bag in the half-sized fridge. Plastic containers filled up the brown paper bag so he could barely close the top. One thing for sure — his lunches had been a lot more interesting the two days since Mother arrived.

He stuck his head into the boss's office on his way to the control room. She bent over her desk, a donut in one hand and a pen in the other. "Morning, Kathy. Everything okay today?"

She lifted her head from the paperwork in front of her to give him a distracted smile. "Fine. Quiet night, even quieter morning."

Eric wisely didn't comment on the donut, though just two days before, she'd mentioned that the doctor told her she needed to drop some weight or risk another heart attack.

"Hope it stays that way," he said. "I could use a stress-free day."

As he slipped into his chair and adjusted the brightness on the three big monitors on his desk, Eric thought how true that statement was. Coming to work today felt almost like a vacation. He'd rather deal with county disasters than get caught in the daggerlike looks flying around his house between Allie and Mother.

The radio squawked its familiar static for a second, then a voice said, "Four fifty-seven, ten-eight."

After three years on the job, Eric knew the officers on the Danville police force by badge number better than by name. He glanced at the giant clock on the wall. Officer four fifty-seven — Chad Palmer — was a few minutes early for work this morning.

From the desk behind him, Molly acknowledged the transmission. "Ten-four, four fifty-seven. Have a safe day." She swiveled her chair around to smile at Eric. "So did you figure out what you're giving Allie for her birthday?"

Working in such close quarters, he and Molly couldn't help but know most everything there was to know about each other. He'd worked second shift for the first three years. Shortly before Joanie was born, an opportunity finally came to move to first, and he jumped at it. He'd worked with Molly several times over the years, but after two months sitting three feet away from her for eight hours a day, he'd learned all about the challenges she faced as the single mother of two lively boys who always managed to be in trouble at school. And she knew he'd been trying to come up with the perfect idea for Allie's birthday present.

"Yeah, I think so." He opened a drawer in his desk and pulled out the phone book. "She told me last night she wants some new clothes."

Molly scrunched her face while she fiddled

with a lock of dark hair that hung free from the ponytail she wore every day. "Never try to pick out clothes for a woman. It's not a good idea. Maybe you ought to get her a gift card somewhere."

He shook his head as he shuffled through the pages. "Too much like handing her cash. I made that mistake the first birthday we were together."

The memory of Allie's furious face hovered before his mind's eye. How was he to know that the Sanderson family made such a big deal out of birthdays? In his family, a birthday meant cupcakes for the kids in his class and money to spend however he wished. Later on, the cupcakes disappeared, and the amount of birthday money increased.

But not in Allie's family. They went all out for birthdays — sort of like Christmas, only just one person got presents. Lots of them. The gift certificate fiasco was not one he cared to repeat.

She had been so down on herself since the baby's birth that he really wanted to give her something special, something that let her know he'd put a lot of thought into the selection. Something just for her, to make her feel good about herself.

The radio squawked again. "Four twenty-three, ten-seven." Anderson, announcing he was coming off his shift and heading for home. A brief pause, and then Officer Baker's deeper voice informed them that he was officially on duty with, "Three eighty-two, ten-eight."

"Then I highly recommend jewelry," Molly said before she acknowledged both transmissions.

"Nah, I got something better than that. The perfect gift for Allie." Smiling to himself, Eric found the page he wanted and jotted down the number. He'd make the call when the radio settled down for the morning.

Allie slipped into her bedroom and shut the door with a quiet *click* behind her. She spread a baby blanket out in the center of the bed and placed her sleeping daughter on it. Then she positioned a pillow against the headboard and picked up the telephone on the nightstand. She dialed a number without looking it up.

"Danville Pediatric," said a familiar voice on the other end.

"Hello, this is Allie Harrod." She spoke quietly, with a quick glance at the closed door. Betty was in the guest room on the other end of the house, but Allie didn't want her to overhear. "I need to speak with the nurse, please."

"One moment."

Classical music played in Allie's ear as she sat on hold. She watched the baby sleep, the tiny nostrils flaring ever so slightly with each breath. Her gaze was drawn again and again to the terrible marks marring the tender skin around Joanie's nose. No matter what Betty and Eric said, Allie didn't think they looked like scratches. Those were welts of some sort, maybe hives. What if they were an indication of something terribly wrong? She could just see the doctor's sad expression, shaking his head as he said, "If only we'd caught it early."

A click on the line, and then a female voice. "This is Theresa Hutton."

Ah, Dr. Reynolds' regular nurse. Good. Allie straightened, leaning forward away from the pillow. "Hello, this is Allie Harrod. I'm worried about my baby."

"I'm so sorry, Mrs. Harrod." The nurse's voice was pleasant. "I have Joanie's file right in front of me. What seems to be the problem this morning?"

"She has a terrible rash." Her words tumbled over each other. "Or maybe hives. I've never seen anything like it. It's horrible."

Nurse Hutton's tone contained an ocean of tranquility. "Where is the rash?"

"On her face." Allie leaned forward to get a better look at the marks. Was that another welt, a new one? Worry tightened her throat so her voice came out squeaky. "All over her face. And it's spreading."

"Does she have a fever?"

Allie had remembered to check. "No."

"Is she eating well and wetting her diaper regularly?"

"Yes."

"What about her breathing? Does it seem labored or at all difficult for her?"

Allie watched the infant a moment, the even rise and fall of her little chest beneath the cotton gown. "No, but I'm sure something is wrong. These hives are definitely not normal. And they're spreading," she repeated, just in case Nurse Hutton had missed that detail.

"Can you hold a moment? Dr. Reynolds just came in. I'll ask what he advises."

The classical music returned before Allie could voice a response. What would the doctor say? Maybe Eric was right. Maybe she was overreacting. But another glance at Joanie's marred skin told Allie that she couldn't risk doing nothing. Her anxiety mounting by the second, she tapped a finger

83

on the back of the receiver pressed to her ear. The click of the nurse coming back on the line made her jump.

"Mrs. Harrod, Dr. Reynolds would like you to come by the office this morning. We're pretty slow right now. How long will it take you to get here?"

A searing flash of alarm sent blood roaring in Allie's ears. The doctor wanted to see Joanie immediately. He must think there was something wrong with her. Allie's motherly instinct had been right!

An iron fist of fear squeezed her chest. If only it hadn't been. "I can be there in fifteen minutes."

"That's perfect. We'll see you then."

For a second after the line went dead, Allie didn't move. Then she sprang into action. Running into the closet, she kicked off her bedroom slippers and jerked a shirt off a hanger. A handy pair of sweatpants lay folded on the shelf, and she hopped up and down as she jammed her legs into them.

Shoes, shoes. Where were her shoes?

All over the place, that's where. But Eric's were arranged in a neat row on his side, so she shoved her feet into his sports sandals and tightened the straps as far as they would go. She dashed back into the bedroom and scooped Joanie off the bed, blanket and all, then ran to the nursery. Stuffing a handful of diapers from the stacker into the diaper bag, she slung the strap over her shoulder and whirled toward the door.

Betty stood in the hallway, a quizzical expression on her face. "Are you going out?"

Allie didn't have time to explain. She didn't want to hear any accusations that she was overreacting, either. "Yes," she said as she zoomed past her mother-in-law. "Be back in a while."

Scooping up her purse from the coffee table on her way through the living room, she rushed out of the house.

Faint strains of the same classical music Allie heard on the phone filled the doctor's waiting room. She spoke to the girl behind the reception counter. "This is Joan Leigh Harrod. We don't have an appointment, but Dr. Reynolds asked me to bring her right over."

Sparkly lavender fingernails flew over a keyboard while the girl watched her computer monitor. "Has anything changed since your last visit? Address? Insurance?"

"No, it's all the same." It had been less than a week since they were here last.

In a moment, the printer beside the girl spit out a form, which she picked up and slid in front of Allie. She plopped a pen down on top of the paper. "Sign this, please."

While Allie scrawled her name in the box at the bottom, the door beside her opened. Nurse Hutton stood in the doorway, a manila folder in her hands. "Come on back, Mrs. Harrod."

Allie cast a glance around the waiting room. Joanie was being seen immediately, though three people had arrived before them. This must really be serious. She bit back a rising panic. What a birthday present. From now on birthdays would hold none of their former joy. They would always remind her of the day she discovered her infant daughter had contracted a terrible disease. The familiar medical scent of antiseptic mixed with rubbing alcohol tickled her nose as she stepped through the door.

"Come right back here," the nurse said over her shoulder.

Allie followed her down a narrow corridor on the left. But the examination rooms were straight back, behind the reception desk. "Aren't we going into one of the rooms?"

"No, the doctor would like to meet with you in his office. Right in here."

She stopped before an open door on the left and waited for Allie to enter. The room was small, one whole wall covered with bookshelves and crammed full. A plain wooden desk, not nearly ornate enough for a doctor in Allie's opinion, sat in the center, its surface covered with folders and books and loose papers.

"Have a seat. Dr. Reynolds will be just a minute."

Allie selected one of two chairs in front of the desk and slid into it, Joanie nestled in her arms. Ignoring the alarm klaxons going off in her mind, Allie tried to think of a reason the doctor wouldn't want to examine Joanie in one of the regular rooms. Her gaze scanned the crowded bookshelf. Maybe what Joanie had was so rare that he needed to compare her to a picture in a reference book?

Or maybe . . . Allie swallowed. Maybe he didn't believe there was really anything wrong with her. Maybe the only reason he'd asked them to come in was because Allie had sounded panicky on the phone.

Maybe Eric was right.

"Good morning, Mrs. Harrod." The doctor swept into the room and closed the door behind him. "Thank you for coming on such short notice."

He smiled at her, looking over the top of his glasses as he tossed a folder on the cluttered surface of his desk. His doctor's coat, with *Patrick Reynolds, MD* embroidered over the left breast pocket, was blindingly white, as always.

"Th-thank you for seeing us." Suddenly she wasn't at all sure she wanted to be here.

He held out his hands toward Joanie. "May I?"

Allie transferred the baby to Dr. Reynolds. He held her expertly, one hand supporting her neck and head, the other cupped beneath her diaper. Her feet, covered by the drawstring gown she wore, rested on his chest. "Good morning, little Miss Harrod." He spoke in a soft voice, one Allie had noticed he reserved for babies and not their mothers. Wide eyed, Joanie stared at the face hovering above hers.

"Do you see those marks?" Allie asked. "All around her nose."

He leaned against the edge of the desk and turned Joanie slightly in his hands, examining her face from all angles. Then he smiled down at her, and tucked her into the crook of his arm before facing Allie.

"Mrs. Harrod, there is nothing wrong with this baby."

"But those marks —"

"Are scratches. It is not uncommon for infants to scratch themselves. It happens all

88

the time. They try to get their fingers into their mouths and they miss. In your daughter's case, it probably didn't even hurt her or you would have heard her cry. Do you own a set of baby nail clippers?"

Allie gulped. Heat crept up her neck. "Yes, but I thought . . ." She stopped. She couldn't go into what she thought. It sounded too stupid.

Dr. Reynolds' smile was kind. "If you're nervous about using them, you might consider infant mittens."

Allie couldn't meet his gaze. "Are you sure? What if you're wrong?"

Standing upright, he handed Joanie back to Allie and then circled the desk to sit in his chair. He picked up the folder he'd tossed down, opened it, and flipped through the pages inside. "Your baby is just under six weeks old, and you've had her in this office three times in addition to her two-week checkup. Once for spitting up. Once for loose stools. And once because you thought her sternum protruded abnormally."

Allie touched the bump in the middle of Joanie's chest and mumbled, "It looked weird to me."

"In addition," the doctor continued, "you've called the office five times with a variety of complaints including peeling skin, irregular breathing, thinning hair, crying, and a case of gas at two in the morning."

Tears prickled Allie's eyes. Hearing them in a list like that made her sound like some sort of maniac. She really had been sorry about the middle-of-the-night emergency call. "How was I to know eating French onion soup would give her gas? I've never nursed a baby before."

"I know, Mrs. Harrod." The tenderness in his voice made Allie risk an upward glance. His gentle smile brought the tears forth. "I don't mind you calling whenever you have a question. That's what we're here for. I'm not chastising you. The reason I wanted to talk with you this morning is for your own peace of mind."

She sniffled. "What do you mean?"

"I want to assure you that your baby is completely healthy. I've examined her multiple times, and I promise you there is nothing wrong with her. I rarely make predictions, but I'll make an exception in this case. Barring unforeseen accidents, I predict that Joan Leigh Harrod will outlive both of us by decades."

Waves of relief washed over Allie as the doctor's words sank in. She drew in a deep breath and smiled down at her beautiful, *healthy* daughter.

Then she looked up and included Dr. Reynolds in her smile. "Thank you. I feel much better."

He placed both hands on the desk and stood. "I'm glad. Now go home and enjoy your baby. And trim her nails."

"I will," Allie promised as she got to her feet.

The doctor opened the office door as she scooped up the diaper bag and her purse, and patted her shoulder as she left. "I meant what I said about calling if you have a question. If you're really worried, don't hesitate."

"Okay." She avoided the nurse's eyes as she made her way down the hallway.

Out in the parking lot, she laid Joanie in her car seat and snapped the shoulder straps in place. Deep blue eyes stared up at her, bringing a smile to Allie's lips. She traced a finger lightly over the scratches, which didn't look so bad now.

"When we get home," she told her daughter, "you're getting a manicure. And we don't have to tell Daddy about this visit to Dr. Reynolds, do we? It'll be a secret, just between us girls."

7

"Tori's here!"

Allie leaped off the sofa where she'd been watching the driveway through the window and ran to the front door of Gram's house. She still thought of it as Gram's house, even though her grandmother didn't live there anymore. Instead, Gram lived in an assisted living center on the other side of town, a snazzy place as fancy as a country club. Joan and Mom still lived here, in the house where Allie had spent her teenage years. A good thing, since Allie couldn't imagine a family celebration anywhere else.

Mom came out of the kitchen, an eager expression on her thin face as she wiped her hands on a dishtowel. "I'm so glad she made it. She's been working long hours lately. I was worried she wouldn't get out of the office on time tonight."

Allie shook her head. "She wouldn't miss my birthday dinner."

The door flew open, and Allie's baby sister burst into the house. She stopped just inside the threshold, threw her arms wide, and struck a pose. "Here I am! The party can start now."

Mom took a step toward her youngest daughter, but Allie jumped in front of her with a playful grin. "What do you mean, the party can start now? I'm the birthday girl, you know. Tonight, it's all about *me!*" Their childhood competition to be the center of attention had become a long-standing family joke.

Tori tilted her bright blonde head back and her playful laughter filled the room. "You know I'm just kidding, Allie Gator. Happy birthday!"

She threw her arms around Allie, and Allie hugged her baby sister for all she was worth. Petite Tori's short hair, artistically moussed to look mussed up in a sexy, little-girl way, tickled Allie's nose. The subtle woodsy scent of what was probably an outrageously priced perfume lingered in the air when Tori left her embrace and stepped into their mother's.

"It's always good to see my baby." Mom's eyes behind her brown-rimmed glasses danced with pleasure as she hugged her youngest. "You make every gathering special when you come home."

Allie agreed with Mom's sentiment. Since Tori moved to Lexington, every homecoming seemed like a party. Allie and Joan had both settled in their hometown, so they saw each other all the time. But when their lively younger sibling came home, it was the three Sanderson sisters, together again. Sort of like the Three Musketeers. Or maybe Huey, Dewey, and Louie.

"Speaking of babies, where's my namesake?" Tori peered into the living room, her face lighting when she spotted Joan in the recliner holding Joanie. She swept in that direction, tossing her handbag to the floor, and stood in front of Joan with her arms outstretched. "Give her up. It's my turn."

Joan's arms tightened around the infant as she turned a mischievous grin upward. "*Whose* namesake is she?"

"Ours." Tori conceded the point with a quick eye roll. "Your first name, my middle name. But you get to spend quality aunt time with her every day if you want, so tonight I am claiming my rightful share. Hand her over."

"Oh, alright."

Joan transferred Joanie into Tori's arms, and Allie watched her little sister coo into the baby's face.

"Is that Tori?" Gram called from the kitchen.

"It is." Tori moved carefully in that direction, whispering to the baby as she walked.

Allie followed, and Joan rose from the recliner to fall into step beside her. Mom joined them, all the Sanderson women crammed into the small kitchen. Tori, holding the baby close to her chest, leaned forward to kiss Gram's wrinkled cheek. Tori always looked professional, like she just stepped off a fashion runway. She'd cinched her belt in to accent her tiny waist, and the form-fitting gray skirt showed off slim hips without an ounce of excess bulk. Though the baby of the family had always been petite, and Allie more curvy — voluptuous, Eric generously called her — she had never felt the slightest hint of jealousy. They were different. All three of them.

Never, that is, until now. At that moment, looking at her little sister's slim figure, Allie felt like a giant blubbery walrus next to a sleek dolphin.

On the counter sat a tray of goodies Gram had prepared to serve after dinner. Allie snatched one and thrust it toward her sister. "Here," she said. "Have a cookie."

Tori didn't even look up. "No thanks. I don't want to spoil my dinner."

"It's chocolate." Allie waved the tempting morsel under Tori's nose. "You won't spoil your dinner. We still have to wait for Eric and Betty."

"Ken's coming too." Joan glanced at her watch. "He should be here any minute."

"Hey, I think she's wet." Tori hefted Joanie up and down in her arms to test the feel of her diaper. Her eyes gleamed as she grinned up at Allie. "Can I change her?"

"Sure. The diaper bag's back in the spare bedroom." Allie tossed the cookie back on the tray as Tori headed down the hallway, her eagerness for diaper duty apparent in her wide smile. Mom followed, and Gram, with the aid of her walker, turned toward the stove to stir a pot.

"It won't work, you know."

Allie peered sideways at Joan. "What won't work?"

A smirk played at the edge of Joan's lips. "Fattening Tori up with cookies won't make you look thinner."

Darn. Joan always could read her like a book. Allie widened her eyes with what she hoped was an innocent expression, and raised her chin. "I don't know what you're talking about."

Joan lifted a shoulder. "Whatever. Listen, if you're worried about fitting back into those size 8 jeans, you should run with me in the mornings. We could bundle Joanie up and take her in that fancy stroller Mom bought. I'll even come to your house a couple times a week, if you want."

Allie didn't meet her sister's eye. She didn't want to admit that the size 8s were so far out of her reach she'd considered donating them to the Salvation Army. She'd be ecstatic to fit into a 10. Twelve was a more reasonable goal. But running? All that jiggling and bouncing? Fine for Joan, who was fit and trim and had always been the most athletic of the three sisters. To Allie, it didn't sound appealing.

"I don't run in public." She tightened her lips. "Not since I hit puberty."

Joan laughed. "They make sports bras, you know. The things work wonders."

"Thanks, but no thanks." Allie gave her sister a smile to show she really did appreciate the offer. "I just need to cut back on the sweets, that's all. Starting tomorrow. *After* my birthday." She pinched off a chunk of chocolate chip cookie, popped it into her mouth, and winked at Joan before she left the kitchen.

"Happy birthday to you! Happy birthday to you! Happy birthday, dear Allllllliiieeeeeeeee.

97

Happy birthday to you!"

Allie giggled at her sisters' awful attempt at harmony. Beneath the table Eric squeezed her left hand while Mom set a chocolate layer cake in front of her. Twenty-eight candles glowed in the darkened room, creating a ring of light that illuminated the faces around her. Joan's boyfriend Ken looked a little bemused at the exuberance of this birthday celebration. This was his first family birthday with the Sandersons, and Allie knew they could be a little overwhelming when they got together. She cast a quick glance at Betty, seated on Eric's left. Her mother-in-law wore a completely blank expression, though she watched everything from the depths of those sad-looking eyes. From what Eric had told her of his childhood, big, loud, noisy family gatherings were completely alien to Betty. What must she think of theirs?

"Make a wish!" Tori said.

Mom stood behind her right shoulder, cake knife in hand. "Hurry, honey, the candles are melting onto the icing."

Allie closed her eyes. She didn't place much stock in birthday wishes, not since her fourteenth, when she wished Mom and Daddy would stop arguing and love each other again. But tradition was tradition, so she needed to pick one.

I wish . . . I wish I'd become the bestselling Varie Cose consultant in Kentucky!

No sense wishing small. Might as well go for the gold. She sucked in air until her lungs burned and then blew out every candle. First try.

"Yay, Allie!" Joan clapped her hands, grinning. "You'll get your wish."

"I hope so," Allie said as Mom flipped on the overhead light. Mom whisked the cake away to the kitchen counter, where she began pulling the candles off.

"I'm sure your wish is going to come true when you open my present." Tori's grin flashed around the table.

"Cake first," Mom said. "Then the presents. Who wants ice cream?"

"Oh!" Gram hopped up from her seat. "Don't forget the cookies. I know Eric will want one."

A dimple creased her wrinkled cheek as Eric nodded. "I can never pass up your chocolate walnut cookies."

"Cake for me," Allie said as Mom placed a full dessert plate in front of her. "And Moose Tracks ice cream, my favorite."

She picked up a fork, then hesitated as it hovered over the plate. How many calories did chocolate cake have? More than iced cinnamon rolls?

Forget it. Birthdays only come once a year.

Brushing away thoughts of caloric intake, she plunged her fork into the fudgy icing and fluffy cake. "Oh, yum. Mom, this is delicious."

Mom patted her shoulder, then looked at Eric's mother. "Betty, would you like ice cream with your cake?"

Betty sat upright as she had all evening, not allowing herself to rest against the back of the chair, her posture so perfect it could almost be called rigid.

Like the queen of England or something. Allie smashed cake crumbs into the tines of her fork, regretting the unkind thought. Betty probably just felt uncomfortable in front of all these people she didn't know.

"It's really good." Allie smiled at her mother-in-law to include her in the family atmosphere.

The corners of Betty's thin lips turned up briefly. "I'm sure it is, but I rarely eat sweets. Don has problems with sugar, you know."

Allie didn't reply. Granted, she had not spent much time around her in-laws, but she remembered Don scarfing down several pieces of cake at their wedding reception. If he had sugar problems, he certainly hadn't seemed concerned back then. Allie wondered if he was taking advantage of his wife's absence to indulge his sweet tooth. Or maybe he was indulging himself in other ways, like leaving his shoes in the living room, or not wiping out the sink after he shaved in the morning. If Allie were in his position, she'd certainly be cutting loose while the Queen Mother was gone.

Allie! Quit being unkind.

She finished her dessert with a final giant bite and pushed the plate back. "Okay, I'm done. Can I open my presents now?"

"Mine first." Tori jumped out of her seat and retrieved a package from the pile in the corner. She flashed a dimple around the table as she set it in front of Allie. "She's going to love it. It's the quintessential Allie present, just perfect for her."

Allie noticed Ken watching Tori, trying to catch her eye with a friendly smile, but Tori ignored him as she had all night. Tori disliked Joan's boyfriend, even though he was a handsome doctor and a really nice guy. Unfortunately, he was also very religious, which, according to Tori, negated all the points on the "pro" side of a relationship with him.

Personally, Allie did consider him a little over the top with the religion thing, but that's what made him and Joan perfect for each other. Eric seemed to like the guy, and that said a lot, because Eric was not big on religious types.

The package was so pretty, so elegant looking with slick white paper and a shiny gold bow. Allie slipped the ribbon off the package and set it aside. Then she turned the box on its end and worked her finger beneath a crease to peel back a piece of tape.

"Oh, come on," Joan said. "Go ahead and rip into it. We know you want to."

Grinning, Allie did just that. The paper tore with a satisfying *shhhhhhhsh,* and she wadded it up in a loose ball before dropping it on the floor beside her. The box was plain, and she quickly jiggled the top off, then peeled back a thin layer of tissue paper inside.

When she caught sight of her gift, she gasped. "Are you kidding me?" Her gaze sought Tori's, and she couldn't help returning the wide grin her sister wore. "You bought me a Kate Spade handbag?"

Tori gave an excited nod as she bent over to lift the bag out of the box. "Don't you just love the ivory and jade, and those front pockets? And look at the 14-karat gold plating on the leather trim. I've been trying to convince myself not to go back and get another one."

Beside Allie, Eric wore a bemused expression. "I don't understand. You already have a purse. Several, in fact."

Allie turned toward him. "This is *Kate Spade*. It's like *the* hottest designer bag out there."

He looked completely unimpressed as he exchanged a glance with Ken, who shrugged. Just wait till they got home and she told him that this bag probably cost about four hundred dollars. They'd see who was impressed then.

"Thank you so much," she said as she squeezed her little sister in a hug. "I love it."

"Okay, mine next," Joan said. "Though I warn you, it's not a Kate Spade handbag."

She rose, selected a small rectangular package from the pile, and handed it to Allie. From the smug grin she wore, Allie suspected she was about to be the butt of a joke.

Sure enough, she peeled back the wrapping to reveal . . .

"A laundry pen." She rolled her eyes upward to catch Joan's gaze. "You got me a laundry pen for my birthday."

"Ah." Joan held up a finger like an orator about to make an announcement. "But it's a Varie Cose laundry pen, far superior to

103

anything you could buy in a store. And twice as expensive, I might add."

Allie couldn't help but chuckle. "Very funny. Just so you know, Tori is way ahead of you in the run for the title of Favorite Sister."

Laughing, Joan picked up a large gift bag and handed it to her. "I'm not even going to try. I'm saving all my campaign tricks for Favorite Aunt. Still, see if this gains me any points."

It was the Varie Cose Salad Slicer, along with several spare blades and the cheese shredder attachment. She grinned at Joan. "Thank you. It's exactly what I wanted. Now I have my first demonstration product. No, two." She picked up the laundry pen and held it aloft. "And while we're talking about Varie Cose, I want you guys to pick a night next week for a party. Just us, so I can practice in front of a friendly audience. You too, Gram."

Seated next to Mom, Gram nodded while she nibbled a cookie. Her blue eyes widened as a thought occurred to her. "Maybe I could bring my friend Myrtle Mattingly with me."

"I have a better idea." Allie hoped her smile was guileless. "You can host another party for Mrs. Mattingly and all the rest of your friends. We'll hold it at your apartment so they don't have to worry about transportation from the center. You could all host parties for your friends, in fact."

She let her glance sweep from Mom to Joan to Tori. Mom nodded, a curl from her wavy blonde hair flying freely beside the rim of her glasses. Joan and Tori both avoided her eyes.

"You *will* host a party for me, won't you, Tori? Joan?"

The two exchanged a glance before they turned brave smiles Allie's way.

"Sure, Allie," Joan said. "What are sisters for?"

Tori nodded.

"Exactly," Allie said. She glanced toward the pile of gifts. "What's next?"

Eric jiggled a foot beneath the table. His anticipation mounted as Allie ripped through one present after another. She was going to love his gift. It was so much more perfect than that ugly purse, though he didn't dare voice his opinion after Allie made such a big deal out of it.

Ken's gift of an ear thermometer was pretty thoughtful, and Allie seemed to appreciate it. Trust the doctor to come up with a medical gift. And Gram, who was actively divesting herself of her possessions since she moved to her assisted living center, had obviously put a lot of thought into her gift before deciding upon a necklace and earring set Allie's grandfather had given her early in their marriage. The skirt and blouse Carla gave her daughter looked nice. Allie even acted graciously when she opened his mother's card and lifted out two twenty-dollar bills.

At last the time came to give her the present he had selected. He reached under his place mat, where he'd slipped the envelope before dinner started.

"This is from me and Joanie," he told her as he laid the envelope on the table in front of her.

Allie's blue-green eyes sparkled, and a dimple creased her cheek. "I'll bet I know what this is." She leaned sideways and brushed a soft kiss on his cheek. "I appreciate it too."

He couldn't stop a smug smile. She *thought* she knew what he'd given her. She had no idea. He'd come up with the perfect gift.

Allie ripped into the envelope and pulled out the card. He'd spent almost an hour selecting just the right one. He wasn't a poetry kind of guy, but the verse on the front was mushy and romantic and told her just how special she was to him. Her smile deepened as she read it.

Then she opened the card. The certificate inside fluttered to the surface of the table. She picked it up, a crease appearing on her forehead as her smile dimmed. She looked up and her gaze searched his face.

"You got me a gym membership?"

"Yeah." Excitement spilled over into his voice. "After what you said last night, I knew this would be perfect. It's a really nice gym, with an Olympic-sized indoor pool and all kinds of equipment. You're going to love it there."

She looked down again, staring at the certificate. Eric felt a growing sense of dismay. This was the part where she was supposed to get excited, jump up from her chair, and shower him with kisses. Why did she look like she was about to cry?

Beside him, Mother broke her near-perfect silence of the evening. "I think that's a very thoughtful gift."

"I . . ." Allie swallowed. She *was* about to cry. Tears sparkled in her eyes. They didn't look like happy tears, either.

She did get quickly out of her chair then, but she didn't turn toward him. Instead she ran from the room. In a moment Eric heard the bathroom door down the hallway slam shut.

What was the matter? What had he done? He looked at Carla, then Joan, hoping someone would explain why Allie was so upset, but neither of them would meet his eye.

At the far end of the table, Tori shook her head, her shiny pink lips pressed tight. "Way to go, Eric."

8

Eric let the heavy dispatch center door slam shut behind him. Molly looked up from behind her desk in the control room, her bright smile freezing on her features when she caught sight of him. He nodded, then headed for the kitchen to stow his leftover fried chicken in the fridge.

"Morning, Kathy," he said as he passed his boss's office.

He didn't stop to chat but went straight to the control room, where he took his time adjusting his monitors and getting his notepad and pen ready for the day. As he went through the familiar daily routine, he let go of the tension in his gut. A knot of resentment remained. He could ignore that here, as long as there was something else to focus on, something he could be successful at. Like dispatching emergency personnel in response to 9-1-1 calls. Much easier than dealing with a difficult wife.

"So how did it go last night?"

Molly's expression was casual, but those dark eyes didn't miss much. He looked at one of the monitors. "It was okay."

"Did Allie like her birthday present?"

Trust Molly to get right to the point. Eric considered how to answer. He didn't really want to talk about it yet, because he still hadn't figured out exactly where he'd gone wrong. He scanned the database and noted which officers had already reported in for the morning, aware that Molly was watching him closely, waiting for an answer.

He shook his head. "Not really."

"What did you end up getting her?"

"A membership to the Danville Athletic Center."

"What?" She rocked forward in her chair. "Did she *ask* for a gym membership?"

He glanced sideways. Molly had all the background on this whole birthday present thing since she'd been listening to him try to work it out for weeks. And she was pretty easy to talk to. Besides, she was a girl. Maybe she could help him understand why Allie was so hurt over what he thought was the perfect gift.

"No. It was supposed to be a surprise. But I think she was expecting me to give her five hundred bucks so she could buy into this makeup sales business." He swiveled the chair sideways so he faced Molly head-on. "I don't get it. She hates it when people give her money as a gift, but apparently this time that's what she wanted."

"Did she tell you that before?"

"Not in so many words, but Wednesday night we did talk about the money and the clothes and her birthday all in the same conversation." He shook his head. "I can't remember exactly what she said. She was upset because none of her clothes fit since the baby was born. I figured she'd appreciate the gym membership as a way of losing some weight."

"Ah." Molly tilted her head back against the headrest. "Eric, you might as well have told her you think she's fat."

Allie's injured expression during the silent car ride home haunted him, and he couldn't meet Molly's gaze. "Yeah, I figured that out. And apparently I made it worse by insulting her in front of her family during her birthday dinner."

Molly winced. "Ouch. At least you made up before you went to bed, right?"

Miserable, Eric shook his head. "I tried, but she wouldn't talk about it. Just kept saying, 'It's okay' and telling me she appreciated how much thought I put into my present." He caught Molly's gaze. "I really did put thought into it. I don't think she's fat, not really."

Molly's eyebrows arched. *"Not really?"*

"Well . . ." Eric hesitated. They were getting close to the heart of the problem here. "She is bigger than before she got pregnant. But she's not fat like —" He inclined his head in the direction of Kathy's office. "I know she's self-conscious about her weight, but she doesn't talk about it, so I don't either. It's not a big deal to me. Allie could never be anything but gorgeous, no matter how much weight she gained."

Emotion flickered in Molly's eyes, and she spoke in a soft voice. "Not all men feel that way, Eric. Does she realize how lucky she is to have you?"

He snorted. "I don't think she feels very lucky right now." Judging by her rigid posture on the far edge of the bed last night, that was a safe assumption.

Radio static filled the room, followed by an officer's voice announcing a ten-thirty-eight, a traffic stop. Eric acknowledged the transmission, and typed a note into the database. When he looked up, Molly had turned back to her monitors.

She watched the flickering letters as she spoke. "Well, there's only one thing for you to do now."

"And that is?"

"Grovel." She grinned sideways at him. "It's the only way."

Eric scowled. "I'm not very good at groveling."

"Sure you are. Tell her exactly what you just told me. You think she's gorgeous, not fat, and then apologize for not realizing the unspoken message you would be sending with the gym thing."

That sounded good. He'd apologized about a hundred times last night, but the hurt still lingered in Allie's eyes. She hadn't really forgiven him. Maybe he could soothe her feelings if he told her how he really felt about her, and especially that he didn't think she was fat. Scratch that. He wouldn't mention the f-word, because that would put her defenses up. He'd just tell her he thought she was more beautiful now than when they first met. That wasn't groveling, it was just communicating, something Allie was always telling him he needed to do more of. He felt better just thinking about it.

"Thanks, Molly." He tapped his pen on his notepad, relieved to have a plan of attack. "You've been a big help."

"You know you can talk to me anytime,

Eric." Molly's tone was soft.

He smiled at her, then pulled his keyboard forward and opened a new window, ready for the next call. Molly was a good friend.

Allie pressed the doorbell button and listened for the chimes to sound inside. She glanced at her watch. One minute before ten. Good. She was on time. Morning sunlight gleamed off a brass plate centered on the door beneath the peephole. The lettering confirmed that she had the right house. *Sally Jo Campbell, Varie Cose Regional Director.*

Weird. Why would someone put her full name and title on the front door? Allie had seen people do that in businesses, but never on their homes.

Of course, Sally Jo worked out of her home. Technically, this was her business.

She shifted the rigid handle of the infant carrier to her left hand and tugged at the hem of her new blouse. Mom had good taste in clothes, and she'd gauged the size perfectly. This style camouflaged the worst of the tummy bulges. Allie's mind zipped from bulges to sit-ups to gyms to Eric.

He thinks I'm fat. Which, of course, I am. She set her teeth and pushed away another wave of melancholy, her fourth or fifth of the morning.

The door whooshed inward, and Sally Jo flashed her toothy smile.

"There you are, honey. You're just in time to grab a cup of coffee before we get started." Her gaze dropped to the infant carrier in Allie's right hand. The wide smile wilted. "Oh. You brought your child."

"I had to. My mom's working so I didn't have anyone to watch her." Allie refused to ask Betty to watch Joanie. She had no desire to get in debt to her mother-in-law. "I hope that's okay."

"I guess so, as long as she's quiet." Sally Jo took a backward step and gestured for Allie to enter. "We've got a regular nursery school going on here today. Darcy brought her baby too."

"Darcy's here?" Allie brightened as she stepped inside. "I didn't know she signed up to sell Varie Cose."

The furnishings in the elegant entry hall, though sparse, were stunning. Allie longed to run a finger over the gleaming surface of a gorgeous hall stand with an etched glass mirror on the wall above it. Was it cherry? Whatever it was made of, it matched an exquisite grandfather clock that stood at the base of a wide staircase. If this was how a Varie Cose regional director could afford to furnish her house, Allie would probably triple her income at the state.

"You have a beautiful home, Sally Jo," she said as she lifted the heavy infant seat in front of her with both hands.

"Thank you. I enjoy it." She waved a manicured finger toward the room on the left. "Go right on in there, and I'll bring you something to drink. Coffee? Tea?"

"Just water, thanks."

She swept down the hallway, and Allie went in the direction Sally Jo indicated. Three women were already seated on the living room sofa, and a fourth in a wing chair that faced it. Allie carried Joanie to the only remaining empty seat, a second wing chair on the far side of a highly polished coffee table, next to the fireplace. From the sofa, Darcy grinned a greeting. Her baby sat in her lap chewing industriously on a teething ring. Drool glistened on his chin and his chubby little fist.

"I was hoping you'd bring your baby," Darcy said as Allie set the carrier on the hardwood floor. She extended her neck, looking over her son's head toward Joanie. "She's so tiny!"

"How old is she?" asked the woman next to her.

"Six weeks tomorrow," Allie replied. "How

old is your baby, Darcy?"

"Almost six months." She picked up the cloth diaper resting across one knee and wiped the child's hand. "Gosh, it's hard to remember him being so little."

"Here you go." Sally Jo entered the room with a glass of ice water in one hand and a coaster in the other. The ice tinkled against the glass as she set them on the table in front of Allie, then took her position center stage at the end of the coffee table. "Do all y'all know each other?"

Allie shook her head, as did several of the other ladies.

"Okay, then let me do the honors. There's Allie, Nicole, Darcy, Kirsten, and Laura." She pointed a lacquered fingernail at each woman in turn. "Welcome to your first Varie Cose meeting, ladies. Let me be the first to congratulate each of you for beginning what I hope will be a highly profitable career. As you can see, it has been for me."

Her gesture encompassed the elegantly furnished room. One thing about her, she wasn't modest. Allie caught Darcy's eye and grinned.

"However," Sally Jo continued, "I want y'all to know that you will get out of this business only what you put into it. It *is* a business. Y'all are businesswomen now."

Kirsten, seated on the sofa next to Darcy, lifted a hand. "How long do you think it will take us to start making money?"

"Honey, that all depends on how hard you're willing to work." Sally Jo rested a hand on her collarbone. "I made back my initial investment with only two demonstrations. But then I took a long-term approach and took out a small business loan to invest in my inventory." Her gaze circled the room. "That's something you might want to consider."

Allie leaned forward to pick up her water glass and didn't meet Sally Jo's eye. A loan? Eric wouldn't go for that. She didn't much like the idea, either. At least, not until she was able to prove that she could make money.

Sally Jo continued. "Today we'll go over the products included in your start-up kit. I'll show you how to demonstrate each of them. We'll talk about how you get bookings and ways to grow your business. Then we'll go over the order process, placing orders and distributing product to your customers. I'll finish by telling you how you'll get paid." That brought a smile to everyone's lips. Sally Jo clapped her hands together. "Okay, did all y'all bring a pen to take notes?"

Allie dug in the bottom of her purse and found a pen as Nicole said, "I have a pencil, but I need something to write on."

"I'll give each of you a pad of paper." Sally Jo flashed her trademark smile. "Trust me. This is the last thing you get for free. Remember, you have to spend money to make money."

Allie set her purse on the floor beside Joanie. She exchanged another glance with Darcy. When the girl rolled her eyes, Allie smothered a grin. As far as she was concerned, five hundred dollars was plenty to spend. The sooner she started making some, the better.

Eric was thinking about heating up his fried chicken when his cell phone rang. He glanced at the Caller ID.

He pushed out of his chair and jerked his gaze toward Molly. "I've been waiting for this call. Can you hold down the fort for a few minutes?"

She nodded. "No problem."

He punched the Talk button while he walked toward the door. Better take this call in private. In the tiny building that housed the Dispatch Center, that meant outside.

"Hey, Dad. I wondered when you'd finally get around to calling me back."

"Yeah, I've been busy. We got a big contract at work last month. I've been putting in overtime trying to make sure we don't fall behind."

Eric closed the door behind him and crossed to his pickup. The light breeze held an October chill, and he wished he'd grabbed his keys so he could sit inside. Instead he leaned against the tailgate and faced the warm sun. "Well, I guess that's good. Keeps you off the streets, huh?"

His father laughed. That was one of his sayings. "That it does." His tone took on a hint of reserve. "How's your mother?"

Eric had called yesterday and left a message on the answering machine, letting Dad know that Mother was safe in Danville. In case he wondered. Though why he hadn't called to talk to her, Eric couldn't imagine.

Yes, he could. The Harrod family wasn't big on talking. Never had been. They operated under the premise that a problem ignored was a problem solved.

"She's fine. Seems lonely, though." A stretch, for sure. Mother had maintained her aloof mask since the moment she arrived. Exactly as she had always done.

"I doubt that." Dad paused. "Has she said when she's planning to come home?"

"No, she hasn't." As far as Eric could tell,

she had not given the matter a single thought. Or if she had, she apparently didn't think it necessary to discuss it with him and Allie.

"Well."

Eric ground the gravel beneath his heel. Dad wasn't making this easy on him. "Actually, I was sort of hoping you could call and ask her yourself. I think she might like that."

"No." Dad's response was quick and firm.

"No? Just like that?" Eric hefted himself off the tailgate and paced toward the edge of the parking lot. Loose rock crunched with each step. "Come on, Dad. She's your wife. Don't you think you should talk to her?"

"What for? She made her point very clear when she left."

Now they were getting somewhere. "What point was that?"

"Said she's tired of being a doormat. Said I didn't *appreciate* her." Dad paused. "I probably didn't," he admitted, "but I thought she was happy. Everything she ever asked for, I gave her. What more does a woman want?"

Eric shoved a cold hand into his pants pocket to protect it from the wind. He didn't know how to answer that question. If he knew how to make a woman happy, Allie wouldn't be upset with him right now.

"I don't know, Dad," he said. "I wish I did."

"Huh."

Dad's grunt held a note of understanding, and Eric felt a sudden affinity. They were both pretty clueless when it came to women. Must be a trait shared by the men in his family.

Regardless, Dad couldn't sit on his duff in Detroit and do nothing about his wife. "What if she doesn't come home? I've gotta tell you, Dad, when she got here the other night, she didn't sound like she was just coming for a visit. Don't you think you ought to call her and find out if she's considering making this, uh, arrangement permanent?"

"She'll come home eventually. Where else would she go?" He paused. "Unless you're planning on letting her move in with you."

Eric ignored the hint of accusation he heard in his father's voice. "Listen, you know Allie and I love having Mother visit." An acceptable lie. "But she can't stay with us forever. Our house isn't that big. Things can get a little strained, if you know what I mean."

"That's women for you." Dad sounded relieved, like he'd been worried Eric might let Mother live there permanently. "Females can't live together. It goes against their nature to have to share their space with another woman. Like she's a rival or something. Men aren't like that."

Eric wasn't going there. "Anyway, I think you should call Mother and ask about her plans. I mean, surely you two have to talk about finances and stuff like that."

He scuffed a foot across a strand of crabgrass that had inched its way over the parking lot. He had no idea about the financial arrangement between his parents. As a kid he couldn't remember ever hearing them discuss the matter, and since he grew up, there had been no reason to ask.

"I have a better idea. She's right there in your house. Why don't you ask her how long she's planning to stay? While you're at it, you can ask her something for me."

Stubborn old man. No wonder Mother left him. Eric struggled to keep the frustration out of his tone. "What's that, Dad?"

"Ask her where she hid the remote control. It's driving me crazy having to get out of my chair to change the channel."

9

Allie gave the heavy box one final shove and scooted it across the threshold. She closed the front door and leaned against it, winded.

"Can I help with anything?" Betty stood in the kitchen doorway, her hands clasped and her face its usual solemn mask.

Allie shook her head. "Not unless you know how to put a set of shelves together."

"I never have, but I doubt it's that hard. I daresay we could figure it out between the two of us."

Allie stared at her mother-in-law. Unless she misunderstood, Betty just offered to help her with a project. Was that the first sign of a thaw from the Ice Queen, perhaps?

"Thanks, Betty. Actually, I thought Eric could do it when he gets home. He put all the baby furniture together, so he has practice reading instructions that look like they're written in a foreign language."

Wordless, Betty gave a single nod and

started to turn away.

"Uh . . ." Allie hated to let the moment pass. "Supper sure smells good. What are we having?"

"Baked chicken breasts. I saw the recipe in a low-calorie cooking magazine, so while you were out I went to the grocery store and got the ingredients." She gave a little sniff. "Much less fattening than fried chicken."

She disappeared into the kitchen, leaving Allie to grind her teeth alone. So much for the thaw. Betty had just managed to insult Allie for her weight and Gram for her cooking in a single comment. Two with one blow.

The handle on the front door turned, and Allie stepped aside to let Eric come in. She managed a quick smile of greeting in his direction. Last night's scene at her birthday dinner was still raw, and she had been waffling between misery and anger all day. The combination left her wretched and unable to meet Eric's gaze.

"What's all this?" His gesture included the box and several full bags she had dropped in a corner.

"Business supplies." She picked up the canvas bag that held the smaller of the products from her demo kit and pulled out a bottle of cleaning spray. "This stuff is guaranteed to eliminate household stains, including hard water stains in the toilet, or you get your money back in full. It's amazing. Sally Jo showed us how to demo it today."

"Do you take an actual stained toilet with you for the demo?" He glanced around the room, as though looking for one.

The sight of the corners of his mouth inching upward lifted Allie's mood. She slapped him playfully on the arm. "No, we invade the hostess' bathroom and clean hers right before her eyes." She bent down and scooped a package out of one of the Wal-Mart bags. "Which is why we need these."

He made as though to reach for the package of rubber gloves, but instead caught her around the waist and pulled her to him. "I love you, Allie."

A burden lifted at the sound of his whispered words. Allie dropped the gloves and slipped her arms around him. Eyes closed, she buried her face in his neck. "I love you too." This was the way life should be, her and Eric together instead of snapping at one another. Tears made her nose itchy, and she sniffled. "I'm sorry I acted like an idiot last night. I know you were just trying to give me something I needed."

"No." His hands grasped her shoulders

and he pushed her gently back. His gaze held hers. "You don't *need* the gym. I thought I was being helpful, giving you something you wanted. I don't care if you lose weight or not." His hands slid up her neck to cup her face. "I think you're beautiful just the way you are."

As Allie searched his face, warmth seeped throughout her insides. Eric was telling the truth. He really didn't care if she was fat. He really thought she was beautiful.

She leaned forward and planted a kiss on his lips that almost threw them both off balance. Was she the luckiest girl in the world, or what?

"Ahem."

At the sound of Betty clearing her throat, Allie pulled back and would have stepped away, but Eric refused to let go of her. He locked his hands around her waist and whispered in her ear, "Story of my life lately."

Betty's eyebrows arched. "Dinner will be ready in ten minutes."

"Thanks, Mother." Eric lifted his nose and inhaled. "Smells wonderful."

Grinning, Allie gently pushed him away with a hand on his chest. "Help me get these bags into our bedroom. After dinner, I have a project for you." She kicked at the long box.

Eric flashed a wry grin. "I can see that. But first, let me say hello to my second-best girl."

While Eric bent over Joanie's infant seat on the sofa, Allie looped her fingers through several bags and headed for the bedroom. He followed her a minute later, Joanie tucked in one arm and the rest of the bags dangling from the other. He dropped them beside hers on the bed.

Allie stood with her hands on her hips, surveying the front wall. "If we move that desk over, the shelves I bought today will fit right in the corner. I think the computer power cord will still reach the outlet. What do you think?"

Eric's lips pursed. "It'll be tight. Why do you need shelves, anyway?"

"To store my inventory. Most of the time I'll place orders with the company through the Internet, but Sally Jo says some products sell at every party and customers appreciate it when you have them already on hand. Which reminds me." She gave him a sideways flinch. "I dropped by the bank and got a credit card today. Just for business purchases. That way I can keep everything separate from our personal expenses."

An anxious breath caught in her lungs.

She'd expected him to react negatively to that, since they had agreed early in their marriage not to succumb to the temptation to build up a large credit card debt. He merely lifted a shoulder.

"Makes sense. Just be sure you pay it off every month, or you'll end up spending all your profit on finance charges."

"I will." She let out a relieved sigh.

He cocked his head and looked at the desk. "It's going to be crowded in here."

"You're right." Allie cast a withering glance in the direction of the kitchen. "But I can't set up my office in the guest room."

"Oh, that reminds me." Eric lowered his voice. "I talked to Dad today."

Allie listened to Eric recount his conversation with his father. "A doormat, huh?"

Eric nodded.

She glanced toward the open door and spoke in a whisper. "Your mother sure seems to like cooking and cleaning and all that. If she's as quiet at home as she is here, I can kind of see why your father would be surprised that she suddenly up and left."

"Yeah, but apparently he isn't going to do anything about it." Joanie wiggled in Eric's arms. He grabbed a waving fist and smiled down at his daughter.

Allie folded her arms across her chest.

"She can't live here, Eric."

"I know." He looked up and whispered, "What do you want me to do? Tell her she has to leave, go to a hotel or something? I will, if that's what you want."

Allie studied his earnest expression. He would do it. He would tell his own mother she had to go to a hotel. And he'd probably take the blame for the move himself, because Eric was too much a gentleman to blame anything on his wife.

She sighed. "I guess we can make it work for a little while. But it's definitely a temporary situation."

The relief on his face made her feel guilty for nagging. She really was lucky to have Eric. If he had a fault at all, it was that he didn't communicate enough. It took a major blowup like last night to open him up. Apparently his father didn't talk much, either. Neither had Allie's own father. Thank goodness it was the only thing Eric had in common with Daddy.

Betty appeared in the doorway and spoke in her quiet voice. "Dinner is on the table." She turned away without waiting for an answer.

"Thanks, Mother," Eric called after her.

Allie grinned as she fell in step beside him. "You know, having someone cook all our meals is one thing I could get used to."

"Mom, please?" Allie shifted the telephone to her right ear and added a note of shameless begging into her tone. "It's just for a couple of hours until Eric gets off work."

Genuine regret sounded in Mom's voice. "You know I'd love to babysit my granddaughter, but I can't leave the hospital."

"Mondays are supposed to be your day off!" Allie wasn't above whining if that's what it took to convince Mom.

"They usually are. I had to switch shifts with someone in order to host your party tomorrow night."

Allie leaned against the back of the desk chair and directed a sullen glare toward her computer monitor. Mom was doing her a favor by hosting her very first party as a Varie Cose consultant.

"You're right," she said. "I'm sorry. I'll figure something out."

"Why don't you ask Betty to watch Joanie?" Mom asked.

"Because Betty hardly ever holds her or anything. She was here with us all weekend, and I think she only picked Joanie up twice. She never offered to change her. Whenever you or Joan or Tori are here, you can't put her down."

"Allie, Betty isn't like us. She's quiet and probably very shy. Maybe you should make it a point to ask for her help instead of waiting for her to volunteer."

Allie tapped a finger against the phone. "Yeah, maybe you're right."

"I've got to go, honey. Good luck. I'll talk to you later."

The phone clicked in Allie's ear. She replaced the receiver in the cradle on the edge of her desk and stared at it as she considered her options. Maybe she could call Joan . . . No. Joan wouldn't be able to leave the furniture store she managed on a couple hours' notice. And Tori had an important job as a marketing analyst in Lexington, so that was out of the question. Gram? Allie shook her head. Gram would probably love the opportunity, but she was in her mid-eighties and hadn't fully recovered from breaking her hip a few weeks before Joanie was born. She still relied on a walker for longer journeys, like the one from her apartment down the hall to the center's dining room.

She shot a glance toward the baby monitor on the nightstand. Maybe she should take Joanie with her. The memory of Sally Jo's expression during Thursday's meeting when both Joanie and Darcy's son started crying leaped into focus. Sally Jo had specifically said that babies shouldn't come to today's makeup demo. Still, if Allie had no choice . . .

She did have a choice, albeit an unpleasant one. With a sigh, she heaved herself up from her chair.

"Betty?" Allie stepped into the kitchen. The older woman sat at the table, flipping through the pages of a magazine.

Betty looked up. That woman held the record for blank expressions. Her face didn't give away a single hint at any thoughts that might have been rattling around in her brain.

Allie slipped into an empty chair. "I've got to go to a meeting at three o'clock today. I thought my mom would be able to watch Joanie, but she had to work. I wondered if you'd mind."

A spark of interest flared into Betty's brown eyes, though she maintained her stoic silence.

Allie went on. "It'll only be for a couple of hours, just until Eric gets home. She shouldn't be any problem. I'm sure you can handle her."

"Of course I can handle her." Betty closed the pages of the magazine. "A child that age just needs to be fed and kept dry. I noticed some bottles of milk in the freezer, and though it has been a long time since I've changed a diaper, I think I still remember how."

"So you'll do it?"

Betty inclined her forehead. "Of course."

Relief flooded Allie. "Thank you. I really appreciate it. I'll have my cell phone on the whole time, so if you need to call me, you can."

Her lips formed that slight smile. "We'll manage."

Allie got up from the table and pushed her chair in, while Betty watched in her cool, detached manner. "Okay. Well, I really appreciate it."

As she turned, Betty asked, "Will you be home in time for dinner? I'm making a low-fat pasta dish."

Another low-fat dish. Allie forced a smile. "I should be home by five thirty."

She left the room and headed to the nursery to check on the baby, not sure whether she should be relieved or irritated.

"Okay, y'all, now we'll apply the final layer — the powder." Sally Jo picked up a cotton ball. "Watch me."

Allie dipped a cotton ball in the powdery pile on the thin foam tray in front of her.

Colorful blobs of makeup and concealer filled the tray's slots so it resembled one of those watercolor paint trays Allie used to have in grade school. She held the face-sized mirror in one hand and, matching Sally Jo's technique, brushed the powder over her skin with an upward sweeping motion. Seated beside her at the table in Sally Jo's spotless kitchen, Darcy stared into her own mirror and dabbed at her nose.

"There. Now for the finishing touch." Sally Jo picked up a clear plastic box and started at one end of the table. "Let's see, Kirsten, I think this color suits you." She set a small lip pencil in front of the brunette and moved to the next seat. "Nicole, you get Chocolate. Perfect for you. Laura, your skin tone cries out for Pearly Peach, and Dusty Gold for Darcy. And for Allie . . ." Allie held her chin high as Sally Jo studied her through narrowed eyes. "Definitely a bright pink. Let's try Candy Coral."

Allie took the lip pencil from Sally Jo's fingers and looked at it. Pretty bright. As a rule, she didn't wear lipstick, just a shimmery gloss that Eric preferred because he said it made her lips kissable. But she couldn't very well sell the stuff if she wouldn't at least try it, could she?

"Now, I want you to start at the top and

draw a V." Sally Jo demonstrated with a finger in front of her own mouth. "Then carefully outline your top lip, working from the center out. On the bottom you're going to do the opposite and move from the edges in. When your whole mouth is outlined, fill it in."

Allie pulled the mirror close so she could get a better look at her lips. She followed the outline carefully, then surveyed the result. "I think my lips are lopsided."

Darcy laughed, but Sally Jo said, "Most people's aren't symmetrical." She returned to stand beside Allie. "Let me see."

Allie lowered the mirror and swiveled sideways in the chair, then tilted her face upward for Sally Jo's inspection.

Her brows drew together. "Oh yes, I see what you mean. Here, let me work on you."

She held out a hand. Allie, feeling slightly offended that she had to be "worked on," put the lip pencil in her palm. Sally Jo's strokes were firmer than hers. Allie felt as though her lips were being pushed all over her face.

"The good thing about lip pencils," Sally Jo said as she worked, "is they can correct any mistakes Mother Nature made. They can make a big mouth small, or thin lips wide and sexy. They can even fix irregularly shaped lips. There." She tossed the pencil on the table and straightened. "Take a look."

Allie picked up the mirror and tilted it to examine her mouth. Did she have thin lips, or lopsided ones? Judging by the amount of color Sally Jo had drawn outside her lip line, apparently both.

"It's really, uh, bright." Those lips didn't even look like hers.

"Trust me," Sally Jo said, "you've got the coloring to pull it off. That shade is perfect for you."

"How do you know that?" Laura looked up from her own mirror. "You picked different colors for each of us. How'd you know which ones to try?"

"Practice." Sally Jo put a hand on her hip and smiled. "And the color charts included in your skin care start-up kit help a lot. They have all kinds of pictures of women with different coloring. After a while, you just sort of know what will look good on someone."

Allie studied her reflection in the small mirror, moving it around so she could see all the parts. One eye looked pretty good, but the accent color on the outside lid of the other one looked a bit off-center. The concealer she'd layered on brightened a couple of dark smudges she had not realized were there until Sally Jo pointed them out. She held the mirror at arms' length, trying to see her whole face at once.

Sally Jo stepped to the sink and pulled a trashcan from the cabinet beneath. She returned to the table and picked up Kirsten's tray. "Why don't you girls run into the bathroom and take a look in better lighting."

Allie trooped down a hallway behind the others and into a bathroom. Laura flipped on the vanity lights, and the five women squeezed close together in front of the sink, examining their reflection.

"Wow," said Laura. "That's a pretty dramatic change."

Kirsten nodded. "It sure is."

"She did a good job picking out eye shadow for each of us." Nicole tilted her head sideways. "I'm not sure about the lip color, though. Do you think mine is too dark?"

Allie stared at her reflection. A stranger stared back. "That," she said, "is a lot of makeup."

Laura nodded. "Way more than I usually wear. Maybe this is evening makeup. You know, they say you're supposed to wear more at night because of the lighting."

"Sally Jo always wears a lot." Kirsten

shrugged. "It looks natural on her. If we were wearing professional clothes instead of jeans and sweats, it would probably look better. Maybe we just have to get used to it."

"I guess so." Nicole's tone was uncertain. "If we're going to sell the stuff, I guess our faces are sort of like an advertisement."

"I really like that moisturizer." Kirsten's fingers brushed at her cheek. "My skin feels so soft under the makeup."

Allie leaned forward to get a better look at that right eyelid. Definitely not even with the other one. But it was kind of amazing how the placement of a darker shade gave her eyes a totally different look. And her lips! She puckered. She could get used to having wide, sexy lips.

She glanced at Darcy, who was staring at the reflection with a look of growing horror.

"What's the matter, Darcy?" Allie asked. "Don't you like the way you look?"

"It's not that. It's just . . ." Darcy's gaze swept down the line in the mirror from Nicole to Allie. "We look like clones. Sally Jo made us over in the Varie Cose image, like Gregory Peck in that movie *The Boys from Brazil.* We're the Cose Clones!"

On the drive home Allie kept leaning to the

side so she could peek at her reflection. The more she saw it, the more she decided she liked the new look. She needed a different image if she was going to make a go as a Varie Cose consultant. The old Allie was okay for a social worker. Allie the successful businesswoman needed to project a totally different image. This makeover was definitely a step in the right direction.

She had everything she needed to make a bundle selling Varie Cose's most popular line of products. Her new makeup start-up kit — correction, *skin care* start-up kit — rested on the seat beside her. All three hundred dollars' worth of it.

Allie winced. The bank said her credit card should arrive within a week. She hoped it didn't take too long. The check she'd just written had taken her account balance dangerously close to zero. Hopefully she'd sell a lot of stuff at Mom's party tomorrow night and could get some money back in the bank before Eric noticed. Besides, she had to have a variety of colors to demonstrate. As Sally Jo said, how could she expect people to buy makeup without trying it first?

A glance at her watch as she hurried from the car to her front porch gave her a shock of surprise. Time had gotten away from her. A flash of guilt shot through her. She had been away from Joanie for almost three hours, and she'd been so busy she hadn't had a chance to worry. Her arm brushed her breast as she reached for the front door, and she winced. Her body was not her own these days. She hoped Joanie was hungry.

"I'm home," she called as she pushed the door open.

The delicious odors of oregano and lemon struck her at the same moment the sound from the television assaulted her ears.

Eric sat on the sofa, his eyes glued to the screen. "Hey, honey," he said without looking up. "Did you have a good time?"

A crowd roared, and Allie glanced at the box. Football, of course. It had claimed Eric's attention all day yesterday too. She wondered if there was a support group for football widows somewhere in Danville.

"Yes, I did." She set the bag containing her skin care samples in a corner. "Where's Joanie?"

"Mother's changing her. She did just fi—"

His words trailed off as his jaw dropped. He stared at her, his eyes going round. "Did you get mugged by a band of renegade clowns on the way home?"

Allie put a self-conscious hand to her cheek. "You don't like it?"

Eric hesitated before responding, staring at her face with as much intensity as he had the television screen a moment before. "Well, it's different."

"Makeup is a top seller." She tried to ignore the hurt that pricked her feelings at his hesitant tone. "My face is my best advertisement."

He continued to stare at her with a sort of horrified fascination. "Couldn't you just rent a billboard instead?"

Allie thrust her nose into the air. "Thanks for the support, Eric."

She stomped between him and the television, heading for the nursery, but he jumped up to step in front of her.

"Aw, I'm just giving you a hard time. Don't be so defensive." He pulled her into a hug.

She sniffled. "I guess I'm just a little self-conscious. I want to be successful, you know?"

"You will be." He dipped his head toward hers, then stopped, his brow furrowed. "I'd kiss you, but I'm not sure where to find your lips in all that stuff."

Allie planted a big Candy Coral kiss on his cheek. "There. Now we're both wearing the same shade."

"Gee, thanks." He fingered the lip marks.

Allie gave him a playful whack on the shoulder. "Go back to your football while I go feed our daughter."

Eric returned to the sofa. "Mother just finished feeding her."

"Oh." Allie halted her progress toward the nursery, a wave of dismay washing over her. She'd missed Joanie's dinner.

"She did fine." Eric's tone was distant, his attention already more on the television set than on her. "Ate like a little piggie, as usual."

My baby didn't even miss me. "She took the bottle okay?"

He didn't answer or look away from his game.

"Eric!"

"Huh?" He glanced up at her, his expression blank. "Oh. Yeah, she took it great." He picked up the remote and punched the volume up in a not-so-subtle hint.

Her feelings smarting for the second time in as many minutes, Allie headed for the kitchen to get the breast pump.

10

"We all know accidents happen." Allie stood in front of the fireplace facing her first set of potential customers, her hands clutching her next demo item behind her back. "When you're all dressed up for a hot date and sitting across the table from a handsome man, the last thing you want to be thinking about is the stain on your skirt where you dropped that meatball. Varie Cose knows that, which is why we developed . . ." She let her smile sweep the room before whipping the item from behind. ". . . the laundry pen!"

To her right, Joan let out an audible groan. Allie cast a glare in her sister's direction, but Joan's attention was suddenly absorbed in playing with her little namesake.

Allie refixed her smile and picked up her demonstration cloth. "I know you've seen these in the grocery store, but the Varie Cose laundry pen contains a concentrated liquid portion of our patented laundry soap, so it really does work better than the commercial variety. Let me show you."

The eight women scattered in various seats around Mom's living room watched as Allie picked up a bottle of mustard and smeared two stains on the white cloth. She held it aloft for the women to see, trying to remember to make eye contact with each one. Mrs. Peterson returned her smile and nodded absently, while Mrs. Faber avoided her gaze by sipping from her glass. Mrs. Vaughn's brow creased with concern at the sight of the yellow stains.

Allie set a foam blotter on the coffee table, in plain sight of them all, and spread the white cloth across the top. Rose Mattingly leaned forward on the sofa for a better look as Allie uncapped the laundry pen and brushed gently at one of the stains, as she'd been taught to do by Sally Jo. The yellow mark faded visibly upon contact, and as she brushed, vanished completely.

Mrs. Vaughn drew a startled breath. "That's amazing."

Allie turned a smug smile in her direction. "It really is. We have the special patented formula in another form as well." She rummaged in her bag and pulled out a box, then held it aloft for them to see.

"Individually packaged wipes for larger stains."

She extracted a small package, ripped it open, and dispatched the second stain as quickly as the first.

"I could use some of those things." Mrs. Peterson brushed a crumb away from her ample bosom. "I have a shelf here that catches everything. Lonnie always says he can tell what I ate by looking at my —" A blush stained her cheeks and she busied herself with a close examination of Allie's now-clean white cloth.

"These items work on all stains and most fabrics," Allie said, "but be sure to try them out in an inconspicuous spot on delicates first."

In the recliner, Joan leaned forward and placed Joanie on her legs. "Do they work on spit-up?" she asked dryly, pointing at her shoulder.

"Definitely." Allie handed her the towelette she'd just used, and everyone watched as Joan dispatched a white splotch on her blouse.

"What did you say that item number was?" asked Mrs. Vaughn.

"Three seventy-two." Allie tried not to smile as three women wrote the number on their order form. Cha-ching! She walked back to the fireplace, dropped the box of towelettes into her bag and turned a wide Sally Jo smile on her guests. "Those are all the products I have to demonstrate tonight, but I encourage you to look through the catalog."

"Can I take it home with me?" asked Mrs. Peterson.

"Sure." Allie kept her smile fixed in place. Those catalogs cost three dollars apiece, but of course she couldn't say no. She just hoped they didn't end up on the floor of someone's car. "My number is on the back if you decide later you'd like to order something else. I've set out an assortment of makeup samples on the kitchen table. We don't have time to do full makeovers tonight, but trust me when I say Varie Cose's skin care products are the best you can buy. And their colors are terrific. Feel free to try them, and if anyone would like to host a makeover demonstration, just let me know. You can earn some very nice hostess gifts. Plus, I offer a 20 percent discount on everything a hostess purchases the night of her party."

Mom stood. "Let's all go into the kitchen and have some refreshments while we fill out our order forms."

Mom winked at Allie as she followed her

guests into the kitchen. Joan remained seated, speaking in a low voice to Joanie, who lay lengthwise on her legs.

"I think that went well," Allie whispered. "Don't you?"

Joan nodded. "You're a natural." She locked gazes with Allie. "But as your sister I feel the need to tell you that you've gone a little overboard on the makeup."

Allie gave her an injured look. "I want everyone to see the products I'm selling."

Joan snorted. "Less is more, I always say. These women don't wear tons of makeup. In case you haven't noticed, some of them aren't wearing any. They might buy a lipstick if it looks natural, but they're not going to paint half their faces Pumpkin Orange."

Allie sniffed. "It's Candy Coral. Sally Jo says this shade is perfect for my coloring."

"Whatever. I'll bet you ten bucks you don't sell a single lipstick tonight."

"You're on."

Joan put a finger in Joanie's waving hand and smiled down at her niece. Then she turned the smile up to Allie. "Don't mind me. I'm just butting my nose in to give you some inexpert and unasked-for advice. That's what sisters are for."

Since Allie had given Joan a fair amount of unasked-for advice over the years, she

148

didn't answer. Instead, she headed for the kitchen. She was going to sell a lipstick tonight if it killed her.

"Three hundred eighty-seven dollars!" Allie could barely contain her glee as she totaled up the order forms after the door closed behind the last guest. She grinned across the kitchen table at Mom. "And three of your friends booked parties of their own."

"Not bad." Mom, balancing a sleeping Joanie in her left arm, slid the stack of order forms across the table with her right hand and glanced at them through her brown-rimmed glasses. "Oh, look. Rose bought the vacuum food sealer. That bumped your total up quite a bit. Odd that you didn't sell any makeup, though."

"Except to my wonderful sister." Allie threw an arm around Joan, who was seated beside her, and hugged. "She bought a lip-stick."

"Yeah," Joan's lips twisted into a disgusted smirk as she tucked a lock of straight brown hair behind her ear. "I'm a sucker. I just torpedoed my own bet and paid fourteen dollars for something that would have cost me six-fifty in the store."

"But Varie Cose's quality is much better," Allie told her. "And it's guaranteed. If you

149

want to return that lipstick for any reason at all, you can."

"Yeah, yeah." Joan heaved an exaggerated sigh and then grinned at Allie. "You did a good job. At your very first party, you've almost made back all the money you paid."

"Well, not exactly." Allie shuffled the stack of carbonless order form copies and slipped them into the accordion folder she'd bought at Wal-Mart. "Only half of the total comes to me. Even less of Mom's order, since she gets the hostess discount. Plus I have to pay for her hostess gift, the *lovely assortment of Varie Cose kitchen utensils in an attractive, unbreakable container.*" She flashed a Sally Jo smile toward Mom.

"You don't have to give me those," Mom said.

"Of course I do! You were my first hostess, and I want to follow all the rules. Besides, Sally Jo says it's a tax-deductible expense."

Allie didn't see any reason to mention the other expenses she'd incurred, like the shelves and skin care demo kit and catalogs and plastic bags with the Varie Cose logo on them and order pads and . . . she could give herself a headache just thinking about it.

"Hey, I thought of something I want to

run by you." Joan turned in her chair to look at Allie, an arm resting on the table. "You could donate some Varie Cose stuff to the auction."

Allie stared, mind blank. "Auction?"

An irritated blast escaped Joan's throat. "The dinner and auction my church group is conducting to raise money for our mission trip to Mexico. I've been talking about it for weeks."

"Oh, yeah." Allie avoided her sister's eyes while she stored the makeup sample pouches into their compartmentalized plastic box. She was a brand-new business-woman and not really financially stable enough to be giving away a bunch of product. But sisters should support each other. "What kind of stuff?"

Joan lifted her shoulders. "Whatever you want. It's a charitable contribution, so it's tax deductible. Plus it would be a good advertisement. I'm one of the auctioneers. I'll make sure to talk you up a bunch when your stuff goes up for bid."

Allie tilted her head as she considered. That sounded like a good investment, actually. Joan's church had been working really hard to publicize this dinner and auction event, so it was likely to draw a large crowd. "Okay, let me see what I can put together."

Joan sat back with a pleased smile. "Thanks."

Allie scooped up the ballpoint pens scattered across the table and dropped them in the file with the forms. "It's getting late. I need to get the baby home and in bed."

"When's your next party?"

"Thursday at Gram's apartment, and Tori's on Friday. Tomorrow night I'm going with Darcy to help with her first party. She was supposed to come tonight to help me, but she couldn't find a sitter."

"Which reminds me." Mom's expression was tender as she looked down into her granddaughter's face. "Though you know I love any and every opportunity to see Joanie, I'd recommend not taking her with you from now on."

Allie looked at her beautiful sleeping daughter. "She did kind of steal the limelight, didn't she?"

Beside her, Joan laughed. "That, and it sort of spoiled the effect of trying to demonstrate your water purifier with a nursing kid hanging off your —"

"I get the point." Allie cleared her throat. "You're probably right. Mom, do you want to babysit tomorrow night?"

Mom shook her head. "I have to work a double shift at the hospital."

She looked at Joan, who shook her head. "Wednesday night Bible study."

Allie shrugged. "She'll get some time with Daddy and Grandmother, then." She stowed her things into her big consultant bag with the Varie Cose logo emblazoned on the side and stood. "Thanks again for doing this, Mom. I really, really, really appreciate it."

Mom stood and came around the table to place a kiss on Allie's cheek. "I was glad to do it. That's what family's for."

11

Allie studied the face turned up toward hers. She'd stayed up late last night studying the color charts included in her skin care demo kit, and she mentally reviewed the pictures of various models and their ideal color options. The problem with selecting a color for Lisa was her hair. It was an artificial bright auburn, but her eyebrows were light brown. What would Sally Jo do in a case like this?

Seated beside Lisa at the round dinette table, Tori pawed through Allie's box of eye color sample packets and pulled one out. "Try this. That pale green is terrific."

Honestly, each of the four girls at Tori's party had tried at least three different color combinations, and they hadn't even gotten to the lipstick yet! At this rate, Allie would have to replenish her demo kit after her very first makeover party. She gave Tori a look that she hoped her little sister interpreted correctly. *Shut up and let me do it!* Tori's bright blue eyes rounded as she returned the gaze without blinking.

"Okay, give it here." Lisa snatched the packet and peeled it open. She reached for a clean applicator in the center of the table, and Allie purposefully turned her thoughts away from calculating the cost of the used foam-tipped sticks scattered around the table.

Seated next to Lisa, the brunette named Carrie finished brushing mascara on her lashes and lowered her mirror. "How's that?"

Allie inspected her work. "Beautiful. That eyeliner really emphasizes the shape of your eyes. I can't believe you don't wear it all the time."

Carrie looked into the mirror again. A smile touched the edges of her mouth. "You're right. I kind of like it."

Allie hid a smile. One sale, for sure. Thank goodness. Last night's disastrous party at Gram's retirement center had her worried that her success at Mom's was a fluke. She selected a lipstick and handed it to Carrie. "Now for the finishing touch. Everybody look here a minute." Four sets of eyes turned her way, and she demonstrated the proper way to apply a lip pencil, just like

Sally Jo had taught her.

Heidi, the girl who worked with Tori at the advertising firm, reached for the box of lip pencils. "Oh, goody. I just love lipstick. Look at all these fun colors!"

Lisa returned to the task of smearing green powder, totally the wrong color for her in Allie's opinion, on her eyelids. The other girl, whose name Allie had promptly forgotten as soon as Tori told her, dabbed a thick layer of powder beneath her eyes.

"Have y'all ever tried putting Preparation H beneath your eyes?"

Tori turned her bright blonde head in the girl's direction and laughed. "Why would you do that?"

Lisa gave a final green swipe to her right eyelid and dropped the applicator on her foam tray. "They say it gets rid of bags and tightens puffy skin. Haven't you ever seen *Miss Congeniality*?"

Allie handed her a dark chocolate eyeliner and instructed, "Not too thick on the bottom." She glanced at the other girl. "Personally, I'm not putting anything on my face that was made to smear on people's backsides. Just use a little more concealer."

"Oooh, I really like this one!" Heidi held up a miniature lip pencil and examined the writing on the side. "Pink Satin. I definitely want one of these. But I'd like to try this one too." She held up another.

Two sales. Allie smiled as she pushed a bottle of remover lotion and a cotton ball toward her. "Go into the bathroom and clean your lips. Be careful not to mess up your foundation, though."

She'd been disappointed when Tori told her she was expecting only four guests. But unlike Mom's party guests, these girls loved makeup, so she ought to sell enough to make the drive to Lexington pay off. With luck they'd all book parties of their own, and Allie's customer base would expand beyond her family.

Allie stepped from the chilly night air into the house. Eric, seated on the couch, glanced up at her for a single second before returning his attention to the television. "Hey. How'd it go?"

Allie looked at the screen. A ball game. She'd figured all the ball games would be over by ten thirty. Of course, then Eric would just watch a recap show on one of the sports channels.

"Fine." She let her purse slip off her shoulder and land on the chair by the door. "I sold almost as much tonight to four people as I did the other night at Mom's house."

His gaze remained fixed on the game, but he nodded. "That's good."

Allie dropped onto the edge of the chair cushion, still holding her demo bag. "Sort of makes up for last night's disaster." Allie had hoped folks who lived in Gram's upscale retirement center would spend a lot of money, but they'd turned out to be tough customers. A shame Varie Cose didn't sell anti-aging products.

"Hmmm."

Allie looked toward the guest room. "Is your mother already in bed?" He didn't answer. She spoke sharply. "Eric!"

He looked at her, his expression blank. "Huh?"

"Your mother. Has she gone to bed?"

"Uh huh. You just missed her."

"What about Joanie? How did she do to-night?"

"Great." He looked back at the television, then straightened. "Oh! Guess what she did? She reached for a toy and managed to grab it."

Dismayed, Allie dropped her kit on the floor. "She did?"

"Yeah, she was lying on the baby gym mat, and Mom was punching the button on that frog dangling above her, the one that sings and lights up. Joanie stared at it for a minute, then she reached right up and grabbed it."

Allie leaned back in the chair, her purse pressing into her lower back. Her baby had taken an important developmental step, and she missed it. She pushed her lower lip out and pulled a sad face. Eric didn't notice. He'd turned his attention back to the television.

Irritation flashed through her. "Eric." Her voice came out more snappish than she intended, but it got his attention. He looked at her, and she went on in a calmer tone. "Could you please turn the television off?"

His brow creased. "What for?"

Allie's fingers tightened on the padded arms of the chair. "I'd like to talk, and it's hard to do when you're obviously paying more attention to that stupid game than me."

His eyelids narrowed. "Let me get this straight. You're gone to a party every night this week, and when you finally decide to come home, you want me to drop everything and focus all my attention on you."

Anger flared. "I was *working* every night this week. You act like I've been out partying without you."

159

"Yeah, well, I worked every *day* this week. The way I look at it, if I want to relax at night by watching a game or two, I'm entitled."

Allie stiffened in the chair. "I think I'm entitled to at least one conversation with my husband every evening."

"Well, then maybe you ought to stay home every now and then." Eric shifted his gaze back to the television.

Honestly, he could be so irritating! Allie stood abruptly. "I'm going to check on the baby."

She marched between him and the television set toward the nursery, her nose in the air. He responded by punching the volume up on the remote control.

As she let herself into the nursery, she gnawed on the inside of her bottom lip. She hated arguing with Eric. Correction. That was not an argument. Both people had to be actively involved in order for it to be called an argument.

She pulled the door shut with a quiet click. It served her right. She knew better than to interrupt him during a ball game. He was just like —

She shook her head and tried not to finish the thought. Mom and Daddy had way more problems than just television. Primarily, Daddy's unfaithfulness. Eric would never be unfaithful. He just had an irritating addiction to sports, that's all.

Allie pushed away the disquieting feelings that soured her stomach and looked into the crib. At the sight of her slumbering daughter, her tense muscles relaxed. She ran a finger tenderly over the soft baby hair. She hated missing any important step in Joanie's development, but at least her daughter had been at home, with her father and grandmother, instead of with a babysitter. And tomorrow was Saturday, the first day Allie didn't have a meeting or party to go to all week. Maybe Eric would go with her in the morning to deliver Tuesday night's Varie Cose orders, and they could grab some lunch or something. Then they could spend the afternoon at home, enjoying family time.

Except Eric would probably be plastered to the television, watching college football games all day.

Sports were definitely the worst invention men had ever made, at least as far as wives were concerned. Correction. Sports were the second worst invention. Bathroom scales topped the list.

Eric's cell phone, plugged into the charger

in the bedroom, rang at 10:20 Saturday morning. Seated on the sofa in the living room, he tore his gaze from the article recapping a high school homecoming game and glanced at Allie over the top of the Lexington newspaper. Danville's paper didn't have a Saturday edition. Beside him, Mother paged through the sale ads, though why she bothered with the ads from another town he couldn't imagine.

"Want me to grab it?" Allie sat in the chair sipping coffee, her feet tucked under her.

Eric would have let her, but she hadn't made a move to get up from the chair. She was quiet this morning, obviously nursing a grudge over last night.

He set the paper aside and heaved himself off the couch. "No, I'll get it."

The phone was starting its fourth ring when he snatched it off the bedside table and glanced at the display screen. *Molly Green.* Weird. Molly never called him at home, though all the dispatchers had everyone else's contact information, in case of a major emergency at work.

Eric pushed the Talk button. "Hey, Molly."

"Eric." Her familiar voice sounded a bit breathless. "I'm so sorry to bother you at home, but I couldn't think who else to call."

He unplugged the charger and walked

back toward the living room. "No problem. Is everything okay?"

"Oh yeah, fine. Well, not *fine.* I'm having toilet problems, and I can't get a plumber over here until Monday. Or rather," she clarified, "I found one who will come, but I can't afford to pay the weekend rates. We only have one bathroom, so I can't wait until Monday. Could I borrow some tools so I can fix it myself?"

Eric leaned against the wall, the phone to his ear. "I'm not a plumber, but I could take a look at it for you."

Allie looked up from the newspaper, a crease deepening on her forehead.

Molly spoke in a rush. "Oh no, I don't want you to spend your Saturday fixing my toilet. I just need some tools, that's all. All I have is a screwdriver and a hammer, and I think this job is going to take a little more than that."

Eric shook his head. "Molly, have you ever fixed a toilet?"

"Well, no. But I'm hoping it'll turn out to be something easy."

"We don't have anything going on this morning," he said. "I'll be there in half an hour."

"Well, if you're sure." Relief made her tone light. "Thanks, Eric."

"No problem."

Eric punched the End button and straightened. Frowning, Allie had dropped the newspaper in her lap to watch him. Mother picked up a pen and circled something on the flyer.

"You didn't have any plans for today, did you?" he asked Allie.

"I have some Varie Cose orders to deliver, and I thought it would be fun if you went along with me."

"Fun? Running around town like a delivery boy?" Eric gave a snort of laughter. "I'd rather fix a toilet if it's all the same to you."

Allie's eyes flashed and her mouth opened to deliver a retort. But her gaze dropped to Mother and her mouth shut again. Something in her face stopped Eric from turning away. She looked disappointed, like she really had wanted him to drive her around town this morning.

"Listen," he told her, "Molly's a single mother. She can't afford to hire a plumber. Just let me run over there and take a look at her toilet, and maybe it won't take too long to fix. I'll probably be finished in time to help you with your stuff before the game comes on this afternoon."

Her mouth became a hard line. "And what time is that?"

Eric returned her stare. Was she irritated that he wanted to watch the game? She knew U.K. was playing Mississippi State this afternoon. He'd been talking about it all week. "Two o'clock."

"Well, I was hoping —" Her mouth shut with a snap.

Mother looked up at Allie. "If you need me to watch the baby while you run your errands, I don't mind."

Allie's lips parted as she stared at Mother. Actually, Eric didn't blame her for looking astonished. That was the first time Mother had volunteered to keep Joanie. Satisfaction settled in his gut. His mother was developing a relationship with her granddaughter, just as he'd hoped. If only he could get Dad down here to meet Joanie too.

"Thanks, Betty," Allie said. "That'll be a big help."

Eric gave a nod and headed into the bedroom to put on some old clothes. Obviously all Allie wanted was someone to tag along after her and take care of Joanie. Mother seemed glad to do it, which suited him just fine. He'd rather be helpful fixing something for Molly than spend the morning on delivery duty. And no matter what, he'd make sure he was in front of the television by two o'clock to enjoy his Saturday afternoon the way a man should — watching what promised to be a great football game.

"Eric, I can't thank you enough. I feel horrible that you've spent so much of your Saturday fixing my toilet."

Prone on the bathroom floor, Eric gave the wrench a final turn. "Don't worry about it. It's really no big deal."

He glanced up at Molly, who stood leaning against the wall, her arms wrapped around her ribs, watching him. She looked different today, more casual, though the jeans and T-shirt she usually wore to work weren't much dressier than those she had on now. Maybe it wasn't the way she looked so much as her attitude. She seemed more at ease here in her home environment. Carefree, even. And embarrassed at having him mess around with her toilet, especially when he'd finally discovered the reason the thing was overflowing.

But Eric was embarrassed too, because a couple of times he'd looked up from his work to find her staring at him. His shirt hung over the towel rack, safe and dry from the mess the malfunctioning toilet had caused. At home he ran around without a shirt all the time, but here, in Molly's bathroom, he felt as though he was inappropriately half dressed.

Which was dumb. This was Molly, a friend and co-worker. Nobody to be embarrassed in front of.

Eric sat up and reached into the bathtub to pick up the Hot Wheels car. He grimaced as he held it out to her. "You probably ought to boil this thing before you give it back to your son."

Her nose wrinkled as she took it between her thumb and forefinger. "Are you kidding? This is going in the trashcan. Serves Josh right for flushing it down the toilet and then not telling me about it. I'm sorry you had to take the whole thing apart to find it."

Eric grinned. "It sure was wedged way down in there. Don't be too hard on him. He's just being a boy." He understood the fascination of the toilet bowl for a little boy. He remembered floating a toy boat in his toilet, pretending it was caught in a storm as it circled around and around in the watery whirlwind. Mother was all kinds of upset when she caught him.

He twisted the shutoff valve. The sound of water rushing through the pipes and into the tank filled the room. When it finished, he pushed the handle down. Molly grinned at him in triumph as the toilet flushed without a problem. The youngest boy peeked out from behind her, then whirled and ran down the hallway, shouting to his brother, "He fixed it. We can flush now."

Eric got to his feet. "Hey, what time is it?"

She glanced at her watch. "Two ten." She winced. "Oh, Eric, your game started ten minutes ago. You missed the kickoff."

"Don't worry about it." He gestured toward the sink. "If it's okay, I'll just wash my hands before I leave."

"You have dirt on your, uh . . ." Her fingers reached to brush his chest, but stopped just short of touching him. Pink spots appeared on her cheeks. "I'll get you a washcloth."

Eric found himself unable to meet her gaze when she returned with the washcloth and a fresh towel. He took them wordlessly and twisted the hot water handle, aware that Molly slipped out of the room behind him.

As he scrubbed at his arms and elbows with the washcloth, Eric wondered at the sudden discomfort between them. Molly was . . . well, she was just Molly. He'd known her for years. They worked side by side in a room so small they could grasp hands without leaving their desks if they wanted. He had a tremendous amount of respect for her. She did a great job raising two boys alone after her ex-husband left her and moved to Arizona. No need to feel awkward.

Once he had dried off, he slipped his shirt over his head. He'd grab a shower later, between games. He headed down the short hallway toward the front room of Molly's small house.

"Look what I found." She stood in front of the television set, the remote control in her hand. "U.K. won the toss and they just got a first down. Why don't you have a seat and I'll fix you a sandwich?"

Eric glanced at the television set as he shook his head. "Thanks, but I should probably get home."

Molly tilted her head. "Please? The boys are playing in the backyard, so they won't bother you. A sandwich is the least I can offer after you saved me so much money."

The quarterback threw an awkward pass and Eric winced. But the receiver nabbed it out of the air just before a Mississippi State player tackled him. "Wow!" Eric looked at Molly. "Did you see that? Another first down."

Molly grinned. "Have a seat. Ham and Swiss okay?"

"Sounds good," Eric told her as he lowered himself onto the sofa. This was going to be a great game.

12

Allie parked her car in Sally Jo's driveway and twisted the rearview mirror to glance at her makeup. Even though her lipstick looked fresh, she pulled the lip pencil out of her purse and went over her lips once more. Satisfied, she snapped the lid back on. The shipment from Varie Cose's warehouse had been short one box of stain wipes, but Sally Jo had offered to let Allie purchase one from her inventory.

Sally Jo opened the door before she could ring the bell.

"I've been hoping you'd get here soon," she said without preamble as she threw the door wide and gestured for Allie to enter. "I've got to leave for a party in twenty minutes."

"Sorry." Allie stepped into the elegant entry hall. She'd waited an hour for Eric to call and tell her if he'd be able to go with her on her calls. But she didn't see a need to explain that. "I had to get the baby settled before I left her with my mother-in-law."

Obviously, Sally Jo was not enamored with babies. The brief smile she flashed Allie looked more like a grimace. She shut the door and brushed past Allie down the back hallway. "The wipes are in here. Why don't you have a party booked today?"

Allie followed, aware of Sally Jo's excellent posture and her long strides, the way she held her head high. Allie straightened her shoulders. "Nobody requested one, but I'm considering taking weekends off anyway. It took my husband a long time to build up enough seniority to get Saturdays and Sundays off. I'd like to reserve those for family time."

Sally Jo stopped with her hand on the knob of a door at the end of the hall to turn her arched eyebrows toward Allie. "Of course, that's your choice. Saturday afternoons are highly profitable, you know. It's a great day for pedicure parties. Women love to have something fun to do while the men are watching their dumb football games all day. Once they've relaxed with their feet in a Varie Cose footbath, their checkbooks flow like fountains."

Allie hadn't thought of that. It made

sense, though, and she'd love to be able to turn a profit as a result of the football obsession shared by every guy over the age of two. Maybe she should buy one of the pedicure demo kits. Tori's friend Lisa had sounded interested in booking a party, but she didn't select a date yet. Perhaps she could be persuaded to do a pedicure party.

Sally Jo turned the door handle and stepped into the room, Allie on her heels. Inside the room, Allie stopped and stared around. This place was like a Varie Cose store! Shelves covered three walls, stuffed full of products. There had to be two dozen bottles of cleaning spray, and at least as many boxes of laundry soap. Box after box of housewares filled the shelves on Allie's left, and through the open closet door Allie glimpsed more stacks of Varie Cose boxes. One whole shelving section was devoted to skin care. Allie stepped close to examine the small pastel green boxes stacked four deep. Sally Jo had several of every shade of foundation, blush, eye, and lip color the catalog offered.

"Wow!" Allie ran her finger over a row of spray cleaner bottles. "You've got your own warehouse right here."

Sally Jo's gaze swept the room as she nodded. "I told you and the other girls I like to

173

keep an inventory on hand. I take a few of the top-selling products with me to every party so people can take their orders home with them. Occasionally someone will buy something I don't have, and then I have to order it. But most of the time I can either give it to them right away, or deliver it the next day." She took a box of stain wipes from a shelf and handed it to Allie. "You should consider building an inventory yourself. It really helps."

Allie looked at the well-stocked shelves one last time before she left the room. "That does make sense."

Allie pulled into her own driveway and shoved the car into Park. She'd finished all her deliveries, and even managed to convince Mrs. Faber to host a makeover party the following Saturday. That made five parties on her calendar in the next two weeks. All in all, a profitable day already, and it was only two thirty in the afternoon.

Eric's pickup was still gone. Molly's toilet problem must have turned into a major repair job, especially if it caused him to miss his ball game. A flash of irritation set Allie's teeth together. He wouldn't miss his precious game to help with her errands, but he didn't hesitate to run out the door the minute Molly called.

That's not fair. Molly was in trouble. I should be glad I have the kind of husband who can handle home repairs.

Allie got out of the car, slung her purse over her shoulder, and headed for the mailbox. She and Eric had never paid a plumber or carpenter or anyone to do anything to their home. Plus, Eric had done many repairs on Gram's house, a couple of them pretty major. He'd saved Gram and Mom a ton of money. And Molly was all alone, without a husband of her own to help.

Allie paused with her hand on the mailbox door. Molly was all alone. And Eric was over at her house. What if . . .

She shook her head. No. That was silly. Molly was a co-worker who needed help, nothing more.

A thick stack of envelopes and catalogs crowded the mailbox. Allie flipped through the pile as she headed toward the front door. A couple of election brochures. The power bill. Something in a window envelope from a post office box addressed to her.

She pulled that one out of the stack and felt the telltale outline of a plastic card. Her credit card! Unable to wait until she got inside the house, Allie ripped into the envelope and extracted a folded piece of stiff paper. The card was attached. Her name in raised gold letters glistened in the sunlight.

It was official! She was a businesswoman with her own company and her own credit card. Now she could make a real investment in her business and start building her inventory. Oh, nothing like Sally Jo had in her spare room, at least not at first. Allie would start slowly. She knew exactly what she'd buy first — that pedicure demo kit. Maybe a few of the top sellers, like laundry soap and cleaner. A few lipsticks. She could easily pay the bill for those items with all the parties she had booked over the next couple of weeks.

She skipped up the front porch stairs. When Eric finished his repair job and got home, he'd be plastered in front of the television, watching ball games for the rest of the day. That meant she had all afternoon to browse through the Varie Cose online catalog and place her inventory order.

The sound of the front door closing drew Allie's attention from her study of the pedicure procedures she'd printed off the Varie Cose consultant website. She glanced at the clock on the bedside table. Almost five o'clock. She'd filled her afternoon with follow-up phone calls trying to convince people to schedule parties and then settled down for a little paperwork. She'd lost track of time after Joanie's last meal.

A moment later Eric came into the room. When he caught sight of the papers spread across the surface of the bed, his eyebrows rose. "What's all this?"

"Just getting some work done." Allie tried not to emphasize *work,* but she still felt slightly offended at his tone last night when he referred to her parties as though they weren't a job. "You're late. That toilet must have turned into a real project."

Eric turned his back on her and stripped off his shirt. "It was, but I finished a couple hours ago. Molly turned the game on, and I got involved."

Allie shifted on the mattress uneasily. She'd assumed he was working all this time. Why hadn't she taken the time to call him, to find out why he wasn't home yet? "You watched the game at Molly's house?"

He opened a dresser drawer and took out a clean T-shirt. "Yeah."

"Were her kids there?"

He gave a single nod. "At halftime we went out in the yard and tossed a football around. Mikey has quite an arm for an eight-year-old."

Allie picked up the papers and shuffled them in a neat stack in her lap, trying to control her rising temper. "I thought you were going to come home and run errands with me when you got the toilet fixed. I waited for an hour."

"Sorry about that." Eric stooped to take a pair of jeans from the bottom drawer. "I didn't get the toilet fixed until after two." He straightened. "Josh had rammed a toy car up in there and it got wedged sideways. Had to take the thing completely apart to get it out." He laughed, shaking his head.

Thoughts raced around Allie's mind as he shoved the drawer closed with a foot. He was acting like coming home hours late was no big deal. "Uh, her kids were there all day, right?"

He gave her an odd look. "I just said they were. They watched most of the game with me." He disappeared into the bathroom.

Allie heard the shower turn on. Disquiet niggled at her thoughts. Even if Molly was a co-worker, she was an attractive single woman, and Allie did not like the idea of Eric spending a whole afternoon in her house, even with her kids there to chaperone. But if she said anything, he would accuse her of being a nagging wife. Or maybe he'd think she was being snippy because she was upset that he didn't take her on her deliveries. What had he said this morning? He didn't want to spend his Saturday running around town like a delivery boy.

She got off the bed and picked up the dirty shirt Eric had dropped on the floor. The sound of the shower told her he was still occupied in the bathroom. With a quick glance in that direction, she buried her face in the fabric and inhaled deeply. No perfume. Just the strong, outdoorsy scent that was uniquely Eric. A quick inspection of the neckline showed no sign of lipstick, either.

Feeling like a jealous shrew, she tossed the shirt into the laundry basket they kept in the walk-in closet. But as she did, she heaved a sigh of relief.

Allie let Tori take the infant seat from her hands when they stepped through the front door of Gram's house Sunday afternoon. She followed Mom, Gram, and Joan into the living room as they swarmed around Joanie like bees around a sweet-smelling blossom. Tori set the seat on the coffee table and bent over it.

"Hello there, my sweet little niece," she cooed. She straightened and turned a delighted grin toward Allie. "She smiled at me!"

Allie nodded. "She's smiling a lot the past few days. The other day she even laughed out loud."

"I want to hear." Joan stepped closer, her shoulder pressed against Tori to shove her out of the way. "Let me have her so I can do something to make her laugh."

"Not a chance." Tori's eyes flashed as she held her ground. "I'm holding her first."

"No, *I* am." Mom used the voice they all knew, the one that said she had the final say. Tori and Joan reluctantly stepped aside.

As Mom unfastened the straps, Gram's gaze slid behind Allie. "Why, Betty, you didn't have to bring anything."

Allie turned to find Betty standing just inside the front door beside Eric, the insulated casserole dish Allie received as a wedding gift in her hands. At least somebody was getting some use out of it.

Betty nodded. "I hated to come empty-handed, so I made a broccoli casserole."

"You didn't have to do that, but I'm sure it will be delicious." Gram used her metal walker to make her way slowly toward the kitchen. "Bring it right in here."

Betty followed, and Eric crossed the room toward the recliner. He settled in, picked up the remote control, and punched the television on. Sunday afternoon football. He was accustomed to making himself comfortable in the family home. Allie bit back an irritated remark about his unsocial behavior. Nobody else seemed to notice, though. They were too involved with the baby.

Behind her the front door opened and Ken stepped through. Joan tore herself away from Joanie and went to him, her brown eyes alight. The couple did not kiss but stood close together, hands clasped, sharing a private glance and a tender smile. Allie's heart warmed as she watched her sister, so obviously in love. The look on Ken's face as he gazed down into Joan's eyes made Allie heave a sentimental sigh. Her sister deserved to be treasured.

Then Ken's gaze rose to the television set, and a different light glinted in his eyes. He crossed the room, pulling Joan along behind him by the hand. Edging around Mom and Tori and Joanie toward the sofa, he asked, "Is that the Raiders game?"

Eric nodded, his eyes not leaving the screen. "They scored while we were in the car on the way over."

Ken released Joan's hand and dropped to the cushion. "I was watching it next door at my place. You should have seen it. A fifteen-yard pass right over the goal line, and he was wide open."

Joan caught Allie's eye and her lips formed an indulgent smile. She shrugged a shoulder as though to say, *Men!*

Allie grimaced. Yeah, men.

"Girls," Gram called from the kitchen, "would you set the table?"

Allie and her sisters trekked into the kitchen to gather the plates and utensils, and then joined in the familiar task they had shared since they moved in with Gram thirteen years earlier after Mom and Daddy's divorce. Allie kept glancing across the counter that separated the dining area from the kitchen. Betty and Gram navigated the small space like they'd been working together all their lives. Betty quietly reached in to help when Gram, hampered by her walker, picked up the roast pan to pour the drippings into a skillet for gravy. Allie couldn't help noticing how Gram accepted that assistance with a grateful glance. Anytime Allie or her sisters tried to help, Gram became irritated and insisted, "I've been doing this longer than you've been alive, missy!"

"Is Betty always so quiet?" Tori whispered as she laid silverware on the napkin Allie had just placed on the table.

Allie nodded and matched her sister's quiet tone. "I swear she doesn't say ten words all day. No wonder Don hasn't missed her. He never knew she was there to begin with."

The table laid, the girls stepped back and admired their handiwork. Gram's imitation Wedgwood china, some pieces showing wear from years of use, gleamed in the light shining through the windows. The smell of homemade yeast rolls blended with the odors of the savory roast and a lingering hint of cinnamon from the apple pie resting on the counter.

"Now, girls," Gram said, "if you'll just get the food on the table, we'll be ready to call the men to dinner."

Joan picked up a basket of rolls from the counter and turned to set it on the table. "I'll bet they'd rather eat in front of the television so they can watch the game."

Gram paused in the act of placing a serving spoon in a bowl of roasted carrots and onions. The fringe of white hair across her forehead accented the blueness of her eyes as she looked at Joan. "We could get out the TV trays for them."

Allie retrieved the bowl, trying not to scowl. "Eric was plastered to the television all day yesterday watching football. At another woman's house, no less."

Joan's jaw dropped, and Tori's eyes went

round as store-bought cookies.

"What other woman?" Tori asked.

Aware of Betty's gaze, Allie wished she'd kept her mouth shut. Voicing the fear that had niggled at her mind all night made her feel foolish. She lifted a shoulder and spoke in a light tone. "Just a co-worker who needed some help with a little home repair project. No big deal. It's just that football has taken over my life lately. Can't we have a family meal without it?"

Joan and Tori both relaxed, and Betty turned toward the sink to wash her hands.

"Oh, don't be such a grouch," Joan said. "Let them watch their game."

Allie set the bowl on the table. If they made Eric come to the table, he'd just bolt his food and hurry back to the television. Might as well let him enjoy himself with Ken. "Fine." She smiled to take the bite out of her tone.

"Besides," Joan said as she headed for the living room, "football hasn't taken over your life. Varie Cose has."

Allie looked up in surprise as she disappeared through the doorway. "I don't know what she means."

Tori laughed. "Are you kidding? That's all you talk about anymore."

"That's not true." Gram's tone held a

184

note of loyalty. She made her slow way around the counter toward the table. "She talks about the baby too."

Betty set her broccoli casserole next to the rolls as Joan returned, followed by Eric, Ken, and Mom with Joanie leaning against her shoulder.

"We got the trays out of the closet," Joan said as everyone went to stand behind their chairs. Betty stood in the same position she'd occupied for Allie's birthday dinner, maintaining her usual silent vigil. With a start, Allie realized she was becoming a regular around this dinner table, just as Ken had a few months before, and Eric even before that. One thing about the Sanderson family — they accepted everyone into their fold.

They bowed their heads and Gram said grace. Eric slipped an arm around Allie's waist, the pressure of his touch uncertain. Allie knew the reason for his hesitation. He wanted to make sure she was okay with his absence from the family table, but he didn't want to mention it in front of the others. She supposed it would feel sort of like asking her permission, and what husband wanted to be seen doing that? But that was exactly what he was doing, seeking tacit assurance that she wouldn't be upset with him if he plastered himself to the television screen once again. Warmth for him rushed through Allie, and she put an arm around him too. The least she could do was not act like a shrew.

When the men had filled their plates, they headed back to the television with an eagerness that made Allie want to laugh. Soon the sounds of a roaring crowd drifted through the doorway from the direction of the living room. Allie kept the portions she spooned onto her own plate moderate and passed completely on the gravy. With a little luck, her willpower would last all the way through dessert.

Joanie was awake and as Mom picked up her fork, she lifted her head from her grandmother's shoulder on her wobbly neck.

"Here, Mom," Tori said, "let me hold Joanie while you eat."

Mom handed the baby over with a grin. "Oh, okay. I guess it's your turn." She sliced a baby carrot and speared a bite on her fork. "Allie, my choir friends have been asking when they're going to get to see my granddaughter. Are you planning to bring her to church soon?"

Allie looked down at her plate. This was not a subject she relished discussing, especially over dinner. She and Eric had talked about taking the baby to church, and she knew her family wouldn't like their decision.

"If you want to show her off, maybe you should just invite them over here one Sunday afternoon. I don't think we're going to start going to church anytime soon."

Everyone around the table became as silent as Betty. Allie avoided meeting anyone's gaze by picking up her roll and tearing it in half. Fragrant steam rose from the soft bread, and she considered the butter dish for only a moment before her resolve reasserted itself.

"Why not?" Gram asked. "You went to church with your parents when you were just a few weeks old. Church is an important family tradition."

Allie glanced up to find herself the focus of Gram's disapproving gaze. "Not in Eric's family. Isn't that right, Betty?"

She looked at Betty more for support than confirmation. Her mother-in-law inclined her head and spoke in her reserved way. "My husband worked long hours during the week. Sunday was our only time together at home."

"That's how Eric feels too," Allie said. "He prefers to wait until Joanie is old enough to make her own decision about religion, and then we'll support her."

Tori's bright head nodded as she smiled down at the object of their discussion, nestled in the crook of her arm.

Across the table, Joan set her fork down. "What do you say, Allie?"

Allie refused to meet her sister's direct gaze. She scooped a mound of mashed potatoes onto her fork. "I agree with Eric. I don't see the point in dumping her in the church nursery every Sunday. When she's old enough for Sunday school, she'll get a lot more out of the experience." When the time came, Allie would be taking her alone. Eric had no use for church, as Joan knew very well. The whole family knew that.

Obviously Joan didn't like her answer. Her lips a tight line, she picked up her fork and stabbed at a piece of meat. Allie sipped from her iced tea glass. She was glad Joan had found fulfillment in the church, but surely her sister didn't expect everyone to become a fanatic just because she was.

Gram didn't like the answer either. Her forehead creased, she said in a petulant voice, "I hoped having Joanie would get you back into church."

"Mother, this is Allie and Eric's decision." Mom spoke to Gram, but Allie saw her give a warning look at Joan.

That effectively ended the subject, for which Allie was grateful. She couldn't help notice Joan was quiet through the rest of the meal.

13

"Four fifty-seven reporting a ten-fifty-four at State Road 33 about a half mile south of Buster Pike."

A ten-fifty-four meant livestock on the road. Old man Dorsey must have another break in his cattle fence. Eric leaned forward and pressed the transmission switch. "Ten-four, four fifty-seven. We'll get someone over there." He glanced at the clock. Almost five o'clock, so traffic would be picking up. He pressed the switch again. "You gonna run interference?"

Static crackled for a moment before Chad's reply. "Ten-four."

Eric grinned at the resignation in the officer's voice. Directing traffic around a bunch of cows on the road wasn't exactly the most exciting aspect of police work, but occasionally it was necessary.

"I'll call him," Molly volunteered, and Eric shot her a look of thanks. Mr. Dorsey responded better to females.

He tapped a record of the call into the database. This made the third time in a month. The guy was going to have to break down and replace that sorry excuse for a fence soon. He half listened as Molly sweet-talked her way through the conversation.

When she hung up, he grinned at her. "You handle him well. He cussed me out the last time I called."

A dimple creased her cheek. "There's a certain amount of talent involved in talking to grumpy old farmers. You obviously don't have it."

"I guess my talents lie in a different direction." He smirked. "Like fixing toilets."

"Oh, I'm sure you're very talented in lots of areas."

She broke eye contact and became interested in the data scrolling across her monitor. Eric picked up the pen and drew a doodle on his pad. The day had been really slow for a Tuesday. Molly had been exceptionally quiet, which made the time drag. In fact, she had been quiet yesterday too.

She broke the silence. "Are you doing anything after work?" Her voice held a note of resolve, which made Eric wonder if she'd been trying to get the nerve up to ask him something.

"Not really. Why?"

"Well, you did such a good job on my toilet the other day, I wondered if you could take a look at the railing on the back deck and tell me what I need to do with it. It's starting to get kind of rickety, and I'm afraid the boys might get hurt if I don't have it taken care of soon."

Eric had noticed the loose railing on Saturday. Josh and Mikey were typical active little boys. He could see them roughhousing on the deck and crashing right through the loose wooden slats.

Allie had another party tonight, so she wouldn't be home until later. And Mother wouldn't mind having Joanie to herself for a while longer. "Sure, I'll take a look at it after work."

"Thanks, Eric."

Her smile lightened her worried expression. Asking for help was probably hard for her, because she was so capable at handling most things on her own. But she shouldn't feel bad. That's what friends were for.

"One more ought to do it," Eric told Mikey.

The boy extracted a nail from the box and held it up. Eric took it and then balanced himself on the kitchen chair as he straightened. The chair legs rested on uneven ground and wobbled a bit as he pounded the nail into the railing. A stepladder would have been safer, but Molly didn't have one.

"There." He grabbed the wood and tried to shake it, satisfied when it held firm. "That one's not going anywhere."

"Are we done?" Mikey asked.

Eric looked down the length of the deck and nodded. "We've tightened them all. You make a good assistant carpenter."

Mikey beamed with pride. Eric put a hand on the boy's head as he hopped down from the chair and ruffled the dark hair before he let go.

The back door opened and Molly stuck her head outside. "The pizza just got here. Eric, would you like to stay for supper?"

The mouthwatering odor of pepperoni wafted toward him from inside the house. Tempting, but . . . Eric shook his head. "I need to be getting home."

"Aw, please?" Mikey tilted his head back to look up at Eric. "I want to show you my Halloween costume. I'm going to be a football player! I got shoulder pads and everything. Then maybe we can throw the football again."

Eric looked down into the boy's eager face. Poor kid. With no father in the picture, how often did he have a man's attention?

Eric's own dad had worked a lot when he was younger, but when he was home he made time for things like playing catch and teaching his son to ride a bicycle. Important stuff to a kid, and Mikey obviously missed it. Allie wouldn't be home yet, and Joanie was fine with Mother for another half hour or so.

Eric looked up at Molly, who stood watching him with an odd expression. Did she want him to stay, or was she just being polite?

She must have seen the question in his face. "I wish you would. Let me repay you a little for your help."

He ruffled Mikey's hair again. "We might have enough daylight left after supper to play for a few minutes."

"All right!" The boy pumped his fist in the air.

Molly laughed. "You two better hurry and get washed up or Josh will start without you."

Eric put a hand on the boy's shoulder as they walked side by side up the stairs. At the top, Mikey ran ahead and brushed by his mother. Molly turned a soft smile on Eric as he approached the door.

"Thank you for letting him help. It means

a lot." She looked into his eyes. "To both of us."

Eric straightened. A few minutes of his time was nothing to him, but it obviously meant the world to a little boy and his mother. He returned Molly's smile. "It really was my pleasure."

That evening Eric sat on the living room floor playing with Joanie. One day she would be old enough to play catch like Mikey and Josh. Dolls and girlie stuff were okay, but sports taught important life lessons, like teamwork and working toward a goal and achieving your best. He intended to help his daughter learn those lessons.

ESPN was recapping a motorcycle race over in Germany, and he half watched while he kept Joanie interested in the toys dangling from the bar on her baby gym. Mother sat in the chair nearest the kitchen with a book, but he noticed she spent more time watching him and Joanie than reading.

"Your father called today."

Eric glanced up. She looked neat, as she always did, with every hair in order and her gray skirt smoothed over her knees. Her expression held no hint of her feelings.

"That's good," Eric said. "What did he have to say?"

"He wanted to know if I've paid the gas bill. There was no hot water for his shower this morning."

"You pay the bills?"

Her eyes widened almost imperceptibly. "I always have. He didn't even know where I keep the checkbook."

Eric remembered Mother sitting at the kitchen table when he was a boy, a stack of bills in front of her, writing checks in her even script. He must have been young, not in school yet. He'd forgotten about that. "Did you forget to pay the gas bill?"

The shadow of a smile touched her lips. "I didn't forget."

He couldn't help it. He laughed. "Mother, did you have the gas disconnected on purpose?"

She closed the book and rested her hands on top of the cover. "Certainly not. I left the bills and the checkbook where I always keep them, in the third kitchen drawer beside the refrigerator. Don needs to learn to take care of those things himself now."

Joanie's waving hands hit a dangling toy and it chimed. She cooed in response. Eric leaned over her and smiled into her eyes, mostly so he could look away from Mother's.

"Aren't you planning to go home at all?"

he asked.

"I haven't decided, but I don't think so."

Eric chewed the inside of his lip. Though he'd begun to suspect this problem between his parents was more than a simple misunderstanding, he'd never considered the possibility that their separation might be permanent. Could Mother seriously be thinking of divorce?

He tapped the toy on the baby gym so it swung tantalizingly above his daughter and spoke in a careful voice. "Thirty-five years of marriage is a long time to throw away."

Whatever reply she might have made was interrupted. The door opened and Allie came in, her arms full.

"Sorry I'm late." She sounded tired. "Those women were the chattiest bunch I've ever seen."

She pushed the door closed by collapsing against it. Eric jumped up from the floor and took the biggest bag, a canvas thing that weighed a ton, from her shoulder. Gratitude flickered in her eyes as she set the briefcase she carried in her other hand on the floor beside the door. He didn't remember seeing it before.

"Is that new?" he asked.

She flashed him a look. "I needed something to carry my paperwork in."

Eric raised an eyebrow at the defensive response. "Okay. I was just asking."

A sigh escaped her lips and she laid a hand on his arm. "I'm sorry. I'm really tired tonight." She looked down at Joanie and a smile softened her lips. She tossed her ugly, expensive purse beside the briefcase and dropped to the floor beside the baby mat. "There's Mommy's precious sweetheart."

Joanie's face lit when she caught sight of Allie, and she let out a delighted gurgling coo. Her little hands waved excitedly and both legs kicked the air.

The eyes Allie turned upward to him gleamed with delight. "She's happy to see me! Did you hear her?"

Eric nodded. "She's been vocal like that all night."

A hurt frown creased her forehead. Eric wanted to kick himself. Allie was so defensive lately, and sure Joanie didn't miss her at all. What was wrong in letting her think her daughter was glad to see her? Sometimes he didn't think before he spoke. "Look at those legs kicking. She knows her mama's home."

"Yes she does!" Allie scooped the baby up and buried kisses in her neck.

Eric dropped to the floor beside his wife and daughter and planted a kiss on Allie's cheek. "I'm glad to see you too."

Allie beamed at him, her smile restored. She sat back against the couch, positioned Joanie in the crease of her bent legs and grabbed both little hands. "Thanks, Betty, for watching her until Eric got home. I hope she wasn't any trouble."

"None at all."

Eric glanced at Mother, whose sedate position had not changed. She watched Allie and Joanie through an expression as unreadable as ever. And she didn't meet Eric's gaze. A tacit signal that she hoped he wouldn't resume their conversation in front of Allie? Probably. But Eric intended to pin her down later.

"Actually, Mother had her until after seven tonight," he said. He watched Joanie plant her feet on Allie's stomach and straighten.

Allie lifted her up to a standing position, her hands holding Joanie's rib cage and supporting the back of her head with her fingers. "Did you have to work late?"

"No, I stopped by Molly's to tighten a few loose boards on her deck."

Allie's head snapped sideways, her eyes wide. "You went to Molly's again?"

He didn't look up, but watched Joanie's attempt to stand and hold her neck steady at the same time. "Just for a couple of hours. That deck was unsafe. I noticed it Saturday."

"Doesn't Molly have somebody else to do things like that for her? Her father, maybe?"

Eric shook his head. "Her father's dead, and her mother is elderly. No brothers. And of course she doesn't have a husband."

"Well, lately she doesn't seem to need one. She has mine." Allie's mouth closed so fast he heard her teeth snap.

"I'm just helping out a friend." Anger flickered at the edge of his mind. Why did he need to defend himself for doing a good deed?

Mother rose silently from the chair and left the room. A second later he heard the soft click of the bedroom door shutting. A tactful exit. Eric didn't look in that direction but studied Allie's profile through narrowed eyes.

"Did you eat supper there?" Her words came out clipped.

"She ordered pizza." From the flush that stained her cheeks, Eric knew she didn't like the answer. "I spent most of the time with her oldest boy, Mikey. The kid is seven years old and obviously starved for male attention."

Allie refused to look at him. "So you spent

200

your evening playing with someone else's child while yours was at home without a parent."

"She had a *grand*parent," he shot back. "Which is a good thing, since her mother wasn't here."

Allie's head snapped sideways, and fury sparked in her eyes. She spoke through gritted teeth. "I was working, Eric."

"I understand that, but I don't see why you have to be gone every night."

Joanie whimpered, and Allie laid her back down on her lap. He saw Allie swallow, and when she spoke it was with obvious effort to keep her tone even. "It takes a lot of work to start up a business. I thought you understood that."

"I do." Eric paused to gather the thoughts that had plagued him at odd times lately. "I guess I just see you throwing yourself into this, and I don't get it."

"You don't get me wanting to be successful?"

He looked over her head at the curtains, choosing his words with care. "I don't get why you're doing it to begin with. You don't have to work. You could stay home with Joanie. I told you that."

"And I told you —"

He held up a hand. "I know you want to

earn money so you can pay your share of the bills. I just don't see why you have to do something that takes so much of your time away from Joanie." He looked down at her. "And from me."

Emotions flickered across her face. Her jaw relaxed and then tensed again. What was she thinking? This conversation had taken an unexpected, and uncomfortable, turn. He didn't want her to think he resented her work with this Varie Cose thing. He really didn't. It's just that Allie was one of those women who threw herself into everything. She was one of the smartest people he'd ever met, and she had three times more energy than anyone else he knew. Whatever she focused that energy on was bound to be a success. But she was also single-minded at times, and lately he was beginning to feel, well, a little ignored.

Her eyelids narrowed and she sucked in a breath. "You changed the subject. We were talking about you spending time at Molly's, and you turned it to attack my job. Almost as though you're hiding something."

So much for communication. Disgust blasted through his lips. "That's ridiculous. I'm not going to listen to this."

He got to his feet and left the room, shaking his head. Women defied understanding.

Sure, he got the fact that she needed to work hard if she was determined to do this sales business. But apparently she thought he had to sit at home waiting for her like a good little househusband. Allie might be smart, but if that's what she thought, she had another thing coming.

14

Allie stood over the changing table and fastened the plastic snaps on Joanie's one-piece jumpsuit. She was growing so fast! Her feet finally filled out the footies on this outfit. They waved in the air as Joanie kicked with energy, cooing, and Allie grabbed them and planted a kiss on each sole. Her baby was nearly eight weeks old! She could hardly believe it. If she hadn't decided to do Varie Cose, she would be going back to work on Monday, in just five days.

Her boss Gina wasn't very happy with Allie's decision not to return, but she understood. She refused to accept Allie's final resignation, though, and said she was going to change Allie's employment status to Unpaid Leave of Absence, so if she changed her mind and wanted to come back, she could.

"I hate to tell her, but there's no way." Allie tickled her daughter's bulging belly, which made Joanie gurgle and kick.

"Anybody home?" Joan's voice called from the front door.

"Your aunt Joan is here," Allie told her daughter. She raised her head and called, "In the nursery."

Joan appeared a moment later and, as Allie expected, scooped Joanie into her arms. "Look at you, little one. You're all dressed and ready for the day." Joan glanced at Allie and went on in a drier tone. "Unlike your mama."

Allie looked down at her flannel pajamas and fluffy bedroom slippers. "Hey, I'm dressed for the day. This is how people who work at home dress."

"Must be nice." Joan wore a navy blue jacket and slacks, appropriate attire for her job as manager of a furniture rental store. "Hey, I stopped by on the way to work to trade that lipstick. You said I could return it if I wanted to, and I don't like the color."

"Sure, no problem. C'mon in here." Allie led the way to her bedroom/office, Joan following along with Joanie.

"Good morning, Betty," Joan called into the kitchen as they passed the doorway.

Allie heard Betty's quiet reply but couldn't make out the words. She had been seated at the kitchen table since breakfast, sipping coffee and looking through an issue of *Cooking Light.* Probably planning another low-fat, low-cal meal for supper. Actually, that suited Allie just fine. She'd be home for dinner this evening because it was Halloween and nobody wanted to book a party on trick-or-treat night. Her diet was going pretty well, and her clothes felt a tiny bit looser. Now that she'd gotten past the initial hurt feelings over Eric's gift, she'd been meaning to go by the gym to activate her membership and check the place out, but there never seemed to be any time. At least with Betty's focus on healthy meals, she was eating sensibly.

"Wow, would you look at that?" Joan stopped just inside the bedroom door and stared open-mouthed at the far end of the room.

Allie let her gaze sweep over the well-stocked shelves with a feeling of satisfaction. Her shipment from Varie Cose arrived yesterday. Though she didn't even come close to Sally Jo's inventory, she had a respectable amount of product on hand. She turned to respond to Joan and saw her sister's eyes weren't on the shelves.

"I've never seen such a mess." Joan shook her head. "How do you find anything?"

Allie followed her sister's gaze to the desk.

Papers littered the surface amid piles of catalogs and file folders and packing slips from yesterday's shipment. She'd dumped the contents of her briefcase there last night, intending to spend today sorting everything out.

"I haven't exactly settled on a filing system yet. But I know exactly where everything is." She rounded the bed and grabbed a catalog. "Here, look through the lip colors and let me know which one you want to trade for."

While Joan, perched on the mattress edge, went through the catalog to the lipstick pages, Allie sifted through the papers on the desk to find her order folder. She dumped the contents onto the bedspread and flipped through them with an index finger to find Joan's original sales slip.

Watching her, Joan cringed. "Allie, you've got to be more organized. You can't run a business by dumping things in a file."

"I know, I know." She spied one from the date of Mom's party and thumbed through the papers until she found Joan's. She held it up triumphantly. "See, I told you I knew where everything was."

"You're so good at computer stuff I'm surprised you haven't developed some sort of computer system to help you get organized."

Joan had always been Miss Organization, but she wasn't very good with computers beyond the basics. Allie loved computers and had even built a couple of databases at work to help keep track of her home visits and clients. She looked at the mess on the bed. Actually, Joan's idea wasn't a bad one. The Varie Cose website had an ordering system, but not much else.

"I like this one." Joan slid the catalog across the mattress and tapped on Soft Sienna.

Allie hopped off the bed. "I have that one in stock."

She retrieved the appropriate box and handed it to Joan, then made a note of the item number on the sales receipt.

"Thanks." Joan pushed the papers out of the way and laid Joanie down on the mattress. She spoke without looking at Allie. "Listen, I wanted to apologize for getting upset about you not bringing Joanie to church. Mom's right. This is totally yours and Eric's decision."

Allie scooped the papers up and shuffled them into a stack before shoving them back in the folder. She'd known Joan was upset, and the fact that she hadn't called or come by for two whole days proved it. From the time they were little, Joan always took a while to work through her emotions, whereas Allie reacted in a flash and got over things just as quickly.

"I appreciate that," Allie said.

Joan put an index finger inside a tiny fist and absently caressed the little fingers that closed around it. "But listen, I do think it's important that Joanie is raised going to church. Even going to the nursery every Sunday is important, because she'll grow up comfortable there. The nursery workers are godly women, so it would be good for her to be around them." She ducked her head toward the baby so Allie couldn't see her face.

Allie studied her sister's profile through the straight brown hair spilling forward to tickle Joanie's skin. Joan must feel really strongly about this, though Allie couldn't imagine why. True, Mom and Daddy had taken them to church every Sunday when they were kids, but she couldn't see that it had made that much difference. Their lives weren't any better off than people who didn't go to church. Daddy still had affair after affair, and her parents' marriage still ended in divorce.

She shook her head. "I don't get it, Joan.

You act like there's something mystical about that building. There isn't. Just going to a meeting every Sunday and sitting in a pew to listen to a sermon doesn't change anything. You can look at our own family and see that."

Joan's head snapped up and she caught Allie's gaze. "Listening to a sermon doesn't change anything. Jesus does. I wonder if Daddy ever really knew Jesus."

Now it was Allie's turn to look away. In the past few months Joan had started to use that name so familiarly. She talked about Jesus like he was a regular guy you could walk up to on the street. It made Allie feel weird. She was okay with praying before meals and all that, but this was getting a little too personal. "Well, if he didn't, then that proves my point. Daddy went to church. It didn't make a difference. It didn't stop him from wrecking his marriage and our lives." She got up from the bed and stepped toward the desk, her back to Joan. "Actually, he's still wrecking our lives."

"What do you mean by that?"

Allie put the folder down and reached up to pull the curtains aside. Clouds covered the sky from one horizon to another, creating a white ceiling that left everything below looking dismal. The October wind blew dead leaves down the street in front of her house. "Just that our parents' relationship continues to affect us even though we're adults. That's a psychological fact."

"Are you and Eric having problems?"

Nothing slow about that reaction. Allie wished she had kept her mouth shut. She was just being paranoid, and now Joan would know it. But this Molly thing was starting to worry her. Maybe talking about it with a totally sympathetic person would help her sort out her feelings.

She turned and faced Joan. "I'm sure it's nothing. A baby changes the family dynamics, you know. I've read up on it. Now that Eric is a father, he's starting to reevaluate himself and his life in terms of his definition of what a father is."

A grin flashed on Joan's face. "You're always psychoanalyzing everyone."

"It's true," Allie insisted.

"I'm sure it is. But I don't think you're concerned with Eric's definition. What is *your* definition of a father?"

The room became quiet as Joan's question echoed in Allie's mind. Her sister was right. Allie had married a fun-loving guy, her best friend, a man who cared about others and loved to help anyone in need, and who shared her passion for life. With the birth of their child, Eric had become something else in her mind. Allie suddenly found herself married to a father. Since her own father had hurt her so much, being married to one was emotionally risky for her.

"Okay." She struggled to sort out her thoughts as she spoke. "That's a valid question. Here's another one. Do you think I've unconsciously married someone just like Daddy? You know, tried to replicate my childhood in some weird way."

"No." The speed of Joan's answer gave Allie comfort. Then she went on. "Daddy wasn't all bad, you know. We had a lot of good times as a family before he and Mom divorced. So if Eric does have a few of Daddy's characteristics, that doesn't mean he's going to end up having an affair and divorcing you." Her voice softened. "That's what you're worried about, isn't it?"

Tears stung Allie's eyes, which surprised her. Did she really think Eric was having an affair? No. Not really. But she couldn't deny the fact that their relationship the past few weeks was stormier than it had ever been. Some of that was her fault, of course. If she was going to make a go of her Varie Cose business, she had to pour a lot of effort into it. Why couldn't he understand that? Why couldn't he be supportive instead of demanding more attention than she could give him right now?

"Listen." Joan reached out and took Allie's hand. "I don't know exactly what you're going through, but we had the same father, remember? You're asking the same questions I asked a couple of months ago. I found the answer. We have a perfect heavenly Father, Allie, one with none of the faults of our earthly father."

Allie looked into Joan's eyes. She was so earnest, so passionate about her religion. And she had found something a few months ago. The difference in her was noticeable. Joan was more peaceful, more at ease. Happier than Allie could ever remember. Tori attributed that change to Joan's developing relationship with Ken, but Allie wasn't so sure. The changes in Joan went too deep to be rooted in a relationship with a man.

She squeezed her sister's hand. "I'm so glad you've found your answer, Joan. But that doesn't mean it's right for everyone. I think we all have to work out our own way around life's problems."

Joan hesitated, then gave a very slight nod. "You're right. We all have to come to our own decisions. Just know that I'm praying for you and Eric. If there's anything I can do, you only have to ask."

Gratitude washed over Allie. She might lack a good father, but she was lucky enough to have a couple of incredibly supportive sisters. She put her arms around Joan and hugged. "Thank you."

Allie spent hours that day in front of her computer. She took a couple of breaks to nurse Joanie and after lunch bundled her up for a walk in the stroller around the neighborhood to give them both a breath of fresh air. The rest of the time Betty seemed more than happy to tend her granddaughter while Allie worked, and Allie gratefully let her. When she finally sat back in her desk chair and smiled at her monitor, her shoulders ached from sitting so long.

Her database was a work of art. She even designed easy-to-use data entry screens and keyed in all her customers' names and contact information, along with the specific Varie Cose products they'd ordered. She could print reports that listed and totaled all the orders by hostess, customer, or product. And she'd had a flash of genius when she realized she could scan in the original order forms with her little all-in-one printer, eliminating the need to keep paper copies. She might have a bug or two to work out over the next few days, but all in all, she thought her database was a breathtaking work of sheer brilliance.

But an examination of her new sales report revealed a disappointing truth. She had not sold as much as she thought. Though she'd conducted a couple of big events, when she totaled up all the sales, she was averaging less than a hundred and fifty dollars per party. Her cost on the product was 50 percent, which meant her profit was less than seventy-five dollars per party. Considering the number of hours she spent preparing for each one and doing the follow-up work, she didn't want to think about how much she was making on an hourly basis. A look at her expenses showed her that she wasn't as close to becoming profitable as she'd hoped. In fact, she was still a long way from breaking even.

The phone rang, and she jumped up to grab the extension on the nightstand before the second ring. Her youngest sister's voice cut her off before she could even finish saying, "Hello?"

"Listen, you have got to stop calling my co-workers. It's getting so I can't walk into the break room without someone telling me you've left a ton of messages on their answering machine."

Allie winced at the irritation in Tori's

voice. "I don't know what you're talking about. I haven't called anyone except Heidi, and that's because of her makeover party."

"So you haven't called Diana or Fran?"

"Well, yes, but they came to Heidi's party, not yours."

"Doesn't matter. They all know you're my sister, so when you start acting like a used car salesman, they blame me."

Allie dropped to perch on the edge of the bed. "I'm not acting like a used car salesman! They all indicated on their customer cards that they might be interested in hosting a party themselves. I'm just following up like any good businesswoman would do."

A grunt of Tori's aggravated breath sounded through the phone. "Do me a favor, would you? Stop trying to do business with the people at my office. It's becoming awkward for me. I wish I'd never had that party for you."

Tori really sounded angry. Allie had never heard that edge in her voice before. Mom did say the other day that Tori was under a lot of pressure at work. The last thing Allie wanted to do was cause more stress for her sister, even though Sally Jo insisted constant follow-up was the only way to ensure that your business continued to expand. "Sure, Tori. I won't call any of your friends anymore if you don't want me to."

"Well." Tori relented a bit. "You don't have to go that far. You can call the girls at my apartment complex. Carrie booked a party, didn't she?"

"It's tomorrow night, in fact. I thought you might be there."

"I have to work." She lowered her voice. "Honestly, Allie, this job is starting to get to me. I didn't get out of here until after nine last night and had to be back for a meeting this morning at eight thirty. When I get home, I'm so keyed up I can't sleep."

Allie knew what she meant. Sometimes she lay in bed at night, and all she could think about were a million and one things she wanted to do with her business. But that would calm down after she got everything running smoothly. Maybe Tori's job was the same.

"Are you in the middle of a big project or something?"

"Yes. There's an account my new boss is trying to land, a big one."

"Then maybe when it's over things will calm down for you."

"Maybe." She sounded uncertain. "I hope so. Listen, I need to go. Uh . . ." A pause. "Thanks for understanding about the phone calls. Sorry I was snippy."

Allie smiled. "Hey, if you can't be snippy with your big sister, who can you be snippy with?"

After she hung up, Allie stayed on the bed and stared at the phone. Her closing words to Tori held a lot of truth. A girl knew where she stood with her sisters. After all, they were stuck with you. No matter how ill-tempered or annoying you acted toward them, they couldn't divorce you. And they always forgave you when you came to your senses.

She heaved herself off the bed and returned to her computer. She wanted to do one more thing before Eric got home. Her new credit card allowed online account access, and she wanted to cross-check that against the records of her purchases. Just to make sure everything balanced out.

The computer took a second to pull up her account after she entered her user ID and password. When it did, Allie let out an involuntary cry of alarm. The balance displayed on the screen was huge, much more than she thought she'd spent. That had to be wrong. She clicked the link to display the detail and scanned down the list of transactions. Had she used the card that many times? A quick review told her that every one of the purchases on the list were valid.

She collapsed against the back of the chair. Why hadn't she kept a running total of her expenditures? She didn't have any idea they would add up to so much money.

If Eric found out, he would be furious. Allie glanced furtively behind her at the door. He would be home any minute. She clicked the logout button and closed the window. The computer's wallpaper picture appeared, a shot of Joanie at four weeks, but this time it failed to bring a smile to her face. She needed to book a lot more parties and hope the ladies bought stuff she had in inventory.

Besides, she didn't need to worry about Eric's reaction. She lifted her chin. This was *her* business. She could handle it on her own without having to answer to him.

A touch of alarm twisted her stomach as her gaze fell on all the products on her shelves. She forced her muscles to relax. She could handle this. So what if she had to make a partial payment to her credit card for a couple of months? Though she hadn't planned on doing that, it wasn't a total disaster. At least the interest was tax deductible. Wasn't it?

15

Eric was pulling out of the parking lot after work on Wednesday evening when his cell phone rang. A group of costumed trick-or-treaters stood on the sidewalk, waiting to cross the street behind his truck. He didn't take his gaze off the road to read the caller ID. Instead, he stuck the earpiece into his ear and punched the Talk button so he could shift gears safely as he talked.

"Hello?"

"Hey, Eric, it's Ken Fletcher."

Ken had become a fixture at Allie's family dinners every Sunday afternoon for the past few months since he and Joan started going out. He was a doctor at the hospital emergency room, and seemed like a nice enough guy, but too religious for Eric's taste. "Hey, Ken. What's up?"

"I'm looking for someone to give me a hand with the auction Joan and I are doing next week. Maybe she mentioned it to you?"

He'd heard Allie and Joan talking about some sort of fund-raiser thing going on at their church, but he hadn't paid much attention. "What kind of help?"

"I need someone with a truck and a strong back to give me a hand moving some furniture that's been donated. Can't get much in the trunk of my old Probe."

Eric got that request a lot. Having a pickup was like an open invitation every time someone moved or bought something big. He didn't mind. "When do you want to do it?"

"Tomorrow night, if that's okay. It's the only night this week I'll be off."

Thursday night . . . Allie mentioned something about a party or a meeting or something. Mother probably wouldn't mind watching Joanie for a couple hours. "No problem. I'll get off around five. You want to come by the dispatch office and we'll go from there?"

"Sounds good. Thanks. See you then."

Eric pressed End and took the earpiece out of his ear, then downshifted as he turned into their neighborhood. The clock read just after five and already he saw several small groups of kids running from house to house up and down the street with bulging bags clutched in their hands. He remembered Mother making him finish his dinner before she'd let him go trick-or-treating when he was a kid. These days it made sense to get home before dark, which was a shame. The world wasn't as safe anymore. Even a small town like Danville had its share of crime, though thankfully it wasn't as bad here as in the bigger cities like Lexington or Louisville. That's one reason he and Allie had chosen to live here.

He pulled into the driveway and got out of the truck. A brisk wind blew across the grass, stirring up the earthy smell of fallen leaves. The weather was cold enough to wear coats and jackets, but he didn't see many on the neighborhood children. Who wanted to cover up their costume with a coat? A group of kids brushed by him as they ran up the front sidewalk and climbed the porch steps. The door opened, and Allie stepped outside, a big bowl of candy in her hand and a wide smile plastered across her face. Eric watched as she exclaimed over the costumes and dropped candy into each bag. She was so great with kids, and she obviously liked them. Why didn't she want to stay home and be a full-time mom to Joanie?

The kids left their house and ran across the yard to the one next door. Allie smiled, waiting for Eric as he walked up the porch steps.

"You should have seen the last group," she told him. "There was this tiny little boy in a cowboy hat almost as big as he was. It kept falling over his eyes." She slipped her free arm around him. "In a couple of years, we'll get to take Joanie." Her eyes sparkled.

Eric kissed her. "It sure is good to have you here when I get home."

She stiffened and stepped away, her expression suddenly cold.

"What?" He spread his hands. "What did I say?"

"Why do you have to start out by taking a shot at my job?"

Eric shook his head. "That's not what I meant. I was just saying it's good to see you."

"That's not what you said."

Why was she so touchy lately? He couldn't say a word without setting her off.

"Well, that's what I meant, but I don't mean it anymore." His voice came out louder than he intended.

Allie's gaze dropped as she looked at something behind him. He whirled to find three preteens dressed like punk rockers standing a few feet away. They stared at him through eyes as round as giant gum balls.

Great. Here they were, standing on the front porch and shouting at each other in front of the neighbor kids. He clenched his jaw and turned back to Allie.

"You have customers," he said through gritted teeth as he stepped by her into the house.

Allie came from the nursery into the living room and slipped onto the center couch cushion beside Eric. Joanie had just finished her last meal of the evening and was fast asleep in her crib. Betty's bedroom door was closed. The television played some stupid sports game, of course, but Allie chose to ignore the rise of frustration when Eric didn't take his gaze from the screen. She saw his jaw bunch, so she knew he was still angry with her.

She had to admit he had a right to be. She stared at the television without seeing anything on the screen, super aware of Eric's tense body beside her. She had been a shrew this evening, defensive because she'd just realized how far in debt she'd gone. His comment about having her at home rubbed her the wrong way, and she snapped before she thought.

She steeled herself, then said the words she found so hard. "I'm sorry I jumped to the wrong conclusion earlier and barked at you."

He didn't look at her. "You didn't jump to the wrong conclusion."

Allie narrowed her eyelids. "You mean you were taking a potshot at my job?"

His voice sounded as tight as his jaw. "I didn't think so at the time. Now . . ." He turned his head to look at her. "Yeah, I think I was. I'll admit it. I don't like your job. I wish you'd quit."

Allie forced herself to remain calm. At least he was looking at her and not the stupid television. "I thought you said you supported me in this. I thought you understood how important it is to me."

"I thought so, too, before I knew what it was going to be like." He cocked his head and his voice lost a touch of its hardness. "Allie, I thought you wanted to stay home with Joanie instead of taking her to a babysitter."

"I do! She isn't in daycare, is she?"

"Only because my mother is here." Eric glanced toward the bedroom door and lowered his voice. "You're taking advantage of her. I don't think you even want Mother to leave anymore."

Allie leaned away from him, hurt. "You're taking just as much advantage of her as I am. You let her fix breakfast for you every morning and pack your lunch like you were ten years old. You've asked her to watch Joanie a couple of times too. The deal was that I'd stay with the baby during the day and you'd watch her at night when I had a party or a meeting. You left her with your mother Tuesday night while you went to Molly's house." She tried to keep the bitterness out of her voice as she spoke Molly's name, but she didn't entirely succeed.

If he heard her tone, Eric chose to ignore it. "You're gone most nights before I get home, so if Mother wasn't here, you'd have to hire a babysitter."

"My mother —"

"Has a job and a life. You can't expect her to arrange her life around your party schedule." Allie opened her mouth to react to his wording, but he held up a hand. "Sorry. Your *work* schedule. And you're right, I did tell you I supported you in this job. That was before I knew that I was going to lose my wife."

"You haven't lost your wife." Allie couldn't hold his gaze. This was the first night she'd been home this week.

"Yes, I have. You might be a stay-at-home mom during the day, but you're not a stay-at-home wife." He covered her hand with his, and Allie felt his warmth seeping into her cold fingers. "You know I want you to stay home all the time, but if you insist on working, I wish you'd go back to your job at the state. At least then Joanie would get to see both of her parents at the same time."

She moved her hand away. Why did she even tell him about Gina putting her on a leave of absence status? Better if she'd kept her mouth shut.

Should she give up on Varie Cose? Put Joanie in daycare and return to the steady paycheck? She'd have to come clean about her debt to Eric, and they'd take a huge loss financially. And what would she do with all that expensive inventory?

No. She couldn't. She was too far into Varie Cose to quit now.

She raised her head and locked eyes with Eric. "I can't quit. I've put so much work into this business. I'm making a lot of progress. Things will calm down once I've established a good client base and gotten a few people signed up as consultants under me. I won't have to do as many parties then, because I'll get a percentage of their sales. That's where most of Sally Jo's income comes from."

Eric held her gaze, and for a moment Allie saw the same sadness in the depths of his eyes that she saw so often in Betty's.

"I hope so, Allie."

The slow way he shook his head before he turned back to the television shot a chill through Allie. She had never heard her upbeat husband sound so pessimistic. His tone reminded her of . . .

She stood abruptly. "I'm going to bed."

He spoke without looking up. "I'll be there in a while."

Allie fought against tears as she closed the bedroom door. For a minute there, Eric sounded just like her father. She rested her forehead on the door, her throat tight. From now on, she needed to focus on signing up new consultants instead of just booking parties. She had to pay off her debt and become profitable soon.

16

On Thursday morning Allie did laundry. It was the one household task Betty hadn't taken over. Though she had offered, Allie refused. There were limits to her comfort level in the household tasks she gave up into her mother-in-law's eager hands. Washing her underwear was one of them.

As she folded the last of Eric's T-shirts and placed it at the top of the neat stack on her bed, the doorbell rang. She glanced at the clock. Darcy called earlier and asked if she had any four-ounce bottles of Stay Clean Spray. A customer wanted one quickly.

She tossed a burp pad over her shoulder and picked Joanie up off the bed. "Come on, sweetie pie. Maybe Darcy brought a friend for you to play with."

Sure enough, Darcy stood on the doorstep with her baby in her arms. At least, Allie assumed there was a baby bundled in the giant wad of blankets she carried. As Allie opened the door, a cold breeze swooped into the house. She stepped sideways so Joanie was behind the door, protected from the wind.

Darcy rushed inside. "Brrr. It's cold out there. I think it's going to snow soon."

Allie shut the door behind her. "I wouldn't be surprised, but it won't stick. Not yet, anyway."

Darcy peeled off a couple of layers of blanket and dropped them in the chair. Beneath them Brandon was still invisible inside a puffy winter coat with a hood and built-in mittens. When Darcy turned him in her arms to face Allie and Joanie, his little face peeked adorably at them from within the hood.

Allie held Joanie against her torso and pointed. "Look who's here, Joanie. Brandon came over to visit."

Joanie could care less. She didn't seem to notice the little boy, but Brandon sure noticed her. A smile lit his face, and he let out an ear-piercing screech.

Darcy winced. "He's started doing that in the last week. I know it's a growth phase, but I wish he'd get over it."

Betty emerged from the depths of the guest room and stopped just behind the chair nearest the doorway. She watched them in her expressionless way.

Allie did the introductions. "Betty, this is my friend Darcy and her son, Brandon. Darcy, this is my mother-in-law, Betty Harrod."

Darcy smiled and dipped her head. "Nice to meet you, Mrs. Harrod."

Betty inclined her own head, then looked at Allie. "Would you girls like a cup of tea or hot chocolate? I got sugar free at the store the other day. Only fifty calories per eight-ounce serving."

Determined not to take offense, Allie smiled. "That was nice of you. Darcy, can you stay for a few minutes?"

"Sure. A cup of tea sounds great. Thanks."

Betty turned. "I'll put the kettle on."

Did they even own a kettle? Allie couldn't remember one, but Betty disappeared into the kitchen and a second later Allie heard water running.

"Get Brandon out of his coat and I'll grab your spray."

Allie went into the bedroom to her inventory shelves. Her desk was much cleaner than when Joan saw it last. All the paperwork had been either scanned and discarded or filed in one of the hanging folders in the bottom drawer. Her sister would be proud of her organization.

"Hey, Darcy," she called. "Come in here a minute. I want to show you something."

Darcy stepped into the room with Brandon on her hip. Her eyes moved as she took in the room and especially all the product stacked neatly on the shelves. "Wow. You're going to catch up with Sally Jo soon."

"Oh, I doubt that." Allie knew her tone sounded dry. "Come over here and let me show you the database I built. It stores all my customer information, expenses, and sales." Allie walked her through the entry screens and pulled up a couple of reports.

Clearly impressed, Darcy eyed the scanned version of a customer sales receipt. "So you're not even going to keep the paper ones?"

Allie shook her head. "No need to. I can always print a copy if I want. Same with packing slips and all that."

"Doesn't Varie Cose's system keep track of all that for you?"

"Some of it, but they don't track sales by customer. And of course they don't track business expenses besides product orders, like office supplies. I can enter all those into my database, and in one report I can see every cent I've spent right alongside every cent I've taken in."

"It's impressive." Darcy turned an admiring glance her way. "I can barely turn a computer on."

"It's really not that hard. It only took me about a day, and it's going to help me stay organized. Plus, it'll save so much time." She basked a moment in Darcy's admiration, then pulled a bottle off the shelf. "Here's your spray."

"Thanks. Let me get my checkbook."

They went into the kitchen and sat at the table while Betty moved around the kitchen getting cups and tea bags. Allie couldn't help but notice that she set the sugar bowl in front of Darcy, but placed a small box of Splenda in front of her.

Darcy noticed too. She nodded toward it. "Are you dieting?"

Allie twisted her lips in a grimace. "Sort of. I'm trying to fit back into my prebaby jeans. It's not looking very hopeful at the moment." She lifted her free hand to pat Joanie's back. "I put on a lot of weight with this one."

There. It didn't sound too awful to admit it out loud.

Darcy nodded sympathetically. "I know what you mean. I gained seventy pounds with Brandon."

Allie gave a low whistle. "Seventy

pounds?" She tilted her head to look at Darcy's trim figure. "You sure don't look like it."

"I take an aerobics class at the gym three days a week. When I started doing that, the pounds just melted off."

Allie kept her gaze fixed on Darcy, but she was aware that Betty had turned from the stove to watch them. "What gym?"

"Danville Athletic Center. It's over on the bypass by the movie theater."

"I'm a member there. My husband gave me a membership for my birthday, but I haven't actually gone yet."

Darcy's face lit. "Then you can go to the aerobics classes too. They're included in the membership fee. Want to go with me tomorrow morning? They have daycare."

Aerobics class? The idea of dressing up in leotards and prancing around with a bunch of other women in front of a mirror didn't sound all that appealing. Leaving Joanie in the gym's daycare for an hour sounded even less appealing. She didn't know what kind of people worked there. She'd need to check references and all that.

Allie shook her head. "I don't know."

Betty stepped forward. "I'll watch the baby for you."

Allie protested. "Betty, you're already

watching her tonight while I go to the meeting at my director's house. Eric will probably be gone a couple of hours."

"I don't mind. I'll be here anyway. I might
as well be useful."

Darcy smiled. "There you go. The class
starts at nine. Want to meet me there?"

No, Allie really didn't want to. But another
glance at Darcy's trim figure made her
hesitate. If aerobics had helped Darcy lose
seventy pounds, maybe she should try it.

She heaved a resigned sigh. "I guess I
might as well."

By the time Darcy left, Joanie had drifted
off to sleep. Allie laid her in the infant seat
in the living room. She'd thought a lot
about Eric's comment last night, and some-
time around three in the morning — after
she got over being mad at him — she realized he was right. She was taking advantage of her mother-in-law.

She returned to the kitchen where Betty
still sat at the table, sipping her tea. She
had used the fancy coffee cups with matching saucers Allie got as a wedding gift, the
first time they'd ever been used. She and
Eric drank from coffee mugs, and if they
entertained, they usually ordered pizza. It
was actually kind of fun, having a friend

over, drinking tea from fancy cups. Allie slipped into her chair and picked hers up. The scent of peaches from the herbal tea filled her nostrils as she finished off the last sip.

She set the cup in the saucer with a soft *clink*. "Thanks for fixing tea for us and for offering to watch Joanie tomorrow." She fiddled with the paper tab on the end of her used tea bag. "In fact, I don't think I've thanked you appropriately for all the things you've done around here lately — the cooking and dusting and running the vacuum and all."

"You're welcome. I don't mind. It's the least I can do to repay you for letting me stay with you."

From the shrewd way Betty looked at her over the top of her cup, Allie suspected she hadn't kept her reluctance hidden well enough. "Well, that's what families are for, right?"

"But you know what they say about house guests and dead fish."

Allie stared at her. "No, I can't say I do."

"They both start to stink after a few days."

Allie laughed. "Don't worry, you don't stink." She sobered. "I admit at first I wasn't sure if you staying here was going to work out. But you have helped me so much with

Joanie. I don't think I could have managed to launch my business without you."

Betty set her cup in its saucer and folded her hands in her lap. "I'm glad I could help. I was so worried when I first moved in that I'd become a burden to you and Eric."

Allie almost choked. Who said anything about moving in? On the other hand, she'd been there two weeks. She was practically a fixture. "Uh, well, of course you're not a burden. Still, I'm sure you miss being in your own home."

A brief smile appeared on Betty's lips as she glanced around the kitchen. "Not as much as I thought I would."

Okay, so maybe letting Betty have free rein of the house had been a mistake. She'd dug herself right in and put down roots. Allie's eyes must have betrayed her shock, because a brief smile appeared on her mother-in-law's lips.

"I know we haven't been close, Allie. I think that's partly my fault."

Partly? Allie fought hard to keep a sudden stab of indignation from showing on her face. She avoided looking at Betty as she spoke with exquisite care. "We've only seen each other a few times since Eric and I married. And we didn't get off to a very good start at the wedding."

"Oh? How so?"

Startled, Allie looked up. "You called me a selfish child. You said our marriage wouldn't last."

"I did?" Confusion creased Betty's forehead.

"In the bride room, in front of all my bridesmaids." How could she not remember?

The creases cleared. "I asked if I could rearrange the name cards for the reception dinner." Her lips pursed. "You said 'no' rather strongly."

A touch of the anger Allie had felt at the time stiffened her spine. "I spent hours on those seating charts."

"I'm sure you did, and you couldn't have known that Aunt Edna and Cousin Gerty fight like barn cats. I was trying to avoid a scene."

"Oh." Allie sniffed. She had been something of a maniac the day of the wedding. "Well, you didn't have to call me names."

Betty's bewildered gaze locked onto hers. "I merely said marriage requires that we leave childhood behind and think of others. It doesn't have a chance if the wife is self-centered." She paused, then conceded, "I suppose that wasn't the most diplomatic thing to say to a bride on her wedding day, was it?"

"Probably not." But looking back on the day from a safe distance of five years, the incident seemed almost silly. Stressed-out bride with a big mouth. Taciturn mother-in-law. A recipe for a verbal volcano. At least on the bride's part.

The brief smile put in a second appearance on Betty's lips. "I watch you with your family, and I realize how odd you must think us. You're so open with one another, so friendly." Her head dropped forward as she looked down at her hands. "I never realized how much Eric missed by being an only child."

A stab of pity cut through Allie's thoughts as she looked at Betty's bowed head. "Why didn't you have more kids?"

"I couldn't. I had complications with Eric's delivery and had to have a hysterectomy a few days later."

"I didn't realize. I thought you and Don chose to have only one child."

"Oh no. We wanted more. We'd always talked about having three or four children."

Allie got up from the table and walked to the stove. Why hadn't Eric ever mentioned the reason he was an only child? On second thought, he probably didn't know. His mother's reserved ways weren't new. She would have thought sharing information like that with her son inappropriate. And from what Eric said, his father's conversation always centered around work or cars or sports.

So spending time with the Sanderson family must have given Betty a glimpse of the family she might have had. Allie could understand why she'd want to become a part of them. But to move in with her and Eric?

Allie picked up the kettle and tapped a cautious finger on the side to feel the temperature. The water was still hot enough. She put the used tea bag back in her cup and poured steaming water on it, then held it toward Betty with a wordless question. Betty nodded, and Allie filled her cup too.

"Well, for what it's worth, I think Eric turned out just fine without siblings." Allie returned to her seat and dunked the tea bag in the water as she poured sweetener in. "So have you made any decisions about Don?"

"No."

Betty's tone held a note of finality, but Allie wasn't about to let the conversation stop there. She had finally managed to pry more than three words out of Betty in one sitting, and she intended to press her advantage.

She had to understand more about what was going on between those two if she was going to figure out a way to shove her mother-in-law out of her nest and back into her own.

"Eric said he called the other day. Didn't you two talk about whatever the problem is?"

Betty shook her head and remained silent, her gaze fixed on her cup.

"So what *is* the problem, anyway?"

At first Allie thought she wouldn't answer. Her face remained expressionless, though a slight movement of her eyelids looked as though she was considering whether or not to confide in her daughter-in-law. When she looked up, she seemed to have reached a decision.

"Don has worked for his company for over thirty years. He can retire with full benefits in three months when he turns sixty-two." She fell silent.

"Are you worried about having him underfoot all day when he does?" Allie prompted.

Betty shook her head. "He informed me the week before I left that he doesn't intend to retire. Not ever."

"What, he wants to keep working until he drops dead on the job?"

Betty lifted a shoulder in a delicate gesture. "I suppose so."

Allie stared at her. Trying to read her mother-in-law's expression was like trying to read an empty whiteboard. The woman obviously needed some practice in the art of communication. "And you want him to retire?"

Betty looked up, mild surprise apparent in her raised eyebrows. "Yes, of course."

"Why? Aren't you happy with things the way they are?"

"I'm happy enough." Betty picked up her spoon and stirred slow circles in her tea. "No, I'm not. Since Eric left for college, the house has been so quiet."

Allie looked down quickly to hide her grin. In a million years she never thought she'd hear Betty Harrod complain of a quiet house. When she was sure no hint of laughter would sound in her voice, she said, "So basically you're bored. You want your husband to retire so you'll have someone to talk to."

"Not just to talk to. To be with. We used to plan all the things we would do after retirement. Don always wanted to travel, to see and do new things we don't have time for now."

"What about you? What did you always want to do?"

"Travel would be nice." The edges of her lips lifted into one of the first genuine smiles Allie had ever seen. She went on in a conspiratorial tone. "I thought we could take ballroom dancing lessons, and then we could go on a cruise to Alaska and burn up the dance floor like Fred and Ginger."

Though Allie could not begin to imagine Betty whirling around a dance floor in the arms of her stout husband, she grinned in return. "That would be fun."

The smile faded and sadness deepened the sagging skin beneath Betty's brown eyes. "Now I don't think we will ever do any of the things we planned."

"Why not?" Allie slapped a hand on the table. "You should make him retire. Just march right up to him and say, 'Don, I'm not going to let you spoil my plans. You're going to retire, and that's that.'"

Betty's gaze became wistful. "That's one thing I've come to admire about you, Allie. You are the most determined woman I've ever seen. If you want something, you do whatever it takes to get it."

Allie fought the urge to preen. Betty was certainly full of surprises this morning. Allie would have sworn that her mother-in-law didn't admire a single thing about her. "Thank you," she said simply.

"In fact, watching you has forced me to rethink the mistakes of my life. I always believed that staying at home when Eric was young was important."

"You don't now?"

"Oh, I still do. I admire you for wanting to stay home and keep Joanie out of day-care, but where I made my mistake was in not returning to work when he went to school. I foolishly kept on as before, thinking I could focus all my efforts on making a comfortable home for Don." Her voice became wry. "I suppose I made it too comfortable. Now he apparently wants things to stay as they are forever." She paused to sip from her cup, and Allie waited for her to continue. "I should have done what you're doing and made sure I had something of my own outside of Don."

"You mean a source of income?"

Betty shook her head. "Not necessarily. I'm talking about a career, a focus. Something that is my own away from Don. I mean, look at me now. I'm almost sixty years old and I don't have anything of my own. No interests. No hobbies other than cooking. No activities except cleaning the house. Everything I am is associated with Don. I'm dependent on him far beyond the finances." She took another sip and then patted her mouth with her napkin. "I can't imagine you ever being dependent on Eric that way."

No, Allie couldn't imagine ever being so wrapped up in Eric that she had no interests of her own. Another reason her Varie Cose business needed to fly. But at the moment they weren't talking about her. They had to solve Betty's problem, and Allie needed to make sure the resolution didn't include living with them. "So if you're not going to call Don and demand that he retire like you guys planned, what are you going to do? Join a club in your community? A big city like Detroit probably has all kinds of things to do." Allie snapped her fingers as an idea occurred. "I'll bet they have cooking clubs. You seem to enjoy trying new recipes and stuff. You've cooked some amazing meals for us lately, all of them really healthy."

Betty gave one of her nearly imperceptible smiles. "I know you want to lose weight, and I thought that was one way I could help you."

Allie leaned against the back of her chair as her mother-in-law's words sank in. So Betty's comments and efforts hadn't been designed to insult her after all. The woman was trying to be helpful. And she hadn't intended to offend her at the wedding, either. Embarrassed, Allie realized she had been too quick to jump on the defensive. "Thank you, Betty. That was very sweet of you."

Betty inclined her head and toyed with the handle on her teacup.

Allie continued. "I think you've enjoyed experimenting with new recipes. I'll bet you'd really get into a cooking club. You could trade recipes and cook for each other and stuff like that. You'd be their star member by the second meeting."

Betty shook her head. "I don't think joining a club is the answer. I've begun to wonder if I need to do something more drastic. Your family has been so kind to include me as one of their own. Now that I've met my granddaughter, I've remembered that I do have family besides Don. Danville is a nice little town. I've been thinking maybe I'll stay here. That way I can be part of Joanie's life. I could help you and Eric, because you're both so busy."

Allie spoke cautiously. "There are some nice little houses over in Gram's neighborhood that aren't very expensive."

Lines appeared beneath Betty's carefully curled bangs. "Oh, I don't think I could afford to buy a house. I've been frugal and made some wise investments, so Don and I have a comfortable nest egg. But I wouldn't expect him to continue to support me forever. If I move out on my own, how would I pay the bills? I haven't had a job since before Eric was born. The only thing I'm good at is being a housekeeper."

Eric and I don't want a housekeeper, Allie wanted to shout. She didn't expect Don to support her, but she expected her son and daughter-in-law to? The situation was far more desperate than Allie realized. Besides, how could Betty even consider leaving Don after being married more than thirty years?

"I understand what you're going through," she said slowly, "and I would love to have you nearby so Joanie can grow up knowing both of her grandmothers. But I'm not sure the answer is to leave your husband. I still think you should call him and talk about this. Tell him exactly how you feel."

Betty pushed her cup and saucer away and leaned back in the chair. That secretive half smile returned to her lips. "Oh, I won't need to call him. He'll call me tomorrow."

Considering Don had only called once in the two weeks Betty had been gone, Allie couldn't imagine how she could be so sure he'd call tomorrow. "Did he tell you that the last time you talked?"

Betty shook her head, a glint of laughter

lighting her eyes. "The electric bill is over-due. Tomorrow they'll shut off the power."

17

The dispatch center door opened a few minutes before five. Eric rolled backward in his desk chair so he could catch Ken's eye and waved him into the room.

"I'm a few minutes early," Ken said as he stepped through the doorway.

"Not a problem. I'm just wrapping up here." He glanced toward the two women in the room. "Ken, this is Molly. She works day shift with me. And this is Rachel, who's on second. Ken's a doctor over at the hospital emergency room, so he treats most of the folks we send there."

Ken stepped forward and shook each of their hands. Molly smiled politely, but Eric noticed a gleam of interest in Rachel's eyes. She had good reason. Ken was an okay-looking guy, though Eric wasn't the best judge of that. The second shift dispatcher held on to Ken's hand about a second too long, her smile a fraction too wide, which made Eric feel the need to further clarify the doctor's position. He caught Rachel's gaze. "Ken's a friend of my sister-in-law."

The gleam faded as understanding dawned, and Eric turned back toward his computer screens to hide a grin. Not only did he work with a bunch of women, they were, for the most part, *single.* Several of them displayed a more-than-average desire to change their marital status.

He stood and bent over to log out of the various systems. If Ken were to break up with Joan because of someone he met through Eric, Allie would never forgive him. Better get him out of here before the other second shift dispatcher, a real looker, showed up.

They left Ken's car in the parking lot and climbed into Eric's pickup. Ken directed him to a neighborhood of high-priced homes on the other side of town. As Eric navigated through the streets, he kept his eyes focused on the road. This was the first time they'd ever been alone, since he'd only known the guy a couple of months. The only thing he had in common with Ken was the Sanderson sisters. And football.

Ken's voice cut into the silence. "So who do you like for the Super Bowl this year?"

"The Steelers, for sure, and I'm betting

the Seahawks."

Ken nodded. "I'm a New England fan myself. And I'm keeping an eye on the Seahawks this year too."

They debated the abilities of various teams and players until Eric pulled into the neighborhood. Ken drew a slip of paper from his jeans pocket. "Says here to take the second right onto Glenellen Drive."

Eric drove slowly down the street, admiring the beautiful and obviously expensive homes. "You know, Allie and I used to go parking in the back part of this neighborhood."

Oops. Probably shouldn't talk about that to a religious guy like Ken.

Ken laughed. "I could point out a few parking places around Indianapolis myself."

That was a surprise. Eric got the impression Ken had always been superreligious. Maybe he'd been normal as a kid.

Eric turned onto the second street on the right, and then pulled into the driveway Ken indicated. Ken compared the number on the paper to the one over the garage. "Looks like this is the place. Mr. Carter is a widower in our church. His wife died a few years ago, and he said he has a few things he'd like to get rid of."

As he followed Ken up the sidewalk, Eric

admired the landscaping. Allie would love this place. The yard was immaculate, with all sorts of shrubs and fancy grasses and the like. Even this late in the year he couldn't see a dead leaf in evidence anywhere, testimony to the fact that somebody spent a lot of time gardening. Of course, if you lived in an expensive house like this, you could probably afford to pay a gardener.

The door was opened by an elderly man in gray slacks and a sweater. "Come in, boys. I've been expecting you."

Ken shook the man's hand. "Thanks, Mr. Carter. We really appreciate your donation for the auction. This is my friend Eric."

Eric stepped inside after Ken and Mr. Carter shut the door behind him. The house was immaculate, and as impressive as the yard. Eric tried not to goggle at the rich furnishings as they followed Mr. Carter down the hallway.

"There it is, boys." Mr. Carter waved toward a desk against one side of the family room wall. "It's not new, but it should fetch a good price. I've got a few other things to go as well, but that's the big one."

It should, indeed, fetch a good price. A beautiful piece of furniture, an antique. Eric didn't know much about wood, but the surface gleamed with a warm, rich color like perfectly browned toast. It had curlicues carved all over the front and side panels.

Ken stepped close and ran an admiring hand over the top. Shaking his head, he turned to Mr. Carter. "Are you sure you want to donate this? It's obviously worth a lot of money."

The older man nodded. "I hope so. It'll help you young people get down to Mexico where you can do some good. When I was younger, I had thoughts of going to Mexico, but I never got the chance. After my time in the army, I had no desire to travel anymore."

Ken pointed to a framed photo on the wall. "You have children, don't you? They might want this desk."

Mr. Carter waved a hand in dismissal. "They're not interested. Both of them have homes of their own, and they've decorated with newfangled stuff. Besides" — he glanced around the room — "if they want antiques, they'll have plenty to pick from."

Eric followed the man's gaze. He was right. This house was loaded with antiques.

"Well, if you're sure."

Eric and Ken each took one side. They carried the desk through the hallway and out to the truck. It was a lot heavier than it looked. Mr. Carter gave them an old blanket to cover it, and a roll of masking tape to wrap around the blanket to keep it from flying off as they drove. Then he directed them to a couple of boxes in the garage, heavy with stuff he wanted to donate. Eric glimpsed an old mantle clock in the box that Allie would probably love.

After they'd gotten everything secure in the back of the pickup, they stood beside the cab. The sun was low in the sky and threw deep shadows across the yard.

"I can't thank you enough, sir," Ken told him. "You've been more than generous."

He held out a hand. Mr. Carter took it and gave it a firm shake, then extended his toward Eric.

As he shook Eric's hand, he said, "I appreciate what you young people are doing. About time that church got a fire going. You just go on down to Mexico and help those people."

Eric gave an embarrassed nod and released the man's hand. The old guy thought he was part of the church.

Ken grinned as he rounded the front of the truck toward the passenger side. "You could come with us, Mr. Carter. We'd love to have you."

Mr. Carter laughed. "No, I think I'd better stay here. But thanks for the invite."

As Eric backed out of the driveway, Mr.

Carter stood on the sidewalk and watched until they turned off his street.

"He was a nice old guy," Eric said. "I can't believe that desk, though. He could probably sell that for a small fortune. And some of the things in those boxes looked like antiques too."

Ken lifted a shoulder. "He doesn't look like he needs the money. Besides, you heard him. This is a way he can be part of our work in Mexico."

Eric let the comment pass. From what he knew of this trip the church was planning, they were going down there to build a house and give medical attention to the poor children. As far as Eric was concerned, those were admirable goals. A shame those people in Mexico would have to put up with a bunch of religious talk at the same time.

They rode in silence during the short trip to the church. Ken directed him to drive his truck around to a back entrance, where they could unload the stuff.

Carrying one of the heavy boxes, Eric followed Ken through a back door and down a short hallway. The last time Eric had been in this church was the day of his wedding. Ken opened the door and reached inside to flip on the light.

"Uh, let's see." He glanced around the

room. "Put that over there, and then let's move some of this stuff around so we have room for the desk."

Boxes and bags lined the walls. Eric helped Ken shuffle them around until they'd cleared a big enough area. "Man, you guys have got a lot of stuff."

Ken's glance circled the room. "The members of the church have been generous. Kind of surprised me, to be honest. When I first started going here, I figured them for a bunch of Sunday morning pew-warmers." He grinned. "They're not as exuberant as the folks at my church back in Indiana, but the way they've supported this mission trip has really opened my eyes. They're a great bunch of people who worship the Lord in their own way."

Eric turned away and headed down the hallway before Ken could see him roll his eyes. Time to get the truck unloaded and take Ken back to his car. Eric could only take so much religious talk in one night.

He hopped up into the bed of the pickup. Ken joined him, and together they stripped off the masking tape and uncovered the desk. Eric took one side, Ken the other, and they lifted it toward the back of the truck.

As Ken hopped down, he commented, "I take it you're not much on church."

Eric let out a snort. "You got that right."

"Why not? Not that it's any of my business or anything."

Eric almost said, "No, it's not, so butt out." But Ken was a nice enough guy, and Eric didn't really have anything against him. No reason to antagonize him, especially since he had to stare at him over the dinner table every Sunday. Besides, if Eric told him how he really felt, it might shut the guy up about religion for good.

When Ken had a firm grip on his end, Eric got down from the truck bed and lifted the other side. They hefted it, and Ken walked backward into the building. They placed the desk in the spot they'd cleared, and as they were returning to the truck, Eric answered Ken's question.

"We didn't go to church all that often when I was growing up. My parents don't have anything against church, but they've never really been into religion. We went with my grandmother every so often, mostly on special occasions like Christmas and Easter. When I was about eleven or twelve, the youth group had a party at the skating rink. The leader made a point of telling me about it and that he'd really like me to come. Sounded like fun, so I went."

Ken's face became guarded, almost as

though he knew what was coming. He didn't say anything, so Eric continued. "Turns out the guy was a pervert. I was pretty strong for my age, so I got away. Called my mother to come get me."

"Did you report him?"

"I never told anyone." Eric gave a humorless laugh. "Didn't have to. The kid he tried it on after I left that night did, and then they started coming out of the woodwork. Last time I checked, his name was still on the child abuse registry."

Ken's expression did not change. "How did your church react?"

Eric shrugged. "No idea. I never went back. It kind of left a bad taste in my mouth for churches, you know?"

"I don't blame you."

Eric shot him a look of surprise. "You don't?"

"Heck, no!" Ken pounded a fist into his other hand. "You better not let me catch somebody hurting a kid, church or no church."

Eric gave him a grim smile. "I'm with you there."

They were silent as they climbed into the pickup and Eric started the engine. He steered through the parking lot and turned onto the street. As the steepled building receded in the rearview mirror, Ken spoke. "You know, not everyone who attends church is like that guy."

Eric glanced sideways at him. "I know. I just never saw much sense in the whole church thing. I'd rather spend my Sunday mornings relaxing with my family."

"Well, that's kind of the point of church too. Only it's getting together with your church family."

"See, that's where you lose me." Eric turned the steering wheel and guided the truck onto Fourth Street. "I'm not interested in claiming any sort of relationship to a bunch of people I don't know. Especially when there are creeps like that guy hiding in the pews. Plus, I don't see the need. I know how to act, how to treat people decently. I'm basically a good person. I don't need a minister to tell me how to act."

"I can see where it might be confusing. But Christianity isn't just about being a good person. It's about a relationship with God, and about how much he loves us."

Whatever. Eric pulled the truck into the parking lot of the dispatch center. About time too. He'd about reached the breaking point with this conversation. In a minute he'd have a hard time being "good" himself.

He parked next to Ken's Ford, and Ken

hopped out. Before he closed the door, he leaned in, and for a minute Eric thought he was going to continue his church lecture. If he did, Eric would be tempted to put the truck in reverse and leave with Ken still hanging on the door.

Instead, he said, "Thanks for your help. Are you by any chance free Saturday? Somebody's donating a bunch of stuff in their garage, and a truck sure would come in handy."

Great. The guy wanted another chance to shove the church stuff at him. Eric was tempted to refuse, make up an excuse. Problem was, he hated to lie. He really didn't have any plans until the college games came on Saturday afternoon. Allie probably had some Varie Cose thing going on. "Around ten o'clock be okay?"

"That'll be great." Ken started to close the door, then paused. "Are you and Allie planning to come to the auction next Tuesday?"

Eric shrugged. "We haven't talked about it."

"I wish you would. We're serving dinner, something easy like spaghetti, I think." Ken grinned. "It's free, but we can be forced to accept a donation to the cause."

Plus, it would give Ken and his buddies a

chance to prove that church people weren't all bad. Eric could see the setup a mile away. "I'll mention it to Allie, but she'll probably have a party or a meeting or something."

Ken hesitated. "Encourage her. I think you'll both have a good time."

The guy didn't give up, did he?

"We'll see," Eric said. That was as close as he was coming to a commitment to go to church.

Allie mounted the steps to Sally Jo's front door. She was dreading this meeting. Not that she didn't want to see the girls or her director, but Sally Jo was going to let them try out the winter skin care products and introduce them to a new line of colors the company had just released. Allie knew she would be tempted to order the demo kit, and she had made a resolution not to buy any more products or kits until she was in the black. As she stood on the porch, she gave herself a quick pep talk and then pressed the doorbell.

"Come on in," Sally Jo said when she threw open the door. "The others are in the kitchen."

Allie followed her down the short hallway and found Darcy and Nicole seated at the kitchen table. She slid into the empty chair next to Darcy.

Sally Jo stood on the other side, so they were all facing her. "Now that we're all here, we can get started."

"Kirsten and Laura aren't coming tonight?" Allie asked.

Sally Jo's lips pressed into a disapproving line. "They quit."

Allie, Darcy, and Nicole exchanged glances, then Darcy asked, "Did they say why?"

"Various reasons." Sally Jo waved a hand in the air. "Too much time involved, their inability to sell the products, not enough customers. It all boils down to a lack of commitment. I can't say I was surprised. I've gotten so that I can predict who will make it in this business and who won't." She beamed at each of them in turn. "I'm happy to say all three of you ladies have what it takes to be successful."

Darcy straightened in her chair, a pleased smile on her face. Her attitude sure had changed since that first makeup demo. She'd bought into Varie Cose as fully as Allie. But Allie noticed Nicole didn't meet anyone's eye. She straightened her notepad in front of her.

I'll bet she quits next. Maybe she'd sell me the manicure demo kit she bought last week when I bought the pedicure kit.

Allie lassoed that thought and reined it in. *No! I'm not buying anything else.*

She reached into her briefcase, which sat on the floor between her chair and Darcy's, and pulled out a stack of her reports. She flipped through them and found a blank page to make notes on.

Beside her, Darcy's eyes lit up and she reached over to snatch a page out of Allie's hand. "Hey, this is what I was telling you about." She held the page toward Sally Jo, then said to Allie, "Before you got here I told them about your computer program and all the cool reports you can do."

Sally Jo took the paper Darcy held out, page one of Allie's customer summary report. She scanned the page, then looked at Allie over the top of it. "You have all your customers in there, with their addresses and everything?"

Allie nodded. "Whenever someone places an order, I pull them up on my computer and record the item. It helps me keep track not only of the products they've bought but of the exact colors too. So if someone wants to reorder, I've got everything at my fingertips without having to go through a bunch of paper files."

Sally Jo's brow wrinkled. "I've got records

for each customer too, but I keep their order forms alphabetized in a file cabinet in my office."

"I don't have that much room," Allie confessed. "My mother-in-law is staying in our spare room at the moment, so my 'office' is a corner of my bedroom. I've started scanning all the order forms and recording the document ID in the customer database."

"She doesn't even have to keep the paper records." Darcy tapped the paper. "She can pull it up and print it whenever she wants."

"That must take a lot of time," Nicole said.

Allie shrugged. "Not much more than keeping paper files organized. Plus, since I've got my customer names and addresses in the computer, I can do mailing labels. I'm going to send them all a Christmas card."

"Not just Christmas cards." Sally Jo spoke slowly, staring at the report in her hand. "You could send postcards announcing new product lines, or sales, or price reductions."

Allie hadn't thought of that. She sucked in an excited breath. "You know what else my program can do? I can print labels only for those customers who have bought the items that are on special. That way I wouldn't waste postage sending cards about skin care products to somebody who only buys cleaning products."

"I've intended to do customer mailing labels," Sally Jo said, "but I just haven't taken the time to type all those names and addresses into my word processing software. I'm not very good with computers, so it would take me forever."

Darcy grinned broadly at Allie. "Me either, but you almost make me want to learn just so I can do all that stuff I saw at your house." She looked at Sally Jo and Nicole. "You should see all the stuff she does on her computer. Inventory reports, sales summaries, and all these cool reports."

Sally Jo held the page across the table to Allie, her expression thoughtful. Allie took it and shuffled the pile of papers she held into a neat stack, embarrassed but pleased at Darcy's praise.

Then Sally Jo's face cleared and her blinding smile found its way back to her mouth. "Time to get started. We're going to have fun tonight, girls." She picked up a package and held it out to Nicole at the end of the table. "Go ahead and use the makeup removal cloths while I heat some moist towels in the microwave. We're going to give each other facials!"

Allie slipped her reports back into her briefcase and took a damp cloth from the package Darcy handed her. As she rubbed her makeup off her face, her mind was already busy planning the mailing label query she would write when she got home.

18

Allie stepped into the Danville Athletic Center and paused to get her bearings. As many times as she'd driven by, she'd never actually been inside the place. She gawked through rounded eyes. To her left was a rock climbing wall. She'd always wanted to try one of those. Not while anybody was watching, of course. Joan had always been the most athletic of the three Sanderson sisters, and Tori the most graceful. Allie was pretty much a klutz and a weakling. She probably couldn't make it two feet off the ground.

Beyond the rock climbing wall, she saw a line of big windows through which she glimpsed the glistening blue surface of water. The indoor pool. Above the windows a row of television sets hung suspended from the ceiling, and facing them were several lines of treadmills and other machines. Allie watched a couple of people walk on a set of moving stairs, and even from a distance she could see the sweat plastering one man's T-shirt to his back. Ee-ewwww. Definitely a machine to be avoided. A staircase led upward, toward a small group of women walking on a track that circled the second floor. Now walking was something she might be able to get into. No learning curve, since she'd been doing it for twenty-seven years.

Directly in front of her stood a rounded reception counter and a metal turnstile guarding the entrance to the fitness center. The woman seated behind the counter smiled at her. "Can I help you?"

"Uh, yeah." Allie approached the desk and fished in her purse for the certificate. "My husband gave me a membership. I'm here to activate it and take an aerobics class."

"Ah, Valerie's class. That's a good one." The woman took the certificate and keyed something into her computer. "Here it is. Just give me a minute." Her fingers flew over the keyboard, and then she glanced up. "Stand on that X."

"Huh?" For the first time, Allie noticed a camera mounted on top of the computer monitor, pointed directly at her. Someone had formed an X on the floor with two pieces of masking tape. As she stepped backward, she ran her fingers through her hair. "I didn't know I'd have my picture taken. I don't have any makeup on at all."

"You look fine. Smile."

Allie did, and then waited a minute while her membership card printed. When the woman handed it over the counter, Allie glanced at it and winced. She'd expected driver's license bad, but this was more like mug-shot bad. The grim face staring back at her looked like a washed-out ghoul.

The woman gave her a sympathetic smile. "Don't worry. Nobody will see it except you."

"You've got that right." No way was she going to show this to anyone, even Eric. Especially Eric.

When the door opened behind her, Allie turned to see Darcy step inside. She hid the card in her palm.

"There you are." Darcy wore tight-fitting pink gym pants that hugged her legs, and a matching top that barely touched the waist-band of the pants. Allie had opted for camouflage clothes — comfortable sweats that were only a little ratty and an oversized T-shirt that covered her hips. Her sneakers were leftovers from college, unlike Darcy's blindingly white gym shoes. Joan had nagged Allie to get a new pair of tennis shoes for years, but Allie hadn't seen the need to spend money on shoes she couldn't wear to work. If she was going to start doing the gym thing, she might have to make an investment. *After* her business was in the black.

Darcy hitched a gym bag over her shoulder and stepped toward a scanner on the edge of the desk. "Come on back here and I'll introduce you to Valerie."

Allie followed Darcy's example and waved her card beneath the scanner. The turnstile let them through. As they walked past the treadmill area, Allie saw another large room on the opposite side of the building. Through the open doorway she glimpsed a bunch of exercise machines that looked like they came straight from a medieval torture chamber. The smell of stale sweat crept from the room. In the back corner a muscle-bound superjock with arms the size of her thighs hefted a barbell.

They came to a wall of glass that looked into the aerobics room. Though Allie had never taken a class, she recognized the place because mirrors lined the other three walls and the carpeted floor was uncluttered by equipment. A group of women stood inside, all of them wearing clothes similar to Darcy's, all of them pencil-thin. She followed Darcy through the door, nerves fluttering in her stomach. Okay, so there was no way she was going to appear in public dressed like that, but at least she might have made sure her T-shirt matched her sweats.

"Hey, everybody, this is Allie," Darcy announced as they stepped inside. "She became a Varie Cose consultant the same time I did, and she has an eight-week-old baby."

A chorus of "Hi, Allie" and "Welcome, Allie" sounded around the room as Darcy crossed the floor to drop her gym bag in the far corner. A girl broke away from the group and approached, wearing a grin almost as wide as Sally Jo's. Her thick dark hair swung in a ponytail from the back of her skull as she walked.

"Allie, I'm Valerie." She stuck out a hand. "I'm the instructor for this class. Welcome."

"Thanks." Allie lowered her voice and glanced around. "Uh, I've never taken an aerobics class before, so I don't really know what to do."

Valerie waved a hand. "Don't worry about it. Just follow along and you'll catch on in no time."

Just follow along? No instructions, no training? Allie wiped damp palms on her sweatpants. Still, how hard could aerobics be? It was just a group of women exercising to music.

Darcy approached and grinned at the instructor as she spoke to Allie. "Valerie hosted my most successful party so far. Seven hundred dollars and six bookings."

"Wow." Allie turned a wide eye on Valerie.

She nodded. "I'm going to have another one too, because I only invited a few of my girlfriends. I've been teaching aerobics for almost twenty years, so I know a lot of people."

Twenty years? Allie took a closer look at the woman. A few lines creased the skin around her eyes, and now that she looked closely, Allie could see a scattering of gray on the sides of her head. But her body looked like a teenager's.

"Not only that," Darcy said, "I actually signed my first consultant through Valerie's party, plus I have a feeling another of them is going to sign up."

Valerie laughed. "You realize you're working yourself out of more sales. If I know several Varie Cose consultants, I'll feel honor-bound to spread my business evenly between all of you."

Darcy caught Allie's eye and smiled. "Oh, that's okay. I want my consultants to be successful too."

She certainly did, because Darcy got a percentage of whatever her consultants sold.

Plus, when she signed fifteen consultants, the company gave her a car. Allie forced a smile to her face, but did private battle with a bout of jealousy so strong it surprised her. She hadn't signed any new consultants at all, and that's when the real money started coming. Darcy was way ahead of her.

Valerie clapped her hands. "Okay, girls. It's nine o'clock, so let's get started."

Everyone moved to form what was obviously a familiar arrangement, with three rows facing Valerie. Allie followed Darcy, relieved when she went to the back row. When they got there, she realized that there was no "back" in this class, because everywhere she looked, her own reflection stared back at her. For the second time she wished she had worn something else. This old brown T-shirt made her look huge, especially next to Darcy and ten others about her size. In fact, Allie realized with a shock as she looked at the reflection of the class that she was the fattest person here. The rest of these women were all Skinny Minnies. She looked like Helga Huge standing in their midst.

Valerie punched a button on a boom box and jogged the few steps to the front of the class. The music began, some sort of techno-sounding song that Allie didn't recognize but had a loud beat. Valerie lifted her hands slowly above her head. As one, the class did likewise. Allie did the same.

"Reach, ladies," Valerie commanded. "And stretch . . . stretch . . . and down . . . down. Don't forget to breathe."

Valerie's words came in sync with the beat of the music. Allie stretched and breathed, and mimicked the girls all around her in bringing her arms down to her sides. They repeated the movement, holding the stretch as long as Valerie told them to, and then stretched side to side.

The tempo of the music changed. At the same moment Valerie shouted, "We're going to pick it up here, ladies. Start with the right in four . . . three . . . two . . . one."

As one, the class began marching in place. A full beat behind, Allie started marching like them, but she had to do a couple of quicksteps to catch up. It was sort of like walking in place, not hard at all. She could do this. But the minute she settled into the routine, Valerie changed the movement again.

"Now take it wide."

Everybody stepped outward, still walking in place but with their feet spaced wider. Again, Allie quickstepped until she caught the rhythm. Valerie shouted, "Pick up those knees, bring them up. That's right. And now take it in. Four . . . three . . . two . . . Now tap it out."

The movement changed again, this time a toe tap, but everybody's arms were bending at the elbow like they were lifting dumbells. Allie's breath came harder. How could she be expected to move her arms *and* her feet at the same time?

"Four . . . three . . . two . . . and turn."

Turn! Allie heard the command and froze for half a second. The entire class turned to the left in unison, never missing a beat with their toe tapping and elbow bending. Allie quickly aligned herself and caught up. How did they know which way to turn?

"Good, and get ready to slide . . . four . . . three . . . two . . . slide."

Slide? What the heck did that mean? Allie kept marching in place, but the entire class suddenly shifted gracefully about three steps sideways. The girl on her right sidestepped around her without missing a beat. Allie rushed toward the place she was supposed to be, and picked up the toe-tapping rhythm again.

"Lift those knees, ladies!" urged Valerie. "And four, and three, and two, and one."

The entire class shifted again, this time to the right, leaving Allie standing on her own. No fair! Valerie didn't even say to slide that time. How did everybody know what to do? She rushed to her place and started toe tapping, but nobody else was toe tapping. They were doing some sort of backward step, their feet coming up behind them while their arms went up and down above their heads.

A drop of sweat slid down the side of Allie's face and her heart pounded in tempo with the beat of the music. This was hard work! Not just the exercise, but trying to keep up with everyone. They'd obviously done this routine many times. Either that or this exercise thing was like line dancing where everybody in the world was supposed to know the moves.

Allie's teeth ground against each other. She had always been lousy at line dancing.

Another drop of sweat dripped off her forehead, this time right into her eye. Ouch! She rubbed her watering eye just as the group turned again, this time swinging their arms right and left in sync with Valerie's counting. The girl beside Allie wasn't as quick this time, and she slapped Allie in the arm. Hard. Double ouch.

"Sorry," the girl said, breathless, and kept right on swinging.

Allie scooted out of slapping distance and turned so she faced the same way as everyone else. She was now on the front row, facing her own reflection with the entire class spread out around her. Darcy caught her eye in the mirror and grinned. Allie returned the grin, but hers looked more like a grimace. She watched herself and realized her marching gait looked clumsy next to their perfectly synchronized movements, a klutz in the middle of ballerinas. Her bangs were starting to stick to her forehead. She raked them back, which was a mistake, because now she looked deranged. While she was messing up her hair, the group swung around again, leaving her staring into the mirror alone.

Panting hard, Allie whirled around and glanced at the clock hanging above the door. Nine ten. They'd only been going ten minutes? The class was supposed to last fifty minutes. No way could she make it all the way to the end.

"And four, and three, and two, and one." As everyone started an in-and-out movement with their legs that looked like a complicated dance step, Valerie shouted, "Remember, if you feel uncomfortable, just march in place until you catch your breath and then join in again."

No doubt who that piece of information was aimed at. Embarrassed but grateful, Allie lowered her arms. She could march with the best of them. She still had to watch the group, or she'd get trampled when they started prancing around the room, but at least she didn't look like an elephant in a tutu when she was just marching.

By the time the class ended, sweat had plastered her hair to her head and run in rivers down her chest until her bra was soaked. The bottoms of her feet tingled and her legs felt like jelly, but she'd made it all the way to the end. True, she had marched through most of it, but at least she didn't quit. And she'd made a decision. Aerobics classes were definitely not her style. She'd rather be fat than go through this humiliation again. Darcy obviously had a firm claim on any Varie Cose customer leads this group had to offer, so there was no business benefit to being here, either.

As she limped toward the door to follow the others out, Valerie called, "We're glad you joined us, Allie. See you on Monday!"

Allie bit back her response. It wouldn't be polite.

19

When she slid behind the wheel of her car, Allie checked her cell phone. Two missed calls from Joan. She pressed a button to re-dial as she pulled from the parking lot onto the street. Joan picked up on the second ring.

"Hey. What do you have going on tomor-row night?"

Allie held the phone with her left hand so she could steer with her right. "Uh, noth-ing." She'd been unable to get a party booked for Saturday night. Yet another reason to worry.

"Good. We're having a Sanderson Sister Sleepover. Mom's working third shift so we'll have the whole house to ourselves."

The sisters made it a priority to get together every so often for sleepovers since the early months of Allie's marriage, when Eric was working second shift and she got so lonely at night by herself. But now . . .

"Oh, Joan, I can't do that."

"Why not? Bring Joanie with you. She's old enough for her first sleepover."

"What about Eric?" Allie pressed the brake and stopped at a stoplight. "I've been gone so much I feel guilty leaving him at home alone when I finally have a night free."

"Isn't Betty still there?"

Allie scowled, then realized the expression was wasted since Joan couldn't see her. "Oh yeah."

"Then he won't be alone. Eric will understand if you tell him how important this is."

"It might help if I knew how important it is."

A moment of silence, and then Joan said, "I'm worried about Tori." Concern made her voice tight. "She hasn't had a day off in forever. She even goes into the office on Sunday afternoons. When I talked to her today, she told me she's planning to work this weekend too." She paused. "She doesn't sound like herself, Allie. I think the stress is getting to her. We need to get her away from that office so she can unwind. That's our job as her sisters."

Allie could certainly attest to the fact that Tori's stress was getting to her. The light turned green and she pressed the accelerator. "I don't know, Joan. I'll have to talk to

Eric and see what he says."

"Allie, please try. I think it would be good for you too. You need some sister time."

Well, she didn't know about *needing* sister time, but she could sure use a relaxing night out without having to worry about Varie Cose, or Betty, or . . . *gulp* . . . Molly. "I'll try."

"Good." Relief lightened Joan's tone. "Listen, I've got to go. I've got customers all over the store. Talk to you later."

When Joan disconnected the call, Allie slipped her phone into the console. She and Eric hadn't exchanged more than a few terse words last night when she got home from her meeting at Sally Jo's house. She'd intended to talk to him about Betty, tell him they needed to come up with a plan to get his mother back to Detroit where she belonged. But when she walked through the front door, the sight of him sitting on the couch staring at the television had set her teeth on edge.

Actually, the dispatch center was only a few blocks away. It had been a long time since she'd been to Eric's work, not since Joanie was a couple of weeks old and she'd taken her by to let Eric show her off to his co-workers.

She flipped the blinker lever and glanced

in the mirror before changing lanes. If he was having a slow day, maybe he could take a break and they could talk. At least there they wouldn't have to hide in their bedroom and keep their voices at a whisper.

Minutes later she pulled into the dispatch center's parking lot. Her car rolled to a stop beside Eric's truck, and Allie twisted the rearview mirror so she could get a look at herself.

Ah. Not good. She rummaged in her purse for a brush and tamed the worst of her flyaway hair. At least the chilly November air had stopped her sweating and freeze-dried her hair so it was no longer plastered to her scalp. No makeup, but she patted her whole face with powder from her compact to dim the red glow left over from the aerobics class. Maybe Eric would be pleased that she'd finally put his birthday present to good use.

The heavy windowless door had a code lock on it, so Allie stepped past it to the window looking into the dispatch room. Eric stood just inside. She raised her hand to tap on the glass. But then she expelled the breath without speaking.

Molly sat at Eric's desk with Eric standing beside her. One of his arms rested across the back of her chair as he leaned forward pointing with the other hand at something on the computer monitor. His lips moved as he said something, then they both laughed, and Molly twisted in her seat to look up at him. Icy fingers gripped Allie by the throat as she watched Molly's eyes cut sideways.

That floozy was flirting with her husband!

Allie stood as though her feet had stuck to the sidewalk, her mind whirling. What should she do? Bang on the window to alert them to her presence, and then pretend like nothing was out of line here? Or wait until Eric let her in, and then snatch him out of that woman's reach? Better yet, march in there and grab a handful of that dark hair and jerk it out by the roots?

She didn't have time to do anything, because Molly caught sight of her. For one second their gazes locked, and a flash of guilt showed on the brunette's face. In the next second it was gone and she drew backward, away from Eric.

Eric looked up and caught sight of her. He straightened. Was that annoyance she saw on his face, or just surprise? He pointed toward the door and headed that way.

Allie stepped inside when he opened the door.

"Hey. I didn't know you were coming by."

Obviously not. Allie forced her jaws to un-clench as she glanced into the other room. She tried to keep her voice light, but when she spoke, the words squeaked out through a tight throat. "I just left the gym and thought I'd stop by to see if you had some free time to talk." She allowed her gaze to stray toward Molly again. "I guess you're busy."

Molly held her gaze for a second and then broke eye contact. A spot of color appeared on each cheek as she got out of Eric's chair and went to her own desk. The few times Allie had met Molly she'd been wearing sloppy jeans and T-shirts, and usually no makeup. With a jolt of alarm Allie realized that the girl had gussied herself up since then. The deep red sweater Molly wore flat-tered her dark eyes and creamy complexion. The plunging neckline showed a little too much cleavage for Allie's comfort. A minute ago when Eric stood above her, looking down . . .

Heat dampened her neck beneath the col-lar of her sloppy T-shirt.

"Good for you," Eric said. "What did you think of the place? Ritzy, isn't it?"

Allie couldn't trust her voice, so she just nodded.

"Since you haven't been home, you

haven't seen the pictures your mom emailed this morning. I was just showing them to Molly. They're from your birthday dinner. Come look at this one of Tori holding Joanie at the table."

They were looking at pictures of Joanie? Allie took a couple of steps to stand beside Eric so she could see his monitor. The camera had caught Joanie wide-eyed, her precious little lips forming a tight *O* of surprise that exactly matched the expression on Aunt Tori's face. It was a totally sweet picture that would have made Allie laugh too if she wasn't focusing all her efforts on trying not to slap the woman sitting at the next desk.

"That's a good one. We should print it and frame it for Tori." Her gaze slid sideways, but Molly had become engrossed in her own computer and didn't look their way. Did she always dress like that? Allie pulled the unzipped edges of her jacket together in the front to hide the sloppy T-shirt. But the jacket wasn't long enough to hide her enormous thighs, which felt about five times the size of Molly's at the moment. What in the world had possessed her to come here wearing sweats and ragged gym shoes?

"There are a couple more good ones too.

Here, look at this one."

Eric leaned toward the keyboard, but Allie stopped him with a hand on his arm. "Do you have a minute to talk?"

The speakers emitted a blast of static followed by a male voice with a bunch of numbers. Molly pressed a switch and answered with more numbers. None of it made sense to Allie, though she had come to understand a few of the codes over the years, since sometimes Eric forgot himself and used them at home.

Eric seemed unconcerned by whatever that call meant, though. "Yeah, it's a slow day." He said to Molly, "Can you hold down the fort for a few minutes?"

"Sure," she replied without looking at them.

A good thing. One crossways look from that woman and Allie would dump her out of the chair.

Eric guided her toward the break room. She shook her head when he started to pull out a hard plastic chair. In this small building every word they said would be overheard.

"Do you mind if we talk outside?"

Eric gave her an odd look. "Kind of cold out there."

"It's not too bad." Allie let her gaze slide

behind him toward the dispatch room.

Eric hesitated, but then shrugged. "Okay, for a minute. Kathy's at a meeting down at the courthouse, so I can't leave Molly alone for long."

Allie looked through the office door at Kathy's empty desk. Her jaw clenched shut as Eric opened the outside door for her. How often did Kathy go to these meetings, leaving Eric alone with That Woman?

Eric held the door for her, and as she stepped through, she zipped her jacket up. Eric let the door slam behind them, then rubbed both hands on his arms. "Cold today."

"Darcy said it's going to snow soon." Allie turned abruptly and walked toward her car. What was the matter with her, discussing the weather with her own husband? She heard Eric's shoes crunch the gravel as he followed her. She leaned against the hood of her car and let the warmth penetrate her thin sweatpants. The smell of the hot engine tainted the crisp fall air.

Eric slid into place beside her. "So how was the gym?"

"Nice. They have an indoor walking track I might try next." She turned a scowl his way. "Aerobics classes are definitely not my thing."

He nodded once, then folded his arms and hugged his chest against the cold. "So what did you want to talk about?"

The reason she'd come, to feel him out about the sleepover and to talk about his mother, seemed insignificant now. The sight of Molly laughing up at Eric, their faces — their lips — mere inches apart, seared her brain with white heat. Her nerves buzzed with a powerful jealousy Allie hadn't felt since high school, and she couldn't hold it in any longer. She blurted, "I want to know what's going on between you and Molly."

From the look he turned her way, he might as well have accused her of insanity. "What are you talking about?"

"I saw that in there, Eric. You were flirting with each other."

He hefted himself off the hood of the car and looked down at her. "I was showing her pictures of Joanie. *Our* daughter," he said as though clarifying the fact for an imbecile.

"That may be what you were doing." A sob rose in the base of Allie's throat. She choked it back with a deep breath before continuing. "That's not what Molly was doing. I saw the way she looked at you. She was flirting."

Eric tilted his head back to look up into the branches of the trees lining the parking lot. "That's ridiculous. We're co-workers."

"You're alone together all day long."

"Not alone. Kathy's usually here."

"She's not here now," Allie shot back. "And she wasn't at Molly's house when you went over there. Twice."

Eric shoved his hands into his back pockets and seared her with a look that bordered on disgust. Allie couldn't meet his eye. Instead, she stared sullenly at the plain brick wall of the building in front of her. She drew in deep gulps of cold air in an effort to hold back the tears that tightened her chest. This was not going well. She should have kept her mouth shut until she could speak rationally. Why was she always jumping in tongue-first before she thought?

"What is up with you lately, Allie? Why have you changed?"

"I haven't." She lifted her chin and glared at him. "You're the one who's changed. What made you decide to become Molly's handyman, her substitute husband? You don't see me running over to some man's house to cook his meals for him or dust his furniture or whatever. I'm not trying to act like somebody else's wife."

The cords in Eric's neck bulged as his jaw tightened. "You're right. I don't even see you doing those things for your own husband lately."

She sucked in a noisy breath as her spine stiffened. "Are you saying I'm a bad wife?"

"No," he snapped. "I'm saying you're an absent wife. Your job has become the most important thing in your life, maybe even more important than your daughter. Definitely more important than your husband."

His volume rose until he actually shouted the last word at her. Allie launched herself off the hood of the car and stood in front of him, glaring, her hands clenched into fists while anger made her head buzz. How dare he accuse her of being a bad mother!

She faced him and spoke through gritted teeth. "My job is not the most important thing in my life."

Now Eric was taking deep breaths. His chest rose and fell, and splotches of angry red appeared on his neck. He opened his mouth to speak and Allie prepared herself to meet another verbal blow, but then he snapped his jaw shut. He spun on his heel, and as he walked away he said without looking back, "I've got to work. We'll talk about this tonight when we're both calmer."

He was walking away from her! He'd never done that before. "I've got a party tonight," she called after him, her voice still tight with anger. When he kept walking, she added, louder, "And tomorrow night I'm taking Joanie to spend the night with my sisters."

He reached the door and put a hand on the knob, then turned to give her a sarcastic smile. "I guess if I want to talk to my wife, I should make an appointment." He snapped his fingers, his eyes throwing darts in her direction. "I know — I'll book a makeup party."

The door slammed shut behind him. Allie's fury fled the moment her husband disappeared from view. What had she done?

She should march in there right now, make him come back outside and finish this argument. Except her hair was a mess, her clothes looked like she'd been Dumpster diving, and the tears she'd worked so hard to choke back in front of him were at this moment running in rivers down her cheeks. While on the other side of that door, Eric was sitting beside a pretty brunette who was flashing cleavage in his face.

With a powerful sniff, Allie unlocked her car door and then slid into the driver's seat. The shock on Eric's face when she asked him about Molly — correction, when she practically accused him of having an affair with Molly — couldn't have been faked. In five years of marriage, Eric had never given her the slightest reason to be jealous. He loved her as much as she loved him, she knew that. Was she overreacting? Had she misread the glance she saw pass between him and Molly?

Doubt wiggled its way into her thoughts as she started the engine and put the car in reverse. On the other hand, even the most trustworthy man in the world could be worn down by a determined woman. Everybody knew men were weak when it came to sex. It really wasn't Eric she should be worried about. It was Molly. No matter what Eric said, Allie recognized the expression she'd seen on Molly's face when she looked up at Eric.

With a shock, Allie realized she'd seen that expression before. And she knew exactly when. She'd been thirteen years old and walking home from her friend's house on a Saturday afternoon. The front door at home was locked, so she headed for the back. She rounded the corner of the house and the sight that met her eyes stopped her dead in her tracks. Daddy and their neighbor Mrs. Nelson stood near the back corner of the house. They were kissing. Shock sucked the breath right out of Allie as she stood watching through dense shrubbery. When they broke apart, Mrs. Nelson looked up into

Daddy's face and her eyes cut sideways as she flashed a flirty grin.

The exact expression Allie had just seen on Molly's face when she looked up at Eric.

An invisible fist grabbed Allie's stomach and squeezed.

Eric let the heavy door slam behind him. In the other room he saw Molly start at the noise. He avoided her gaze and stomped across the break room to jerk open the refrigerator. The noisy motor kicked on as he stood looking inside, and the fan blew cold air into the room. He snatched his lunch bag and rummaged in it for the bottle of orange juice Mother had put in the bottom. He wasn't really thirsty, he just didn't want Molly to see his face until he got himself under control.

Allie was way out of line with her accusations. He'd never given her any reason to doubt his fidelity, not since the first night he laid eyes on her at that pizza place on campus. How could she think he'd be unfaithful to her? Especially since the birth of their daughter?

Maybe that was a clue. Allie had changed since Joanie's birth, and not for the better. Hormones, maybe? Eric tossed the lunch bag back into the fridge with a shudder. The mysterious *H* word was enough to send any man running for cover. Whenever a woman got weird, she blamed it on her hormones, and how could a man answer that? Since marrying Allie and becoming the only man in a family full of women, Eric had learned a thing or two about hormones — mostly he'd learned to keep his head down whenever he sensed they might be present. There had been times when just stepping through the front door at the Sanderson house felt like taking his life into his own hands.

He twisted the cap off the OJ bottle and took a couple of big gulps. Sweet citrus juice tingled in his throat on the way down. Allie's behavior wasn't like normal hormone stuff. It felt like she was pulling away from him. She always threw herself into anything she undertook, and that was one of the qualities that first attracted him to her. But she was taking this Varie Cose thing to some sort of unhealthy extreme. It was starting to affect her. Them. If only he could convince her to give it up. Maybe if he —

"Is everything okay?"

Molly's voice from nearby startled him. Eric jerked around and found her standing in the doorway, watching him. After Allie's ridiculous accusations, he found it hard to meet her gaze.

"Yeah." He put the cap on the bottle and twisted it tight, then yanked the refrigerator door open again and set the juice back inside. "She just had, uh, something to ask me."

"Okay." She pitched her voice low. "Eric, if you ever want to talk, you know I'm always available."

Shock wrenched Eric's eyes upward to lock with hers. Was that a come-on? No way! This was *Molly*. His brain a blur, Eric stood with his mouth hanging open, trying to make sense of the weird stuff happening to him today.

In the dispatch room static announced a call, and Officer Baker's voice informed them of a traffic stop and a request for a license search. Eric blew out the breath he'd been holding.

"Uh, I'll take care of it."

Molly did not move as he edged by her in the doorway. He didn't look at her, but felt the weight of her eyes as he keyed the license number into the NCIC link.

Were all the women in the world acting crazy lately, or was it just the ones he knew?

20

Allie shut off the engine and sat in her car, staring across the dark yard at the front window of her house. Flickers of light danced in a crack between the curtains. The television. Probably another stupid ball game. What games were played on Friday night? Football? Ice hockey? She was so tired she couldn't remember.

When had Eric become a sports junkie? He'd always been a basketball fan, which was why he'd chosen the University of Kentucky for college. Many of their dates during the fall had been spent at someone's apartment in front of the television watching football games. She hadn't minded so much back then. In fact, she'd gotten into the whole fantasy football thing with him. But after the wedding, her enthusiasm for ball games flagged. She'd grown up, realized there were more important things in life than sports. Like just about everything.

Family. Friends. A job you enjoyed.

She clutched the top of the steering wheel and rested her forehead on her hand, her eyes closed. Tonight's party had been a total disaster. Sally Jo said the pedicure parties were always huge successes, but Allie didn't even sell a hundred dollars' worth of product tonight. At this rate, her business would never get into the black.

Maybe she should chuck the whole Varie Cose thing. Come clean to Eric about the credit card and cut her losses now, before she got any further into it. Go back to work at the state and use her paycheck to chip away at that debt. She wouldn't even have to put Joanie in daycare, because if Betty carried out her plan, Allie would have a built-in babysitter.

A tear slipped between Allie's closed eyelids. She didn't want Betty to raise Joanie any more than she wanted a babysitter doing it.

Maybe Eric was right. If they really tried, they could pay the bills on his salary alone.

But then Allie would be totally dependent on him. Just like Betty was dependent on Don. Just like . . . pain squeezed her throat as she struggled to swallow a sob. Just like Mom had been dependent on Daddy before their divorce. Look how that turned out.

Please, don't let Molly turn out to be Eric's Mrs. Nelson. Don't let Eric have a Mrs. Nelson.

Allie didn't whisper the prayer aloud, but she sent it upward mentally. It might not do any good; none of her prayers about Mom and Daddy had worked when she was a teenager. But it couldn't hurt, could it? She knew God existed, and that he heard prayers. Apparently he just chose to ignore hers.

She straightened in her seat. Nobody was going to come along and fix her problems for her. She had to stand on her own two feet, carry her own weight. Hers and Joanie's. The income potential for Varie Cose was enormous compared to her job at the state. She just needed to work harder so she could be as successful as Sally Jo. That way, if anything happened between her and Eric, she and Joanie would be okay. Safe and secure.

The snatch of a song flashed into her mind. *Safe and secure from all alarms.*

The phrase was from an old hymn, one they used to sing in church when she was a kid. *Leaning on the Everlasting Arms.* They probably still sang that song at Christ Community Church. According to Joan, not much had changed since the last time Allie went there.

But a lot had changed for Allie. She couldn't even remember what it felt like to be the girl who sat in the pew beside her mother and father on Sunday morning.

For a brief moment, Allie envied Joan. She was so happy lately, and she had so much enthusiasm for her church group and her mission trip. No, it went beyond enthusiasm. Joan seemed peaceful. Was it because of her relationship with God, as she claimed?

With a sigh, Allie pushed the thought away and opened the car door. An icy breeze made her gasp, and she clutched her briefcase to her chest to create a windscreen during her dash to the front porch. She opened the door just enough to slip inside and shut it quickly.

Eric sat on the couch with Joanie on his shoulder. He glanced up from the television and locked eyes with her. She searched his face for any hint of regret after their argument, but at the moment his eyes were as unreadable as his mother's. He held her gaze for a moment and then looked back at the television.

Still mad, then. The apology that had half formed in the back of her mind during the party died unsaid.

In her usual chair, Betty looked up from

her book. "Are you hungry? I could heat something up for you."

"No, thanks."

When Betty returned to her book, Allie tossed her purse and briefcase in the corner and stripped off her jacket. So Eric had decided to give her the silent treatment. There was nothing Allie hated worse, and he knew it. Her stomach churning, she crossed the room and stood between him and the television. His eyebrows arched as he looked up at her, but instead of saying any of the dozen things that came to mind, she silently held out her arms for her baby.

Joanie kicked her legs with excitement when Eric handed her over. Allie hugged her daughter tight and headed toward the nursery. At least one person in her family was happy to see her.

Eric grabbed his jacket and gloves when he saw Ken's car pull up to the curb in front of the house Saturday morning. "I'm outta here," he called toward the nursery.

Like Allie would care. She'd been sulky all morning, probably because he'd forgotten to tell her about helping Ken today with another load for their auction.

At least they were speaking this morning. Eric knew last night's silence was as much his fault as hers, but when she came home from work, his mind had still been reeling over their fight, and Molly coming on to him. Besides, he was the injured party. She should have made the first move.

Allie came out of the nursery, hugging Joanie to her chest. Hurt lingered in her eyes, and he steeled himself against it. She had no right to look like that. He had done nothing wrong.

"When will you be home?" she asked.

He shrugged. "No idea. You?"

"I'll probably be finished by three." She shifted from foot to foot. "Um . . . don't forget about the Sanderson Sister Sleepover." She paused, then asked in a too-casual tone, "Do you have plans tonight?"

In other words, *You're not planning to go over to Molly's house and fix anything, are you?*

How nice to be trusted. Fighting a wave of irritation, he shrugged into his jacket and turned toward the door. "No plans."

"Eric."

Her soft tone stopped him with his hand on the doorknob. The soft swish-swish of her slippers on the carpet as she crossed the room sounded loud in the silence. When she drew near, she raised up on her toes and placed a soft kiss on his lips.

"I love you," she whispered.

For a moment he didn't know how to respond. Then he wrapped both arms around her and drew her close. Joanie squirmed between them as he breathed in the musky scent of perfume that lingered in Allie's hair. What an infuriating woman. She sure knew how to send his brain into a tailspin.

"I love you too." His whisper was hoarse.

When she pulled away, her eyes shimmered with unshed tears. A smile trembled on her lips. "That's what matters."

A knock sounded on the door beside them, and Allie stepped back while he swung it inward. Ken stood on the doorstep. He started to say something to Eric, then smiled when he caught sight of Allie.

"Good morning."

She cupped a protective hand around Joanie's head as cold air blew into the house. "Hi, Ken."

The doctor grinned at her. "Joan sure is looking forward to tonight. It's all she talked about last night."

Allie's gaze shifted toward Eric, and he saw her uncertainty. To be honest, he wished she would stay home tonight. With sudden longing, he realized they hadn't spent a night at home alone in weeks, not since

Mother arrived on their doorstep and Allie decided to do this business thing. But he'd learned a long time ago that the Sanderson sisters drew strength from each other. Maybe a night with her sisters was just what Allie needed.

"Since the girls are going to be tied up, you can come over to my place and watch the U. of L. game." Ken grinned. "I traded shifts with another doctor at the hospital who didn't realize what time the game came on. A couple of other guys will be there."

Probably from his church. Eric started to make an excuse, but then he pictured his night at home without Allie. He and Mother sitting in front of the television yet again. He couldn't remember the last time he'd watched a game with a bunch of guys.

"Maybe I will." Eric zipped his jacket up. "You ready to get going?"

Ken stepped back from the doorway and started down the steps. Then he stopped and swung around to face Allie again. "You are planning to come to the auction Tuesday night, aren't you?"

Allie looked at Eric, her eyebrows high. "We haven't talked about it."

Ken's glance slipped from Allie to Eric. "I really wish you would. Joan may not say so, but I know it means a lot to her to have you there. Tori too. Please tell her to try to come."

That guy just didn't give up. Eric leaned forward to place a goodbye kiss on his wife's lips. When his face was shielded from Ken's view, he rolled his eyes. A real smile touched the corners of her mouth, which lightened his mood considerably.

"See you later," he said.

Allie leaned against the closed door. Eric's kiss went a long way toward loosening the knots that had been lodged in her stomach since yesterday even if they hadn't completely made up from their fight.

Had he kissed Molly? Had things gone that far between them?

The knots tightened again, as did her grip on Joanie. She couldn't think that way, or she'd become one of those jealous maniac wives who drove their husbands into the arms of other women by their possessive behavior. No, she just needed to focus on taking care of herself and Joanie, on making sure they would be okay no matter what. She was strong, independent, capable. Eric always said that's what attracted him to her to begin with. Yet another reason to make her Varie Cose business succeed.

Betty appeared in the kitchen doorway.

"Is Eric gone?"

Allie steeled her expression to hide her turmoil. She could take a lesson from her mother-in-law in keeping a straight face. She nodded.

"Good." Betty stepped into the room and lowered herself into the chair Allie had begun to think of as hers. She sat primly, with her knees and ankles together, her hands folded in her lap. "I want to talk to you about something."

Ooh, this sounded important. "Okay." Allie sat on the couch, legs crossed Indian-style, and propped Joanie in her lap.

"Don called last night."

Allie grinned. "Did his electricity get shut off?"

"Oh yes. He was quite angry about it. He had to pay a reconnect fee, and when I spoke with him at eight o'clock, they hadn't restored the power yet. He had to eat a cold dinner in the dark." A small, satisfied smile hovered around Betty's lips.

"I guess he's starting to realize how much you did around there."

"Yes." She examined her folded hands in her lap while the creases in her forehead deepened.

Joanie's fists waved in the air. Allie leaned forward to grab a rattle off the coffee table and held it in front of her. "So," she prompted, "did you talk to him about retiring?"

Betty nodded. "I told him I was tired of keeping house all the time, that I want to travel and see the world."

Her lips snapped shut. Joanie's rattle as she batted at the toy sounded loud in the silence that followed. Allie fought down a wave of impatience with her mother-in-law. Honestly, it's a wonder Eric ever learned how to talk at all since his mother had never mastered the art.

"And?"

Betty looked up from her examination of her hands. "He told me I should go. Travel all I want if that would make me happy."

"Did you say you didn't want to go alone, that you wanted him to go with you?"

Betty shook her head. "I shouldn't have to tell him that. He knows what we planned. We talked about it years ago."

Allie struggled to keep the smile out of her voice. "Betty, maybe you need to talk to him more often than once every couple of decades. He probably has no idea that you've been counting the days until he retires. You might have to remind him of the stuff that's important to you."

"He should remember his promises." Her

chin rose. "I shouldn't have to remind him."

"We all need reminders every so often," Allie said. "We get busy with our jobs and all the *stuff* that crops up in life, and we lose sight of what's important." She ran a finger over Joanie's soft baby head. "We lose sight of what's important," she repeated quietly.

All the tasks that had taken her energy and focus lately cluttered her mind. So many things to do, urgent things. So easy to lose sight of what's important.

She scooped Joanie up and hugged her tight. "Betty, do you want to leave Don? Throw away your marriage and move in with us?"

Betty's gaze rested on Joanie, and her expression softened almost imperceptibly. "I would love to watch my granddaughter grow up." Her eyes moved as she looked up into Allie's face. "But no. I want my husband to retire so we can spend our last years doing all the things we planned."

"Then I have an assignment for you." Allie stood. "Before this day is over, you need to call Don and tell him what you want. All of it. Don't hang up the phone until you've told him exactly what you want and what you expect him to do about it."

For the first time ever, Allie saw an honest-to-goodness emotion on her mother-in-law's face. Fright. Her droopy eyes went wide and she shook her head. "I can't do that. I wouldn't know what to say."

This poor woman. Somebody needed to give her some communication tools. "Then write it out first and read it to him. But do it, Betty. Your marriage depends on it."

As Allie headed for the nursery to change Joanie's diaper, she had to bite back a bitter laugh. Who was she to be giving marriage advice?

21

Woof, Woof. The deep bark of a big dog sounded through the door before Eric could even knock.

"Come on in, but don't let the monster out," Ken called from inside the house.

Eric knew the monster. Ken's horse-sized mutt, Trigger, held a place of honor in Allie's family ever since he pulled a Lassie and alerted Ken that Gram had fallen and broken her hip next door. That had been a couple of months ago, right before Joanie's birth, and every Sunday when he came for dinner, Eric glimpsed the dog loping across Ken's backyard. Gram always fixed a separate plate of goodies for her hero.

He opened the door cautiously. As soon as the crack was big enough, a gigantic nose pushed through, slobbery tongue at the ready. "Get back, Trigger." He stuck his hand inside and got a grip on the dog's collar before opening the door enough to slip inside.

Trigger allowed himself to be shoved backward, but Eric's hand was slimy by the time he'd said a proper hello. He wiped it on his jeans as Ken came around the corner.

"Grab something to drink in the fridge," Ken said. "Joan stocked up for us when she shopped for their sleepover."

Eric had never been in Ken's house. Not much furniture, but there wasn't room. Ken had put a few folding chairs around the television, since the only other place to sit was the couch. Three steps took Eric across the living room and through a wide doorway into the kitchen. This place wasn't as big as his and Allie's, but seemed about the right size for a single guy. Of course, if that dog grew any bigger, Ken would need to upsize. As he opened the refrigerator, Trigger rushed up to shove his head inside and stepped on Eric's foot. That dog weighed a ton! Eric hauled him backward by the collar when his nose started inspecting the contents on the top shelf.

"This is one huge dog." He directed his voice toward the other room.

"Isn't he?" Ken's voice answered. "Trigger, come!" The dog obediently disappeared into the living room. At least he minded.

Eric scanned the contents of the fridge. Coke or Sprite. No beer, not that he'd expected to find any in the refrigerator of a religious nut. Eric remembered the games he'd watched with his college friends. Four of them rented a run-down old house near campus. On Saturdays the place overflowed with guys crowding around their tiny television set. Beer flowed freely back then, an absolute requirement for a day of football.

He grabbed a Coke and headed back to the living room as the front door opened and two guys came in.

"Twenty minutes to kickoff," one of them announced as he stepped inside.

Ken turned from his corner entertainment center. "Watch the —" His voice cut off abruptly as Trigger, seeing an opening and an unwary guardian, darted outside. The second guy was nearly knocked off his feet as the animal dashed past.

Ken let out a sigh. "I'll be right back. Gordy, Ryan, this is Eric."

Eric shook their hands as the door closed behind Ken.

"So are you a doctor too?" Gordy collapsed onto one end of the couch.

Eric claimed the other end while Ryan wandered off toward the kitchen. "No, I'm Joan's brother-in-law."

"Oh yeah. I know Allie from way back. She used to come to church, but she was a few years ahead of us. I was a year ahead of Joan's class."

Ryan returned, a Sprite in one hand and a bag of chips in the other. "I didn't know Allie well, either. Haven't seen her in a couple of years. Where do you go to church now?"

A gulp of Coke burned Eric's throat all the way down to his gut. Great. They hadn't been here thirty seconds and already he was getting the third degree. "We don't go to church." He clipped the words short. Hopefully they'd get the message and drop it.

They both nodded, but Eric didn't see any other reaction. His tense shoulders eased up a bit.

"So where do you work, Eric?" Gordy asked.

Safer subject. "I'm a dispatcher for the 9-1-1 center."

Ryan tore open the chips and grabbed a handful, then tossed the bag onto the empty spot on the couch beside Eric since there was no coffee table. He stuffed a couple of chips in his mouth as he sat on a folding chair. "That's up on Fourth Street at the top of the hill, isn't it?"

Eric nodded. "How 'bout you?" He let his gaze slide to Gordy to include him too.

"I'm a telephone technician," Gordy said, then stood and wandered toward the kitchen. "What does he have to drink in there?"

Ryan munched a chip. "I work for a hardware supplier, but I'm in school at night. Not sure where I'll land."

The door opened and Ken hauled Trigger back inside. "Mangy mutt." He released the dog, who slunk out of the room with his tail drooping. "Every time he gets loose, he heads straight next door to Joan's. He likes her better than he likes me."

"I don't blame him," Gordy said as he stepped back into the room. He popped the top on a can of Coke. "She's a lot prettier than you."

"No argument there." Ken grabbed a folding chair and flipped it around so he could straddle it. "But she wouldn't appreciate him coming for a visit tonight. She's been looking forward to having her sisters over, and Tori isn't crazy about Trigger. Says animals who weigh more than she does make her nervous."

Ryan, in the process of reaching for the chip bag, straightened and turned an interested look toward the door. "Tori is next door?"

"She will be soon." Ken punched him on

the arm. "Forget it. It's a sister sleepover. No guys allowed, right, Eric?"

"That's right." He leaned forward to rest his forearms on his knees and spoke to Ryan. "And don't even think about a panty raid. I tried it once when Allie and I were dating. She came out of the house swinging a baseball bat. Nearly took my head off."

They all laughed, then Ken said, "Hey, speaking of baseball, you guys should see the stuff Eric and I picked up today. Mrs. Caldwell donated a whole box of baseball cards. I tried to talk her out of it, told her she could probably make a bundle selling them on eBay, but she insisted she wanted to support our mission trip."

"Baseball cards, huh?" Gordy's eyes lit. "I might bid on those myself."

"I took some stuff by the church yesterday." Ryan rubbed his hands together. "We're going to rake it in Tuesday night."

"I hope so. Medical supplies are expensive." Ken glanced at his watch. "We're missing the pregame show. Eric, the remote is over there somewhere."

Eric found the remote control shoved between the couch cushion and the arm. He pressed the On button and relaxed against the soft back. He might not have much to contribute to a conversation about mission trips, but he spoke football fluently.

"I don't know how we can have a Sanderson Sister Sleepover without pizza. Carrot sticks just don't make the same statement." Tori glared at the orange strip in her hand.

Allie snatched the carrot from her sister and bit it in half. Tori had been grumbling about one thing or another all evening. Joan was so right to insist that they get their little sister away from work. If only she would relax and enjoy the sleepover.

"Well, not all of us are a perfect size 2, you know." She eyed Tori's designer jeans. Allie hadn't worn a size 2 since 2Ts. And she was only one then.

"Oh, don't be a grouch." Seated on the love seat beside Tori, Joan leaned sideways to shove Tori's shoulder with her own. "Dip the veggies in that spinach dip. It's yummy. I've got some more good stuff in the kitchen too. Apples and baked tortilla chips with salsa, and air-popped popcorn to eat during the movies."

"All of it sounds extremely healthy." Tori's dainty nose wrinkled. She looked down at Joanie in the crook of her left arm. "I was hoping to feed my niece her first pepperoni."

"Do it and die." Allie pointed the half-sized carrot stick at Tori like a weapon. "Besides, I appreciate Joan's efforts. It's hard to diet when the smell of pepperoni fills the house." She leaned forward to dunk the other half of her carrot into the low-fat, low-cal spinach dip.

"Hey, no double-dipping." Tori grabbed a stalk of celery off the tray on the coffee table and scooped a huge mound of dip. She lifted it to her mouth, leaning away from the baby in case she dripped, and paused with the food in front of her lips. Her round blue eyes caught Joan's and then shifted to Allie's. She heaved a sigh. "I'm sorry to be such a grump, you guys. You just can't imagine the stress I'm under at work."

Joan picked up her glass and leaned back. "Tell us about it."

Tori stared thoughtfully at the celery for a moment. "I work for Attila the Hun." She put the stalk in her mouth and sucked the dip off without biting. "They hired her last month from some high-powered New York marketing firm. The word is she's being groomed to take over when the chief marketing officer retires next year. You've seen *The Devil Wears Prada*?" Allie and Joan both nodded. "That's her. A total demon draped in designers and three-inch heels. She scares

316

the daylights out of everybody, including me."

From the wide-eyed look on Tori's face, Allie figured the woman must be a corporate monster. Her baby sister wasn't intimidated by many.

"So why don't you quit?" she asked. "You can find another job."

Tori's shoulders deflated. "I don't know. I've thought about it. I just hate to give up, you know? I don't want her to beat me. Quitting feels too much like failure."

Allie let out a sarcastic snort of laughter. "I know the feeling."

Both sisters' heads whipped toward her, surprise etched on their faces. "Isn't the Varie Cose thing working out?" Joan asked.

Allie didn't meet either of their eyes. Instead, she leaned forward and grabbed an olive off the relish tray on the coffee table. "It's not as easy as I thought."

"Is that what's been bothering you lately?" Joan asked. "You haven't seemed yourself for a while now."

Tori nodded. "I figured you were suffering from a touch of postpartum depression." She jiggled the arm holding Joanie.

Allie looked from Tori to Joan. Why should she feel any surprise that these two, of all people, had noticed something wrong with her? They were her sisters and the best friends she had in the whole world. They'd shared everything with each other since they were little girls.

A lump formed in her throat. She could tell these two anything. Her darkest secrets. Her deepest fears.

"I . . ." She stopped, and flashed an apologetic grimace at Tori when the words came out in a squeak. "I don't think I'm depressed. Not clinically, at least. I just need . . ." She swallowed.

Joan got off the love seat and slid onto the couch beside her. She put an arm around Allie's shoulders and squeezed. "Go on. You can tell us."

And Allie knew she could. That's what Sanderson Sister Sleepovers were all about.

"I've gotten my business into a financial bind. I owe tons on my credit card, and I'm not making money as fast as I thought I would. Eric will kill me when he finds out." She rolled the olive between her thumb and her forefinger. "It's not as much fun as I thought, either. In fact," she paused as a painful fact she'd been ignoring dawned clear in her mind, "I pretty much hate it."

"So quit," Tori said. "Eric is not going to kill you. You two can figure something out together."

Without warning, the memory of Molly's flirty smile loomed vividly in her mind. A hot tear slipped down Allie's cheek as she shook her head. "I can't tell Eric."

Joan's arm tightened on her shoulder. "Are you still worried about Eric having an affair?"

More tears spilled over. Allie tried to gulp them back as she nodded. Tori shot off the love seat like a rocket. She stood rigid, Joanie still tucked in the crook of her left arm, her mouth so wide she could have shoved an orange in it. "No way. I don't believe it. Eric is devoted to you."

A deep sob heaved in Allie's chest. She thought so too. Once. Now she wasn't sure about anything.

Joan's arm tightened around Allie's shoulders. "Did something else happen since we talked?"

Allie nodded and gasped some air, trying to get her emotions under control so she could speak coherently.

Tori's lower lip protruded. "You talked before? Without me?"

"You weren't here," Joan told her. "And you're already stressed enough." She turned on the couch cushion to face Allie. "What happened?"

"It's his co-worker Molly. She's slim and

pretty and he works with her all day and then comes home to my elephant thighs. I think she's after him." Allie told them what she had seen the other day when she walked into the dispatch center. "The worst part is that I remember Mrs. Nelson looking at Daddy the exact same way that woman looked at . . . ," she drew a shuddering breath, "at my husband."

Tori drew herself up, outraged. "The hussy! Let's go pay her a visit right now."

She looked so fierce Allie couldn't help but laugh, though tears dropped off her jaw to splash onto her pants. Petite Tori wouldn't be able to lift a finger against Molly, but Allie believed she would risk bodily injury trying to defend her sister.

"Listen, Allie, are you sure?" Joan shook her head. "Have you considered what I said the other day about the whole father thing?"

Allie nodded. "I'm sure. It has nothing to do with Daddy. Or," She grabbed her lower lip between her teeth. The olive squashed as her fingers tightened around it. "Maybe it does. Maybe I've picked a man that has the qualities of our father because I'm trying to relive a childhood where I couldn't fix the problem. Maybe subconsciously I was trying to give myself a second chance to make it work."

Joan shook her arm. "Stop that. You can't psychoanalyze everything. Sometimes you just have to trust that God can work everything out."

Tori caught Allie's gaze and gave a quick eye-roll that Joan couldn't see, but Allie found herself wanting to talk it through. She twisted sideways so she could look Joan in the eye. "I know God is there. He exists. But Joan, I'm not so sure he 'works everything out' for people. He didn't for Mom and Daddy. What makes you think he will for me?"

"Because he has for me," she shot back instantly. "He's the Father I never had, the one Daddy couldn't be because he wasn't perfect." She covered Allie's hand with her own and lowered her voice. "He loves you, Allie. You can count on that."

Tori broke into the moment with a matter-of-fact voice. "Well, here's what I think." Allie and Joan both turned to her, and a laugh burst from Allie's mouth. Tori had grabbed a handful of black olives and covered each fingertip on her right hand like they used to do as kids. At the moment she was shaking an olive-covered pointer finger at them like a conductor with a baton. "I think God helps those who help themselves."

"That is not in the Bible." Joan's tone

danced with laughter.

"Doesn't matter. It's true. If Allie sits around and waits for God to drop a pile of money in her lap, she'll never get that credit card paid off. She has to take care of it herself." She stuck her finger in her mouth and ate the olive.

Allie grasped at her words. "I think Tori's right. I can't rely on someone else to get me out of a mess I created on my own. Not God, and not Eric. I have to rely on myself, which is why I can't quit my business. I have to make it work."

A struggle appeared on Joan's face, and silence fell in the room while Allie and Tori watched and waited for her to say something. Her mouth tightened and pursed while she stared at the coffee table with unfocused eyes. Allie wondered if maybe she was praying, and a thrill shot through her. She found herself eagerly waiting for Joan's words.

Which was ridiculous. It was *Joan* sitting next to her. Her sister. Not an oracle from God.

Finally, Joan heaved a sigh and her lips softened into a smile. She caught Allie's gaze and spoke quietly. "You're wrong. You can rely on God because you're his precious child and he loves you. I *know* he solves our problems, and he even drops the solutions in our lap if we ask him to. He's done it for me. But you have to ask, Allie. And then trust him."

Allie felt her gaze caught by her sister's. Trust. Yeah, that was the hard part. There was such certainty in Joan's brown eyes, such . . . peace. She shook her head slowly. "I wish I could be as sure as you."

Warm fingers squeezed her hand. "I wish you could too."

Allie woke to the sound of Joan's slumbering sigh. The television screen showed bright blue, the end of the DVD. Joan had arranged a Mel Fest and they'd spent several hours eating popcorn and sighing over Mel Gibson in *What Women Want* and *Maverick.* They never got to Allie's favorite, *Braveheart.* She fell asleep during *Chicken Run,* and since the *Braveheart* DVD case still sat on the coffee table unopened, apparently the others didn't make it much longer than she did.

In the sleeping bag on the floor next to Allie, Tori had curled into a ball with only the top of her bright blonde head sticking out. Joan lay beyond her, dark hair spilling over her pillow and an arm thrown above her head. Allie sat up slowly, noiselessly, and glanced through the mesh sides of the portable crib. Joanie slumbered with the peace of an infant, her little chest rising and falling in a comforting even rhythm. Allie smiled. Her daughter's first sleepover.

Her throat was dry, which meant she must have been snoring. She wiggled out of her sleeping bag without unzipping it and tiptoed around her sisters. A dim yellow light illuminated the kitchen with a soft glow, the same seashell nightlight that had lit the darkness during Allie's teenage years in this house. She filled a glass with water from the faucet and drank deeply, her gaze circling the familiar room.

They had moved into this house with Gram and Grandpa when Mom and Daddy divorced. Allie was fifteen. She closed her eyes, remembering her first nights here. Full of pain, confusion, guilt. She'd been the one who told Mom about Daddy's affair, and about the bag of marijuana she found in the garage. If she'd kept her mouth shut, maybe . . .

No. Years ago Allie had accepted the fact that she was not to blame for her parents' divorce. Her college psychology classes had reaffirmed that. Daddy was the one who had been unfaithful. It was his fault, not hers. She'd discovered later that the affair with Mrs. Nelson wasn't his first, nor was it his last. But the pot had been the last straw for Mom. Allie didn't blame her, nor did she blame herself. She had realized long ago that her father was unreliable in every way that mattered.

But she never thought Eric would turn out like him.

Pain gripped her insides and squeezed. Her marriage was falling apart. She was going to end up like Mom, struggling to raise her daughter alone. A sob rose from deep in her chest to lodge in her throat. She doubled over, both hands pressed against her mouth to keep it in. She could not give in to despair. She had to be strong for Joanie. For herself.

What a blessedness, what a peace is mine, leaning on the everlasting arms.

She raised up, grabbed her glass off the counter, and slung the remaining water into the sink. Why did that ridiculous song keep coming to mind? She'd never liked it to begin with. It was stupid. What did it mean, even? Leaning meant depending on God to take care of you, to solve your problems. But Tori was right. God helped those who helped themselves. Besides, when you depended on someone else, you opened yourself up to disappointment, betrayal, and pain. Like Mom had done with Daddy. Allie gulped against the painful lump in her throat. Like she had done with Daddy. And with Eric.

But what if Joan is right?

That look in Joan's eyes, that certainty, haunted Allie. Tori didn't have that. In fact, Tori was almost as stressed out as Allie. What had Joan said? That Allie could rely on God because she was his precious child and he loved her. That she could trust him. With a sudden longing that threatened to overpower her grip on her emotions, Allie wanted to be that precious child. If only she could be as sure as Joan.

You have to ask.

That's what Joan said. God had the answers to her problems, but she had to ask.

She raised her eyes toward the ceiling. "I know you're there," she whispered. "I guess I've always figured you were watching to see how I'm handling things down here." The slow breath she drew shuddered. "Not so good, huh? I thought I could handle everything on my own, without you, without Daddy, even without Eric if I had to. But everything is such a mess right now I'm not sure I even know what to ask. What I really need is —" a sob broke her voice — "to know somebody cares."

The silence in the room deepened with an expectant hush. Something was happening. Her ragged breath suddenly stilled, Allie waited while a sense of anticipation danced around the edges of her mind. She closed her eyes and tilted her head back. Her tears dissolved as if . . . as if an invisible hand had gently wiped them away.

She felt loved. Like someone had tenderly placed a warm blanket around her tense shoulders and hugged her tight.

Safe and secure from all alarms.

New tears sprang to her eyes, not tears of pain, but of joy. With a certainty that Tori would call insane, Allie knew she was being hugged tight by someone who loved her. Someone who cherished her as his precious little girl. Someone on whom she could rely. Someone who could drop the answers to all her problems right in her lap, crazy as that sounded.

An unexplainable peace flooded her soul as Allie realized she could lean all the weight of her burdens on the everlasting arms that encircled her.

22

"Oatmeal?" Tori eyed the round container resting on the kitchen counter with disgust. "You want us to eat oatmeal for breakfast after a sleepover? Where's the chocolate donuts? The leftover pizza?"

Seated at the kitchen table while Joanie nursed, Allie looked at her sister's tiny waist as she reached up into the high cabinet where the cereal bowls were stored. Hip bones protruded through the soft pink PJ bottoms Tori wore. With a rush of envy, Allie realized she hadn't seen her own hip bones since shortly after her marriage.

"How in the world do you stay so skinny the way you eat?" she asked. "It is totally unfair that you got all the skinny genes while my genes suck up every fat gram that comes within a twelve-inch radius of my mouth and store it on my hips."

Tori picked up a spoon and used it to emphasize her words. "I don't eat very much as a rule. I know you think I do, because you only see me on Sundays when I'm pigging out on Gram's cooking. But during the week, sometimes I forget to eat at all."

Allie stared at her. Junk food tempted her forty times a day, and her little sister forgot to eat? "I want to hit you."

"No hitting." Joan pulled a yellow box of sweetener off the top shelf of the pantry and set it on the counter. "Besides, Allie, you have no one to blame but yourself. The minute you found out you were pregnant, you ate everything in sight." She smiled to soften her words. "You're not as big as you seem to think you are. You could drop that extra baby weight if you wanted to. What about that gym membership Eric gave you? Have you checked it out?"

"Yeah. It's a pretty swanky place, but I don't know. All that fancy equipment scares me, and I *don't* want to take aerobics." Allie shuddered. "Besides, what would I do with Joanie while I worked out?"

Joan snapped her fingers. "Oh, I meant to tell you. One of the girls in my Sunday school class works in the daycare out there. You remember Sara, don't you? She's so sweet, and she loves babies."

"Really?" Allie looked down at her baby.

If Joan knew someone who worked in the nursery . . . "They do have a pool and a walking track."

"Perfect." Joan scooped raw oatmeal into three bowls. "I wouldn't mind joining a gym, especially during the winter. I'll go with you a few mornings a week to help you get into the routine."

Allie shifted Joanie to the other arm. Her heart felt tender this morning after her middle-of-the-night . . . encounter? She didn't know what to call it, but when she'd awakened, the peace she felt in the night still lingered. She'd been half afraid to go to sleep, afraid that she'd wake up and find the stress of all her problems pressing down on her again. But her first conscious thought before she even opened her eyes had been, *Good morning, God! I'm so glad you're in control.* Her mood was lighter than it had been in . . . well, forever.

Joan's offer to go with her to the gym struck her as particularly touching, and she battled a wave of tears. Joan walked with Ken every morning, so coming to the gym with her meant her sister was willing to sacrifice time with her boyfriend. She waited until she was sure the catch in her throat wouldn't sound in her voice. "You'd do that for me?"

Joan turned a look of surprise her way. "Of course I would. You're my sister."

Allie lowered her gaze to her nursing baby. Was this the answer to one of her problems, dropped right in her lap? Was Joan's offer God's way of taking care of one thing that made his precious little girl unhappy?

She gulped, and couldn't look up until she got a firm grip on her emotions. This feeling, this awareness of her heavenly Father's presence, was still too new. She didn't want to talk about it, because what if admitting it aloud made it go away?

So instead she just said, "Thanks. I'd like that."

Tori added water to one of the bowls and set it in the microwave. The *beep-beep-beep* as she punched the buttons sounded loud in the kitchen where the only other sound was Joanie's soft murmur while she nursed. Joan refilled her coffee mug and brought the carafe to the table to warm up Allie's. Joan yawned as she poured, and Allie did too. She'd only gotten a couple of hours' sleep after her middle-of-the-night encounter before Joanie woke them all for her 6:00 a.m. feeding.

"So what's the plan this morning?" Tori asked as she stirred water into the second bowl of dry oats.

"I'm going to run over and pick up Gram around eight so she can start Sunday dinner." Joan switched her gaze to Allie. "Are you staying here while we go to church, or are you going to go home and come back for dinner with Eric and Betty?"

Allie looked down. "Actually, I thought I might go with you this morning."

Joan's jaw dropped, and Tori stopped stirring to stare at her.

"Really?" Joan asked.

Allie nodded. "Except all I brought to wear today is a pair of tan slacks and a shirt that isn't very dressy." She bit her lip. "I could go home and get some nicer clothes, but . . ."

She really didn't want to face Eric with the news that she wanted to go to church. He'd let her, of course, but she knew how he felt, and why. He'd require an explanation, and at the moment she didn't know if she could articulate how she felt. All she knew was that she wanted to go.

If Joan saw the struggle in her face, she didn't mention it. "That'll be fine. I'll wear slacks too, and we can dress up your top with jewelry. Tori can wear slacks too."

Tori's lower lip pouted. "I didn't bring slacks. I brought an absolutely darling wool skirt I got last week that I wanted to show off."

"Slacks." Joan's tone refused to tolerate any argument on the subject. "I'm sure you can find something in the ton of clothes you have stored in the upstairs closet."

Tori heaved a loud sigh. "You guys are just as bossy now as you were when we were kids."

At eleven o'clock Allie sat between her sisters in the sanctuary of Christ Community Church. The strong floral scent of Mrs. Caldwell's perfume lingered on Allie's skin, applied by the enthusiastic hug the elderly lady had given her when she placed Joanie in her care in the nursery. Or maybe it was from one of the other many hugs of welcome she'd received. A glance around the sanctuary showed so many familiar faces, so many delighted smiles of recognition. Gram sat on the other side of Joan, her gaze fixed on her hymnal. At least her lips were no longer clamped together in disapproval at her granddaughters' choice of clothing. Allie wondered if Gram had noticed, as she did, that many of the women in the congregation wore slacks, even some of the seniors. Allie had glimpsed a couple of teenagers in jeans, something that would never have happened when she attended this church during her high school years.

Deep, rich music filled the sanctuary as the organist began the prelude. In response, unexpected tears prickled Allie's eyes. It had been so long since she'd heard the sound of an organ. The music brought with it the sense of holiness she remembered feeling as a little girl. *I've come home,* she thought. *Like a prodigal.* More tears threatened, and she fought against them. She would not cry here.

The choir filed into the loft from a side door at the front of the sanctuary. Allie searched each face as they stepped through the doorway. Some were familiar, some new. Mom led the second row. When she got to her place, light glinted off the lenses of her glasses as her gaze searched the congregation. A smile lit her face when she caught sight of them.

Movement in the aisle caught Allie's attention, and she turned her head to watch Reverend Jacobsen make his way down the center aisle toward the pulpit. The same aisle Allie had walked down during her wedding. Only then Eric had been here, waiting at the front, his face radiant with love.

Allie shut her eyes against a wave of angst. What should she do about Eric? Ask him to transfer back to second shift so he wasn't alone with Molly every day? Let Betty watch Joanie at night while she did Varie Cose parties? But Betty needed to return home to Don, Allie knew that. So she'd have to hire a babysitter, and if she was going to do that, she might as well go back to her state job.

Her stomach muscles tightened as familiar worries threatened her newfound peace.

God, can you really handle this? Because I know I can't.

Her worries took wing and fluttered away as she remembered the unspoken promise of last night. Safe and secure.

Reverend Jacobsen reached his seat at the front of the sanctuary as the organist finished the prelude with a powerful musical flourish that vibrated Allie's heart in her rib cage. The choir director stepped up to the altar, his arms held wide as he invited the congregation to stand.

Allie got to her feet along with everyone else as the strains of the first hymn filled the sanctuary. Joan handed her a hymnal already opened to the right page. When Allie looked down at the title, chills rose on her arm. The awe from the dimly lit kitchen last night returned as the familiar tune the organ played registered in her mind.

Leaning on the Everlasting Arms.

There was no holding back her tears.

Allie winced as Eric followed her into their bedroom and slammed the door. During Sunday dinner Joan had unwittingly broken the news that she'd gone to church with the rest of the family. All afternoon Allie had sensed Eric's growing anger as they worked in the yard at Gram's house, getting the last of the leaves raked up and the rosebushes ready for winter. He had barely spoken two words to her.

She planted her back against the desk chair and faced him. The fury in his eyes snapped at her across the room. She was glad she'd placed the bed between them.

"I can't believe you took Joanie to church without asking me."

Anger flickered in the back of her skull at his word choice. "Without *asking* you? Are you saying I have to beg your permission to go to church?"

"If you want to take my daughter, yes."

The serenity she'd found at church left her in a rush that stiffened her spine. The day she begged permission to do anything, like she was some sort of servant, would be the day she walked out of here. She drew an outraged breath to tell him so when he raised a hand, fingers splayed, and clarified his point. "Not *begged* me, but you should have talked to me first. We've discussed this. I thought we were in agreement that we'd wait until she was old enough to make her own decision about religion."

Calm down. I knew he'd be upset. With an effort, Allie bit back another angry retort and forced a measure of calm into her voice. "You're right, Eric. I should have called you this morning. But I knew this would happen," she gestured between them, "and I didn't want to start the day off with an argument. Besides, she just spent an hour in the nursery, that's all."

"That's all?" His hands clenched into fists at his side. "You left our helpless child in the care of a complete stranger. Who knows what could have happened to her there?"

"That's not true. I've known Mrs. Caldwell my entire life. Her grandson graduated from high school in my class. Joanie was perfectly safe."

She met his glare with one of her own. The sight of his jaw bunching sent an unexpected shot of compassion through Allie. Poor Eric. Because of the incident with that pervert, he really was afraid for Joanie when it came to church. She should have realized how angry he would be. She'd been so focused on herself and her new awareness of God's love that she had not given a thought to her husband's feelings.

"Eric, I'm sorry. You're right. I should have called you this morning. But last night I . . ." She stared at the multi-colored pattern of lines and squiggles marching across the comforter and tried to gather her thoughts. How to explain what happened last night? The peace she'd felt, the certainty that she could rest in the arms of her heavenly Father and trust him to take care of her? She swallowed and started again. "I realized something last night. I hate selling Varie Cose."

That was *so* not what she intended to say.

A scowl wrinkled Eric's upper lip. "What?"

Allie rushed on, her frantic thoughts becoming a torrent of words. "I hate it, but I have to keep going because I owe too much for all this." She waved at the boxes lining the shelves. "And we need to figure out a way to get your mom to go back home, but that means I'll have to find a babysitter. And I'm worried about us too, you and me."

He looked at her like she'd lost her mind. No wonder. She was making a mess of this. She clamped her mouth shut and whispered a frantic prayer. *Now would be a good time to give me a hand here.*

"Let me get this straight." Eric's effort to keep calm showed in his tense shoulders. "You went to a sleepover with your sisters, and now you've decided you hate your job and you want to kick my mother out of our house, so you have to go to church to set things right?"

Mockery laced his tone. She steeled herself against voicing an angry retort. "No, that's not it. Church doesn't set things right, God does." She clamped her jaws shut and shook her head. "I'm not explaining this well."

"No, you're not." Eric's stare hardened. "Back up a minute. You owe too much to quit? How much do you owe?"

She gulped. Now's when things would get nasty. She really didn't want to tell him about the credit card, not when he was already so mad. But things were tumbling out into the open now, and she didn't see any way to stuff them back under wraps. Unable to meet his gaze, she turned her back on him and rummaged in the stack of folders on the desk for the credit card statement she'd printed out yesterday. Wordlessly, she held it toward him.

He reached across the bed and took it. When his eyes moved to the bottom of the page, they widened. "Allie! How could you do this so quickly?"

Tears flooded her eyes. "I didn't mean to. It just happened."

"Debt like this doesn't *just happen.*" He stopped. Silence hung heavily between them for what seemed like hours before he went on. "Okay, we can deal with this. Just cut up the card before you do any more damage. Call that woman who roped you into this scheme and tell her you quit."

"I can't just quit. I've got over two thousand dollars in inventory I have to sell."

"Return it. They'll probably charge you a restocking fee or something, but that'll be better than owing thousands. You can stay home with Joanie and I'll work out a budget that —"

"No!" Panic rose up in Allie's throat. She couldn't do that, couldn't let Eric fix things. She'd be more dependent on him than ever. She was supposed to depend on God, not Eric. "I can handle it. I'll get it paid off. Just a few more parties and I'm sure I can turn things around."

"What if you can't?" Eric peered at her with an intensity that made her want to look away, but she couldn't tear her gaze from his. "Why don't you want my help, Allie?"

"Because I have to make it on my own in case . . ." The gulp of air shuddered on the way into her lungs. She swallowed. "In case you leave me."

There. Her deepest fear was out in the open. Now would be when he was supposed to come around the bed, take her in his arms, and assure her of his undying love.

The silence deepened between them. Eric stood motionless, staring at her with eyes as deeply sad as his mother's. Allie waited for his words of reassurance, his promise that he would never leave her. Horror choked her like a fast-growing vine. They did not come.

Instead, Eric shook his head slowly. "I thought I knew you. But I'm married to a stranger."

He tossed the credit card bill toward her, turned on his heel, and left the room. The paper fluttered to the mattress.

Allie stared at the door, her mind numb. Was this God's idea of taking care of things? She'd come clean to Eric, opened herself up. And she'd lost him. Was this God's answer?

She sank to the bed. No. She didn't believe that, wouldn't believe it. She was God's precious child, and he loved her. He didn't want her to lose her husband.

A new thought snaked into her mind. But maybe he wanted her to trust her husband.

Maybe that was part of the answer he was trying to provide.

A sob rode a wave of panic from deep inside and lodged in her throat.

Lord, I can't do that! What if he leaves me, like Daddy did, then where will I be? I need your help!

23

Eric jumped into the pickup and jammed the key savagely into the ignition. The instant the engine roared to life, he shoved the shifter into first and sped out of the driveway. The house receded in the rearview mirror. When he turned the corner and lost sight of it, he blew out a breath. He'd left all the women in his life — and all the problems — in that house. He navigated the truck out of the neighborhood and turned onto the bypass. The minute he left the Danville city limits, he stomped on the accelerator and headed into the country. The sun dipped low on the horizon to his right, a big orange ball that shed little light and no warmth.

What had happened to Allie? Everybody said becoming a mother changed a woman. He never really believed it. Oh sure, little changes here and there. They got more protective, maybe. More homey. But Allie had undergone a total personality transplant.

She didn't trust him. Anger gnawed at his gut. He had never done a thing to make her think him untrustworthy. Not in any area. He'd supported her in everything she ever wanted. He stepped up as the man of her family when her grandfather died, before they were even married. He'd maintained her sisters' cars, dug her grandmother's flower beds, even unstopped their toilets and fixed their leaky roof. When Allie wanted to quit her job and do this crazy makeup sales stuff, he'd supported her decision 100 percent. He had not looked at another woman since the day he first laid eyes on her. And still, she didn't trust him.

Maybe he'd never go back. Yeah, that's it. Just hit the road and disappear. That's what Allie apparently thought he'd do anyway. Call it quits, like Mother and Dad seemed prepared to do. If they could walk away from thirty-five years of marriage, five should be no big deal.

The old days, the pre-Allie days, loomed like a sweet dream in his mind as the town receded in the distance. College buddies partying late into the night at that house they'd rented and then dragging themselves to class the next morning. Walking in a pack to the stadium for the home games, whooping and hollering down Alumni Drive until the cops chased them out of the road and onto the sidewalk so traffic could get by. Calling to the women they passed, trying to catch their eyes and maybe hook up for the night.

And he hooked up plenty. Women always liked him, picked him out in the crowd, much to the disgust of his roommates. If he wanted a date with a woman, he always got it. Probably still could, if he wanted.

Like Molly.

His foot lifted slowly off the pedal, and the truck ceased its mad dash forward. Okay, truth time now. Alone in the swiftly darkening cab of his truck, he could be honest with himself. Molly was available, had been for some time. He'd have to be deaf, dumb, and blind not to notice the looks she gave him, the unspoken invitations. She was not a bad-looking woman, either. Six years ago, before he met Allie, he'd have accepted one of those invitations without a second thought. Not anymore.

Eric pulled off the side of the road and let the truck roll to a stop. An ancient stone fence ran along both sides of the curvy two-lane road. Farms spread out beyond it as far as he could see. The fields around him were littered with tobacco stubble, dried-out stalks left over from the harvest. A white farmhouse sat well back from the road at the end of a narrow dirt driveway that carved the fields on either side into uneven pieces.

Okay, the truth. Allie was the only woman for him. He'd known it the moment he laid eyes on her. He loved everything about her. The way she psychoanalyzed everybody and was almost always right. The way she approached a task like a linebacker ready to knock any obstacle out of her way. Her intelligence. Her compassion. Her looks. Everything. He couldn't believe his incredible luck that he'd managed to find a woman like her.

The porch light up at the farmhouse came on, and he could make out a man's figure as it stepped through the front door, staring intently his way. Eric noticed a sign nailed to a wooden post that stood sentry to the driveway. No Trespassing. He put the truck in reverse, backed into the dirt driveway, and then pulled out onto the road heading slowly back toward town.

There was only one catch with leaving his problems behind. He'd also be leaving behind everything he cared about. Everything he loved. Every*one* he loved. He couldn't do that.

The sun had sunk out of sight behind the gentle swell of the hills, and his truck's headlights carved two bright beams through the deepening twilight. They'd just have to work it out, that's all. If Allie wanted to keep doing this makeup sales stuff, he'd shut his mouth and let her. After he watched her cut up that credit card, that is. But she'd figure it out. She might make a mistake or two, but in the long run she would succeed. He couldn't imagine Allie doing anything else.

So what about this church thing? His teeth scraping across each other sounded loud in his ears. All day long as they worked in the yard alongside her family, he had sensed a change in her. A couple of times he heard her humming a song as she raked leaves, and Allie never hummed. He'd attributed her good mood to spending time with her sisters last night. But what if it was something else? What if going to church was what made her happy today? He wanted her to be happy, didn't he?

The first buildings of town came into view. Eric drove past without seeing them. He kept his eyes fixed on the road, his mind skipping all around their argument. What had Allie said? "Church doesn't set things right. God does."

Sounded like something Ken Fletcher would say. Or Joan. That was probably it — Joan had gotten to Allie last night with her God-talk. Eric's wife had found religion. He was married to a religious makeup saleswoman. A shudder passed through his shoulders. Could he live with that?

Without really paying attention to where he was going, Eric steered the truck through town. He followed a path he'd traveled more frequently in the past few days than in all the years since he moved to Danville. Down Main Street past Constitution Square with its restored log cabin and historic statues. Past the courthouse. The fire station. Toward the Centre College campus. With no surprise at all, Eric turned onto the drive of Christ Community Church. He pulled the truck around to the back of the building and got out. A lone car sat on the other side of the lot, covered in darkness.

Eric leaned against the door of his pickup and stared at the building. A tall spire thrust into the sky. Moonlight glimmered off the cross that topped it. What was it about this place that had drawn Allie here this morning? Why did an intelligent man like Ken choose to spend time here? And Joan was no dummy, either. What about this place had grabbed her attention a few months ago and made her want to go off to Mexico like some kind of missionary?

The back door opened and a man exited the building. Uh oh. Though it had been a few years, Eric recognized the guy even across the distance. Reverend Jacobsen performed their wedding ceremony.

It was dark. Maybe if Eric didn't move, he wouldn't be spotted.

No luck. Reverend Jacobsen's head turned toward him on the way to his car. He changed directions and headed straight for Eric.

Terrific.

Eric hefted himself upright as the older man approached, squinting in the darkness. He probably wouldn't remember him, anyway.

His face brightened with a smile as he drew near. "Hello, Eric. What a surprise to find you here."

So much for not recognizing him. Nothing wrong with the guy's memory.

Eric took the hand that Reverend Jacobsen thrust toward him. He pocketed his own as soon as the man released him. "Hello, sir. I was just out driving around and decided to stop for a minute." Lame excuse, but it had the benefit of being the truth.

"I had the pleasure of seeing your wife

and your beautiful little girl this morning."

"Yeah, she told me. I was at home. Uh, with my mother. She's visiting for a while." His mouth snapped shut. What was the matter with him? He didn't need to make excuses for not going to church!

Reverend Jacobsen nodded. "I understand you've been helping out with the auction our mission team is conducting."

Fletcher. What else had he told the minister?

Eric lifted a shoulder. "Not much. Just picked up a couple of donations. Not a big deal."

"Well, we appreciate your help. It's an important project, one we hope will spread the love of God not only in Mexico but here as well."

"Excuse me?"

The older man smiled. "When people like our singles group promote a project with such enthusiasm, it demonstrates God's love in a real and tangible way. Projects like this have a way of catching a community's attention. We hope people who don't normally come to church will come out Tuesday night, and that they'll get a glimpse of God's love in action."

"People like me, huh?" Eric didn't mean his words to come out sounding as bitter as they did. He wished he could take them back.

Reverend Jacobsen didn't seem to notice. His smile held a touch of mischief. "Naturally I hope you'll want to come, and that you'll like us enough to join your family next Sunday morning."

"Do you get, like, a commission or something? The fuller the pews on Sunday mornings, the higher your bonus?"

The guy might have taken offense at the accusation, but he raised his head and laughed. "Not the kind of bonus you're thinking about." Then he sobered. "You're not very fond of churches, are you, Eric?"

Was that a reference to Eric's past, compliments of Ken? Looking at Reverend Jacobsen's guileless face, he didn't think so. "Let's just say I haven't had good experience with people who are fond of churches."

"Ah." The minister nodded. "It's so easy for people to disappoint us."

Eric looked at him sharply. "Something like that."

"I'm sure you've heard what Jesus said on that subject. 'It is not the healthy who need a doctor, but the sick. I have not come to call the righteous, but sinners.' "

Oh, great. He was getting his own private sermon, right here in the church parking lot. "Well, seems to me if Jesus is looking for sinners, church is a good place to start."

Instead of flaring up, the guy laughed again. "I have no doubt of that." Reverend Jacobsen cocked his head, deep shadows from the building hiding his eyes. "Do you mind if I ask you a question?"

Yeah, actually, he did mind. He minded this whole conversation. But he couldn't be rude, not to the guy who performed his marriage ceremony. "Shoot."

"Forget church for a minute. Forget people who may have hurt you. Do you believe in God?"

Eric did. He'd never been able to accept the big bang theory, that the universe and the earth just happened to pop into existence. You didn't throw a handful of nuts and bolts into a blender and expect a car to pop out. Somebody put it all together. "Yeah, I believe in God."

Reverend Jacobsen nodded. "Do you believe that he loves the people he created?"

A slow-moving cloud crept across the moon, deepening the darkness around them. The minister's question hovered in Eric's mind. He had seen so much pain in his job, so much suffering. And yet, he knew deep inside that God didn't cause the misery he'd seen. People did.

The snatch of a tune crept up from the dredges of his memory, one his grandmother had taught him before she died. *Jesus loves me, this I know, for the Bible tells me so.* He'd forgotten. She used to rock him in that old rocking chair, the black one with the gold leaves painted on the arms. She sang to him and told him how Jesus loved him so much he had died just so little Eric could live forever in heaven with God. Eric had believed her, had accepted her words as fact. Then she died. Did he stop believing when she was no longer there to tell him? Or did he believe still?

"Yes." His voice came out in a whisper. "I believe that."

Reverend Jacobsen placed a hand on his shoulder. "Then focus on that, Eric. Don't let imperfect people take your eyes off of the most important thing — God's love for you."

Warmth from the man's hand spread from Eric's shoulder downward. For a moment, he felt like he was a little guy snuggling in his grandmother's embrace. He could almost feel the rocking motion, hear the rumble of music in her lungs as his ear rested against her chest. Could feel the certainty of the words she whispered as they took root in his soul. *Jesus loves me, this I know.*

Then Reverend Jacobsen released his shoulder and stepped back. "I've got to get home or my wife is going to wring my neck. I told her I'd be home over an hour ago." He turned to head toward his car, speaking as he walked away. "I hope to see you at the auction Tuesday night."

"Maybe. I have to talk to Allie about it."

That is, if he and Allie were speaking by then. The engine of the minister's car roared to life, his headlights illuminating the brick side of the church. Eric climbed into his pickup. Instead of starting the engine, he sat in the rapidly cooling cab, his thoughts firing from one side of his mind to the other, like bullets fired across a battlefield.

He wasn't ready to go home yet. He needed time to think about this conversation. And about Allie. And about her job. And her credit card. And why she didn't trust him.

24

Allie stood in the middle of the room, watching Eric shrug into his jacket as he prepared to leave for work Monday morning.

"Have a nice day." Her voice sounded pitiful in her own ears. Whiney. She glanced at Betty seated in her chair reading the newspaper and tried not to think about her husband going off to spend the day alone in a small room with That Woman.

"You too."

He didn't look at her. Still. He'd avoided looking at her since their argument. When he got home last night, he'd been sunk into himself, silent and distant. To be honest, Allie didn't try very hard to draw him out. She didn't want a repeat of their argument, and besides, she had a lot to think about herself. She'd laid in bed for hours after Eric fell asleep, listening to his even breathing. Thinking. And praying. Finally, she'd reached a decision.

When he picked up his lunch bag from the chair and turned toward the door, Allie hurried across the room. She couldn't let him leave like this, go to Molly while angry with her. She stopped him with a hand on his arm and spoke in a low voice, acutely aware of Betty's presence.

"I want to finish our discussion."

Exasperation creased his features. "Right this minute?"

Allie let out a sigh. "No. But tonight, okay? I . . ." She wet her lips and lowered her voice. "I love you, Eric. I don't want you mad at me."

Dark eyes bored into hers. A flicker of emotion dashed across his face in the second before he crushed her to his chest in a fierce embrace.

"I'm not mad at you." His voice was the merest whisper in her ear. "We'll talk tonight."

Then he was gone. Allie shut the door behind him, her hand resting for a moment on the knob. They had a lot to talk about, but at least Eric wasn't angry with her. Her mood rose like a balloon, tugging the corners of her mouth up with it. It was going to be a good day. A productive day. As a result of her sleepless and prayerful night, she had several positive steps to take, tasks that she would enjoy doing for once.

She turned to find Betty watching her over the newspaper.

"Uh," she stammered, suddenly embarrassed. "We had a little argument last night."

"I heard." Betty's face remained as impassive as ever.

Heat rose into Allie's cheeks. "You did?"

"The walls aren't soundproof." She lowered the newspaper to her lap. "Do you need money? I have some put back for a rainy day."

Warmth for this aloof woman flooded Allie. Tears stung her eyes. "Thank you, Betty, but no. This is something I need to work out for myself." She stopped, her resolution of last night washing over her. "No, that's wrong. Eric and I need to work it out together." She sank onto the couch and clasped her hands between her knees. "I've been thinking about our conversation the other day. You remember how you said you wished you weren't so dependent on Don?"

Betty nodded, and Allie went on.

"I'm all about being independent and having your own interests. But if I wanted to be completely self-sufficient, what's the point of getting married?" Allie stared at her clasped hands, speaking slowly as she

357

searched for the right words. "I believe God put me and Eric together." She glanced up, to see if her mention of God had any effect on her mother-in-law. Betty's expression remained dispassionate. "We're a team. Sort of like one of Eric's ball games. The quarterback can't win the game by himself. He needs his teammates working with him. If one of them goes off and does their own thing during the game, they're going to lose."

"Are you saying you're going to quit work? Close your business?"

Allie's teeth snagged at her lower lip for a moment. She took a deep breath and blew it out. "Yes."

There. She'd said it out loud. That made it real. A curious sense of lightness rose up in her, like all her burdens had been lifted.

"Will you go back to your job at the state?"

She shook her head. "I don't know. Eric and I need to talk about that. Maybe . . ." She swallowed. "Maybe I'll stay home."

Betty leaned against the back of the chair, shaking her head slowly as she studied Allie. "You have a college degree, a career. You're smart. Independent. How can you throw that away?"

From the nursery, the soft sound of a baby's first cry upon waking floated into the room.

Allie smiled. "I'm not throwing away my independence. I'm just doing my part for our little team."

She rose and headed toward the nursery. On the way, she stopped by Betty's chair to rest a hand on the older woman's shoulder. "God will take care of me. And Eric. And Joanie. I'm not going to worry about that." She took another step, then stopped. "By the way, have you called Don yet?"

A peachy flush edged its way up Betty's neck as she shook her head.

Allie let out an exasperated grunt. "Do it, Betty. Just do it!"

Allie perched on the edge of Sally Jo's elegant sofa. Joanie sat in her infant seat on the cushion beside her, watching the flicker of a red jar candle on the coffee table through wide blue eyes. The scent of cinnamon apples pervaded the entire house.

"I have to admit, I'm surprised." Sally Jo shook her head, staring at Allie from one of the upholstered wing chairs. "I thought Nicole would be the next to drop out." Her eyelids narrowed. "You've got the drive and ambition it takes to succeed. I think you could rise high in the ranks of Varie Cose,

Incorporated. Are you sure you want to do this?"

Allie nodded. "I'm sure. I might have what it takes, but frankly, I don't enjoy sales. Never have. When I was a kid, I dropped out of Brownies because I hated selling cookies." She rummaged in her briefcase — the one that cost eighty-seven bucks and would probably end up collecting dust on the top shelf of the closet — and pulled out a copy of the list she printed that morning. "Here's a list of items I have in inventory. Before you place your orders, if you don't mind taking a look to see if I have it on hand, I'd appreciate it. I'll sell it to you at cost, and that will save me the restocking fee. I'm going to run a copy over to Darcy's house too."

Sally Jo took the paper. Her eyes moved as she scanned the items. "This won't be a problem. I've got over thirty sales consultants under me. I'll let them know what you have."

Relief wilted Allie's spine. She leaned back against the soft cushion with a sigh. Why hadn't she thought of selling her inventory to other Varie Cose consultants before last night? That would take care of a huge part of the credit card balance. She hid a grin as a thought occurred to her. Maybe God had just dropped a pile of money in her lap. Wouldn't Tori be surprised? *Thank you, Lord.*

Sally Jo set the papers on the table and tapped the arm of her chair with a shiny pink fingernail that exactly matched the hue of her lips. Candy Coral, if Allie was any judge.

"What will you do now?"

Allie shook her head. "I haven't decided." A couple of days ago that admission would have set her stomach churning with anxiety. She grinned as she realized she wasn't worried. She was in good hands.

After she left Sally Jo's, Allie navigated her car through the streets toward Darcy's house.

"This is going to work out, Joanie." She glanced in the rearview mirror at Joanie's car seat. Her daughter was invisible, facing the other way in the center of the backseat.

Allie's mood was lighter than it had been in weeks. Strange, because her problems really weren't gone yet. But a big chunk of the credit card debt had just disappeared, or was about to. The coolest part, the thing that made her insides jittery, was that she sensed the hand of God in that solution. If he could take care of several thousand dollars of debt so quickly, Allie had complete confidence that he could handle the rest. She could hardly wait to tell Eric tonight.

She sobered at thoughts of talking with Eric about God again. Their last conversation had been awful, and it was totally her fault. She'd botched everything. Somehow she had to come up with the words to describe this new feeling she had, this peace. If only Eric could feel this too.

Thoughts of Molly rose up to threaten her newfound serenity, but she pushed them away. She refused to worry about Eric's attractive co-worker. Attractive and *thin.*

Thanks to Betty's focus on cooking light, and Allie's determination to avoid ice cream and cinnamon rolls, she had already dropped a few pounds. And she and Joan were meeting at the gym in the morning to begin their new workout routine. Her goal was to be back into her prebaby jeans for real by Christmas. Since God was batting a thousand in the area of solving her problems, maybe he'd even give her a hand in the weight department. A heavenly diet and exercise plan.

Chuckling, she punched the radio's power button as she headed down Third Street. Darcy lived out in the country, a ten-minute drive from the center of Danville. Allie had never been to her house, but today was a sunny November day, a good day for the drive out to Buster Pike. The disco beat of a seventies oldie blared from the radio and set her toes tapping as the car glided around the gentle curves of the road.

She turned onto Buster Pike as one song ended and another began. The road arced widely to the right, and then to the left to complete a giant S-curve. At the bottom of the S, Allie slowed her car to read the number on a rusty metal mailbox. She was getting closer. Darcy had told her the house was right beyond a wide curve. Another wide curve loomed ahead. Allie slowed even farther and turned the steering wheel to the right.

The moment she rounded the curve, her breath caught in her throat. Her grip tightened on the wheel. Moving obstacles crowded the road. Cattle? She jerked the wheel to the right. What were cows doing —

The car gave a violent jerk as the front bumper met an immovable wall of meat and muscle.

Lord, protect my baby!
Allie's vision went dark.

25

The emergency line buzzed. Eric glanced at Molly, who was intent on her daily report. She had been quieter than normal today, probably because he'd answered her questions about how his weekend went with clipped, one-word responses. She apparently took the hint that he wasn't interested in dealing with her come-on today.

"Your turn," she said with a touch of the old chumminess they enjoyed when he first transferred to this shift.

They took turns answering calls throughout the day, and she had taken the last one. Eric leaned forward and punched a button on the console, then spoke into his headset. "9-1-1 Center. What is your location?"

As he spoke, he swiveled around to check the other monitor for the last reported locations of the officers on duty.

"Two seventy Buster Pike." A woman's voice, tight with hysteria. "There's been an accident. My friend ran into a cow. I heard the crash, and now her baby's crying."

Old man Dorsey's cattle fence again. It was bound to happen sooner or later. Eric glanced at Molly, who nodded and reached for the controls to dispatch emergency personnel while he kept the caller on the line.

He kept his voice calm. "We're sending an ambulance right now, ma'am. Are you at the site of the accident?"

"Yes. I'm on my cell. I can see my friend through the window, but her door's locked. She's . . . she's not moving. I don't see any blood."

Molly's voice, low and steady beside him, broadcast a ten-fifty, an injury accident, to the active duty officers, and then put out a call for a ten-fifty-two, an ambulance request. She disconnected and nodded at him.

"Help is on the way, ma'am. They'll be there in just a minute. What is your name?"

"Darcy Wilson. Can you hear the baby crying? Should I try to break the window and get her out?"

Eric jotted the name on his pad. Darcy. He'd heard that name recently, but couldn't remember where. The muffled cries of an infant in the background stirred his new parental instincts. The urge to pick up a crying baby was strong, but he knew better than to let a civilian touch an accident victim. "I'm sorry, Ms. Wilson. It's best if you wait for the EMTs."

"She looks okay. She's in her car seat. Oh, and my friend is moving. Thank goodness."

"Tell her to stay where she is," Eric warned. "She needs to stay put until the —"

"I hear the sirens." Relief saturated the woman's voice. Eric heard a loud knock on glass, and then Darcy's voice calling to someone. "Don't move, honey. The ambulance is almost here."

The next minutes were a flurry of activity as Officer Baker arrived, followed quickly by a second officer, Chad Palmer, and then the EMTs. Eric disconnected the call with Ms. Wilson and waited for an update from Baker, the first official on the scene. He opened a new incident report screen and began typing the specifics into the database.

The landline rang. The line's display showed Chad's cell number. Eric glanced at Molly. An officer on the scene would use his phone only if he needed to report something he didn't want the media and others who listened to police scanners to hear. Eric leaned forward and punched the speaker button. "What's up, Chad?"

"Uh, Eric? We have a situation here." Chad sounded worried, something Eric had not heard before from the seasoned officer. Molly raised her eyebrows and lifted a shoulder.

"Go ahead."

"Eric, the driver is Allie."

The world dropped out from beneath Eric. He was vaguely aware that Chad's voice continued, but he couldn't concentrate. The blood drained from his head in a flash. He felt dizzy. All moisture evaporated from his mouth.

Allie was hurt. And the crying baby was Joanie. His daughter.

His whole world was in that car.

If anything happened to Allie, to Joanie . . . He closed his eyes, nausea settling in his stomach in an instant.

"Eric." Molly's warm hand on his arm pulled him from the terrible place his mind was slipping into. He looked up and saw that Kathy had stepped into the room and stood nearby. "Did you hear Chad? They're fine. Just shaken up."

Eric shot forward in his seat and grabbed the receiver. "Let me talk to her," he managed to croak through a dry throat.

"Eric?" Tears laced his wife's voice, and he heard an edge of panic. But she was talking. Thank goodness, she was able to talk.

His grip on the phone tightened. "Allie, are you okay? Is Joanie okay?"

"I th-think so. She's crying, but I think she's just scared." Her voice squeaked. "So am I."

He closed his eyes and lowered his head to the edge of the desk. He had never felt so helpless in his entire life. "I know, baby. As long as you're okay, that's all that matters."

She sniffled. "My arm hurts. And my chin."

Chad's voice came back on the phone. "The ambulance is going to take them both down to the ER to be checked out. You want me to come pick you up?"

Eric stood so quickly the seat went rolling away behind him. He had to get to the hospital. Waiting for Chad to come get him would drive him crazy. He cast a frantic look at Kathy. "I've got to get to the hospital."

She nodded. "Go. Molly and I can manage things here."

He ripped the headset off and tossed it on the desk. He was on his way out the door when Molly's voice called after him, "Be careful. I don't want to have to send an ambulance after you too."

■ ■ ■ ■

Allie reclined on a rolling hospital bed. A terrible smoky taste like gunpowder clogged her throat and clung to the inside of her nostrils. Her left arm lay motionless on the mattress beside her. A dull ache throbbed in it, and a niggling pain in her head answered. The last time she had been in this hospital was two months ago, when she'd given birth to the precious infant who slept peacefully in the crook of her right arm. Only then she'd been here for a joyous occasion.

Mom sat in a molded plastic chair on one side of the bed, dressed in pink nurse's scrubs. The anxiety she wore when she first rushed down from the fourth floor had left after she checked over her daughter and granddaughter, which went a long way toward soothing Allie's own. If only somebody would calm Eric down.

She shifted her gaze up to him, where he hovered at her right side. He kept stroking Joanie's cheek. He looked like somebody had strung a tight wire through his nervous system. When Joanie let out a soft sigh, he started.

"She's fine," Allie repeated for what must

be the tenth time. "Ken checked her out. Mom checked her out. She's perfectly okay."

Eric looked unconvinced. "I still think they ought to X-ray her or something, just to be sure. I've never seen her cry like she was crying when I got here."

"She was frightened, that's all." Allie snuggled the infant closer. "Probably sensing my fears, and all the activity, and the ambulance siren. That's enough to scare anybody."

The curtain surrounding the bed opened. Ken, dressed in a white doctor's coat and carrying a large manila envelope, came through and announced, "You have a visitor."

Joan stepped into view and rushed to the bed. She cupped a hand gently around Joanie's head and then carefully bent over to brush a kiss on Allie's forehead. A lock of dark hair tickled Allie's nose.

"How are you feeling?" Joan's whisper held a threat of tears as she searched Allie's face.

Allie instilled her smile with assurance. "A little sore, but otherwise fine."

Joan gave a slight nod, then straightened. She planted a hand on her hip, her lips twisted in a wry smile. "You ran over Elsie the cow?"

Allie's mouth twitched with a grin. "Yeah, well, this diet is getting to me. I was in the mood for steak."

Eric frowned. "It's nothing to joke about. You could have been seriously hurt. A thousand-pound cow can total a car."

Allie had forgotten about the car. She turned her head to look at him, ignoring the dull pain the sharp movement caused. "Is my car totaled?"

He ducked his head. "Well, no. Chad says it's drivable. Moderate damage, mostly bodywork."

Mom rose from the chair and stepped up beside Joan. "What about the cow?"

"Its injuries were too serious. It's headed for the slaughterhouse as we speak."

Allie winced and Joan laughed. "Way to go, Allie. You committed cowicide."

Mom nodded toward the envelope Ken held. "Are those the X-rays?"

He nodded. "No fracture. Her arm is just bruised. I'm guessing you were in the process of turning the wheel when the collision happened?"

Allie closed her eyes, trying to remember. "I think so. There were cows all over the road, and I think I jerked the wheel toward the right."

"So your left arm was across the front of

the steering wheel." Ken demonstrated with his. "When the airbag deployed, it thrust your arm into your body and probably connected with your chin, which is why you're sore there. Rocked your head on your neck a little, but I don't see any signs of concussion or other permanent injury in the cervical spine or thoracic films. No blood reported in the urinalysis, so your kidneys look fine. In fact, everything looks good."

"What is this terrible smoky smell all over me?" She smacked her tongue against the roof of her mouth and grimaced. "I can taste it. Yuck."

Eric grabbed a cup of ice water and held the straw to her lips. "It's chemicals they use in the airbag inflation mechanism."

Allie glanced with alarm at Ken. "Chemicals?"

"Sodium hydroxide. Might cause minor skin irritation if you get it into a cut or your eyes, but it's not harmful," he assured her.

"You smacked yourself in the chin?" Joan tried to cover her laugh with a hand.

One of those old black-and-white movie actors loomed in Allie's mind, punching himself in the face. Laughter bubbled up from her chest. "Yeah, maybe I should go into slapstick as my next profession. Groucho, Chico, Harpo, and —" She made a fist and imitated slugging herself in the chin. "— Bonko." She sucked in a hissing breath as the throbbing in her arm increased with movement. Eric placed a hand on her shoulder and squeezed.

The curtain parted again, and another white-coated man stepped through. It took a second for his identity to register, but then Allie straightened in the bed. "Dr. Reynolds? What are you doing here?" She cast a suspicious look up at Eric.

He released her shoulder and spread his hands. "Hey, he's Joanie's doctor. I thought he should be called."

Allie looked at Ken, a silent apology in her eyes. Would he be offended that Eric had called in another doctor? Ken shrugged. "I agree with Eric. In fact, I placed the call."

"And that is perfectly fine." Dr. Reynolds crossed the short distance to the bedside in two long strides and reached for Joanie. "Mrs. Harrod, this is one of those times we talked about. Remember, whenever you have questions." He winked at her as he lifted Joanie into his arms. "Besides, I was already planning a trip to the hospital to check out a brand-new patient who arrived an hour or so ago."

They watched as he laid Joanie on the foot of the bed and examined her. Eric grabbed

Allie's hand and held it tightly as the doctor listened to their daughter's heart and moved every little limb. Awakened from her nap, Joanie started to fuss when her arms and legs were pulled and pushed, but no more than normal. Allie was aware that Eric's breath had stopped while he watched.

His examination finished, Dr. Reynolds slipped Joanie's hands through the sleeves of her ruffled pink shirt, snapped it closed, and handed her to Eric. "She's fine. Not a mark on her."

Eric's breath blew out in a blast. He cradled Joanie in his arms and soothed her with a gentle rocking. At the sight of the tenderness in his eyes as he gazed into their baby's face, a rush of emotion flooded Allie.

On the other side of the bed, Joan whispered, "Thank God."

Allie remembered her frantic prayer at the moment of impact. She looked up into her sister's eyes and smiled through a rush of tears. "Exactly."

When Dr. Reynolds left the room, Ken grabbed the curtain and held it open. He spoke in his official doctor's voice. "Okay, ladies and gentlemen, it's time to clear this room. We need it for sick people."

Allie laughed, and even Eric smiled. Mom lowered the side rail and helped Allie out of bed with a hand under her arm.

"I'm sure Joan has to get back to the store, but do you need me to come help you at home?" she asked. "I can get someone to cover for me upstairs."

Eric shook his head. "No thanks. I'm not going back to work today. If we need anyone else, Mother's there."

Mom nodded and placed a gentle kiss on Allie's cheek. "I'll call later to see if you need anything. You take it easy for a couple of days. You're going to be sore."

Joan leveled a glance on Allie and then spoke to Eric. "You'd better drive. She looks pretty hungry. She might aim for more livestock on the way home."

Allie groaned. "I'm never going to live this down, am I?"

Her sister flashed a wicked grin as she followed Mom through the curtain. "Not a chance."

Allie lowered herself gingerly into the chair to put her shoes on. Ouch. Sore was right. She felt like she'd been punched around the ring by a heavyweight contender. Or maybe an overly exuberant aerobics exerciser.

Standing at the break in the curtain, Ken watched as Joan retreated down the hallway. When she was out of sight, he spoke in a low voice. "You're still planning to come to the auction tomorrow night, aren't you?"

If the soreness she was feeling right now was any indication of how she'd feel tomorrow, Allie doubted she'd be able to get out of bed at all.

Eric shook his head. "I don't think that's a good idea."

Ken's lower lip disappeared as he chewed on it. "Try, okay? We're going to take turns being the auctioneer, and Joan's up first. So you can leave when her turn is over." He caught Allie's gaze. "Trust me. It will really mean a lot to her to have you there."

Allie glanced at Eric. He looked unconvinced. But Allie knew how much Joan had been looking forward to this auction, how hard she had worked on it. And sisters supported each other no matter what. "We'll try," she told Ken.

"Good enough." He tapped the X-ray envelope against his thigh. "Let me grab the nurse. She's got some paperwork you need to sign."

"You'd better not be grabbing any nurse," Allie called after him when he disappeared down the hallway, "or I'll tell my sister on you."

Her shoes tied, Allie leaned against the back of the chair and looked up at Eric.

They were finally alone.

"Eric, I —"

"Allie, when —"

They both stopped, and Allie gave a quiet laugh. "You first."

He looked down at Joanie, who had drifted off to sleep again, her thumb in her mouth and her fingers splayed across her nose. "When I heard that it was you and Joanie in that car . . ." He paused, his struggle to retain his composure clear. "I've never felt so alone in my life." He looked up at her. "It sort of made all the stuff we've been going through lately fall into perspective. I did a lot of thinking last night, and in that instant when I thought you might be hurt or even —" he gulped — "dead, the only thing I could think was that you'd never know what I realized." The intensity of his gaze sharpened until it seemed to pierce into her very soul. "I don't care what you do, Allie, as long as we're together. Work or don't work. Sell makeup or used cars or whatever. If it makes you happy, it doesn't matter to me, because I love you. I will always love you."

Tears pricked the back of her eyes as she rose and went to stand in front of him. "I love you too. And I want you to know I quit my job today."

He reared back, eyes wide. "You did?"

She nodded. "I'll tell you about it later." She stepped nearer and pressed her face into the warmth of his neck, snuggling close when his arm encircled her. She closed her eyes and breathed in the familiar scent of his skin, outdoorsy and clean with the faint hint of soap. "Right now I just want to go home and stay like this all day long. You, me, and Joanie."

Eric heaved a sigh. "And my mother."

Allie laughed at the resignation in his voice. "I have a feeling that situation is going to work itself out soon."

"I hope so." His arm tightened. "She's my mother and I love her, but I miss being alone with my girls."

Allie could have stayed in that moment forever.

26

The phone rang Tuesday afternoon, shattering the peaceful stillness that permeated the house. Allie tried to jump up from the couch to grab it, but Betty glared her down.

"Don't move an inch. I'll get it."

For a quiet little woman, her mother-in-law could be pretty fierce looking when she tried. Allie settled back into the pile of pillows and adjusted the fuzzy blanket around her legs. As Mom had warned, her body was stiff and sore today, but at least the throbbing in her head had ceased and the yucky gunpowder taste in her throat was gone. She picked up her novel, a Christian romance Joan brought by on her way to work this morning.

Betty appeared at her elbow as she opened the book. "It's someone named Sally Jo Campbell."

"Thank you, Betty." Allie took the cordless phone from her and covered the mouthpiece with her palm. "You really don't have to wait on me like this, you know. I'm fine."

Betty raised her chin. "I promised my son I'd keep you quiet today, and that's what I intend to do."

She returned to the kitchen as Allie held the phone to her ear. "Hi, Sally Jo. I guess Darcy told you about my run-in with the milk machine."

Allie had resigned herself to living with cow jokes for a while, so she figured she might as well face the issue head-on. So to speak.

Sally Jo's laugh sounded in her ear. "She sure did. Honey, if you wanted a hamburger, you could have just asked before you left my house."

"Yeah, but you would have cooked it. I've never tried steak tartare before."

"Eeewwww! I never did see how anybody could eat raw meat." Her voice became serious. "How are y'all feeling? How's your baby?"

"We're fine, really." Allie tucked a bookmark into her book and slid it onto the coffee table. "I've got a nasty bruise on my arm and a blister on my collarbone where the seat belt rubbed me, but that's about it. Joanie doesn't have a mark on her."

"Thank goodness!"

Allie smiled. *No, thank God.*

Sally Jo's tone took on a businesslike professionalism. "I had another reason for calling. After you left here, I got to looking at your list and thinking about your computer program. I could really use a program like that to help me stay organized. With all my records on the computer, tax time will be a breeze."

Allie plucked a few loose pieces of lint off the blanket and rolled them absently between her fingers. "I'll be happy to give it to you and show you how to use it."

"Oh, I don't have time to learn something like that, much less keep it up." She cleared her throat. "I would never have dreamed of asking while you were working so hard to establish your business, but now maybe you'll consider an idea I had."

A flicker of excitement tickled inside Allie. She glimpsed where this was leading. "Go on."

Sally Jo hesitated. "Would you do it for me?" She rushed on. "I would pay you, of course. We could agree on a fair amount. I'd give you all my customer receipts and sales records, and you could scan them in like you talked about. Then if I wanted to send announcements or postcards, you could print address labels for me like you said."

Allie couldn't stop a grin from creeping across her face. This might be the perfect solution, a way to stay home with Joanie, generate a little income, and do something she really enjoyed. Her mind zipped through the process she'd follow to configure her system to handle Sally Jo's customers and inventory. After the initial setup, it wouldn't take much time to keep it up-to-date. Allie straightened on the couch, her eyes going wide. She might even branch out, offer to keep other people's accounts. Darcy's, for instance. Maybe if she did a good job, Sally Jo would recommend her to those thirty consultants who worked under her. It wouldn't take much to set up a database for email addresses, so they could send product announcements that way. Maybe —

Slow down, girl. Don't get in over your head. Again.

She realized Sally Jo was waiting for an answer. "I'd love to do that for you."

"That's great!" Sally Jo's voice held enough enthusiasm for five people. "Maybe we could get together for coffee toward the end of the week. We can work out the details then."

When they'd agreed on a time to meet,

Allie pressed the button to disconnect the call. She settled into the pillows again, a feeling of unmistakable awe settling over her. This was the answer to yet another problem. No doubt in her mind where the solution had come from.

She raised her eyes toward the ceiling and let a giddy giggle bubble up from deep inside. "Thank you," she whispered.

"I still can't believe we're going to this thing."

Allie reached up to squeeze Eric's hand where it rested on the gearshift knob of the pickup. "I want to go. Joan has worked so hard on this auction."

He scowled. "You should be home in bed, resting."

"I rested all day." She rolled her eyes. "If your mother brings me one more cup of tea with a side order of celery sticks, I can't be held responsible for my actions."

Eric steered the truck into the church parking lot. Allie was pleased to see cars crowding nearly every space. They were going to have a good turnout.

"Hey, there's Tori's car beside Mom's. I'm glad she got off work to come." Tori had said on Sunday that Mom practically browbeat her into promising she would be here tonight. Looked like Mom knew how much Tori needed a break from the stress of her job too.

Eric parked the pickup in a space two rows from the end. As Allie opened the door to climb out, he dashed around the front of the truck and grabbed her arm to help her down. She giggled at the serious expression on his face, then softened her voice. "Thank you. You take such good care of me."

She stood on her tiptoes to plant a tender kiss on his lips. His arms came around her to pull her close, and their kiss deepened into something way beyond tender.

Allie pulled back reluctantly. "Not now, lover boy. They're waiting for us inside."

Eric let out an exaggerated sigh. "Story of my life lately."

She leaned close to his ear and whispered, "Later."

Her step light, Allie glided across the parking lot hand in hand with the love of her life. As they approached the door, it opened and a familiar figure flew out.

"Allie!"

Tori stopped her mad dash forward just short of Allie, and then wrapped her in a careful hug. "Are you okay?"

"I'm fine." Allie returned the embrace firmly. "No cow's going to keep me down for long."

Tori pulled back, an impish dimple creasing her cheek. "So you decided to bypass the middle man and go straight to the source for your T-bones. That's taking the low-carb diet a bit far, don't you think?"

"Laugh all you want, but Mr. Dorsey called to check on me this afternoon and promised to fill my freezer with meat from the cow who got fatally intimate with the front of my car."

The elderly man had sounded so rattled on the phone that Allie felt sorry for him. The promise of fresh beef was no doubt a blatant effort to avoid a lawsuit.

"He called me too," Eric told Tori. "Said he was having a new fence put up so his cattle can't cause any more problems."

Two couples passed them and went into the church.

"We'd better get in there," Tori said. "Mom's saving seats at a table right up front." She scrunched her nose. "Right beside the minister."

"Terrific," Eric mumbled.

Tori leaped in front of them and opened the door. She gestured inside with a graceful hand and flashed a dimple at Allie. "Age before beauty."

Allie aimed for her toes as she walked by,

but her sister was too quick. Tori leaped backward with a laugh, which Allie mirrored, shaking her head as they entered the church. She squeezed Eric's hand as they followed Tori downstairs to the Fellowship Hall. Allie caught a glimpse of Joan in the kitchen through a serving window as she followed Tori up to the front of the room where Mom and Gram were already seated. Joan looked really busy, bustling around with about ten other girls and guys her age. Some of them looked familiar, like the girl who'd hosted the Varie Cose party where Allie met Sally Jo and Darcy.

Dinner was lasagna and a green salad, served with a roll on paper plates. As Reverend Jacobsen stood to deliver the blessing, Allie felt Eric's hand slip into hers. She risked a glance at him and saw that his head was bowed, his eyes closed. With a happy smile, she did the same.

When they began to eat, Ryan Adams approached their table. "Hey, Eric. I thought that was you."

Eric stood and shook Ryan's hand. "Good to see you again."

"Yeah, you too." Allie noticed that Ryan's gaze kept sliding to Tori, though he spoke to Eric. "Uh, do you play basketball?"

Eric shrugged. "It's been a while."

"Some of us have been getting together on Thursday nights with a few of the kids who live out at Shadow Ridge Apartments. If you ever want to join us, we could use another guy."

"Thanks." Eric put a hand in his pocket. "I might do that."

"Okay. Give me a call. I'm in the book." Ryan nodded at Tori. "Glad you could make it tonight."

Tori tilted her head and caught him in a flirtatious gaze. "I wouldn't miss it. I just wish I could go to Mexico with you." She batted her eyelashes just once as she drew out the last word.

Allie hid a grin when Ryan's jaw went slack. He looked like a fish on a hook.

"It's not too late." He gulped. "I'm sure there's still room in the group for one more."

Tori's lower lip extruded in a pretty pout. "I can't take off work that long. Maybe next trip."

Someone called his name from across the room, and he stumbled away, dazed. Eric sat down and continued his dinner.

Allie punched Tori's arm. "That was mean," she hissed. "You have no intention of going on a mission trip, you little flirt."

Tori's eyebrows arched. "I might. Someday." She giggled. "He's kind of cute, isn't he? I never noticed before."

As they finished dessert — which Allie staunchly refused — the group who had been serving them filed up to the front of the room and stood in a row. Joan stepped up to a lectern that Ryan and Ken moved forward. She had been so busy Allie hadn't had a chance to talk to her, but she smiled in her family's direction as she waited for the chatter in the room to quiet down.

"Thank you all for coming tonight," Joan began, speaking into a microphone mounted on the lectern. "We're really excited about the opportunity this mission trip will give us to work with some people in Mexico who desperately need our help. We're going to build a house for a large family that is currently living in a broken-down bus that crashed in a ditch a few years ago."

The audience gave a collective sigh of sympathy.

Joan continued. "We're also going to take medical supplies and set up a temporary community clinic." Allie's gaze slid to Ken. "And we're going to conduct Bible school for the children and teach them a little English. Most of all, we hope to show them how much God loves each one of them. We want to get to know them so we can love each of them personally, the way our heavenly Father does."

Everyone in the line behind Joan nodded. The hair on Allie's arm stood up as she noted the determination in her sister's eyes and saw it reflected on the face of every one of the people who stood with her. Behind Allie someone started to clap, and then someone else. Allie found herself joining in with enthusiasm. Even Eric, she noticed, applauded this group whose faces radiated with their shared passion.

Joan raised a hand and the room fell silent. "Of course, we'd love to have each of you join us, but even if you can't fit a trip to Mexico into your schedule, you can still participate. And that is why we've asked you here tonight." She grinned. Several people in the room chuckled. "If you've enjoyed dinner, you'll find a donation jar in the serving window. Whatever you feel led to give will be put to good use. And now, we'll begin the auction. This is how it's going to work."

She explained the details of bidding and payment. Beside Allie, Tori leaned forward and rubbed her hands together. "Here comes the good part. We get to shop!"

Eric leaned sideways and whispered in Allie's ear. "We're just here as observers, right?"

"I don't know. They might have some good stuff." Allie widened her eyes innocently. "Do you think they take credit cards?"

That earned her a pinch on the leg beneath the table and a mock scowl from her husband. She laughed and linked fingers with him, then directed her attention to the lectern. Joan auctioned off her first item — a brand-new television set still in the box — like a pro.

Ken and the others carried each item into the room and paraded it across the floor as Joan read details for the bidders from a stack of index cards. Tori really got into the action when the item up for bid was a silver tennis bracelet donated by a local jewelry store. Allie watched her sister exchange competitive glances with a woman on the other side of the room as the price rose higher and higher. Tori won the bracelet, but Allie was sure she ended up paying more than she would have if she'd bought it directly from the store.

After about forty minutes, Allie started to fidget. She glanced down the table and caught Gram covering a yawn with her hand. Allie checked her watch. Eight twenty.

Gram was normally in bed by nine, so she had to be about ready to leave. In another ten minutes Betty would bathe Joanie and feed her a nighttime bottle. If they hurried, Allie could nurse her instead. How many items was Joan going to auction? Surely they'd showed enough support for one evening.

To her relief, Joan answered her question as a box of used dishes was delivered to the new owner. "That's it for me, folks. I'm going to hand the gavel to Brittany now. Thanks for —"

"Wait a minute, Joan." Ryan stepped into the room with something small cradled in his hands. "You're not finished yet. There's one more thing here you need to take care of."

Joan shuffled through the stack of index cards, confusion creasing her forehead. "I don't think so. Maybe someone else has the details on that item."

Ryan's little-boy grin was so wide Allie wouldn't have been surprised if he'd started skipping. "Oh, this one's yours, alright. It has your name on it."

Allie looked at the small black box in Ryan's hand. She sucked in a loud hiss of air. She knew what that box held. She had one just like it at home. Beside her, Tori had recognized the item herself, and her eyes went round as blue saucers. Allie's gaze connected with Mom, who wore a knowing smile. On her left, Eric straightened in his chair and grinned as he, too, recognized the box. Allie clutched his hand beneath the table and squeezed.

"My name is on it?" Joan shook her head, clearly confused.

"That's what it says right here." Ryan practically danced across the room and deposited the box in her hand, along with another index card.

Joan looked down at the card. "It says here . . ."

Her voice trailed off as she read. She grew very still. A movement at the doorway drew Allie's attention. When Ken stepped into the room dressed formally in a black tuxedo, tears filled her eyes. She had to brush them away so she could watch.

Ken crossed the floor to stand in front of Joan. Allie saw the love shining in his eyes as he gazed down into her sister's face. He gently took the box from her hand, sank onto one knee in front of her, and opened it. The diamond nestled on black velvet inside caught the light and twinkled with a flash of icy fire.

Ken held the box toward Joan. "The card

says that this ring is yours, if you will do me the honor of becoming my wife."

Allie's tears slid freely down her cheeks as Joan bent to throw her arms around Ken's neck. She caught him in a kiss that rivaled the one Eric and Allie shared in the parking lot.

When Ken came up for air, he grinned toward the audience. "I think that's a yes."

Joan nodded, her face alight with more joy than Allie had ever seen. "That's definitely a yes."

The entire room erupted into applause.

27

Allie stood in the dark parking lot surrounded by her family. The night air held the unmistakable touch of winter. She hugged Eric's arm and snuggled close, trying to capture as much warmth as she could from his body.

Joan tore her gaze away from her fiancé long enough to beam at her family. "I am so glad you were here. That made tonight even more special. Were you all in on the surprise?"

Everyone except Mom shook their heads.

"I knew," she said. "Ken shared his plan with me a few weeks ago and enlisted my help in getting Tori here."

"Well, he didn't tell anyone else." Allie pretended to give him a sour look. "Just kept saying we needed to be here because it would mean a lot to you."

Joan cast an adoring glance upward at him. "He was right."

Gram shuddered visibly. "I'm happy for you, Joan, but I'm cold. I need to get home."

Tori stepped close to Gram and put a sheltering arm around her shoulders. "I'll take you on my way back to Lexington." Allie didn't think Tori looked overly pleased about Joan's engagement, but that was to be expected. She wasn't crazy about Ken because of how much he talked about his faith. Allie would corner her after their family dinner on Sunday and outline all the reasons Ken was perfect for Joan. Though one look at the joy on her sister's face should be convincing enough.

They said their goodbyes with hugs and kisses all around, and Allie climbed into Eric's chilly pickup. When he started the ignition, she looked at the glowing blue clock on the dashboard.

"We missed Joanie's bath." She shivered and huddled inside her jacket.

Eric flipped the heat dial all the way to the red side. "We're not going home yet."

She looked at his profile. "We're not?"

The truck pulled out of the church lot onto Main Street. Eric shook his head. "We haven't finished our talk yet. We can't do it at home without worrying about Mother overhearing."

That was certainly true. "Where are we going?"

"You'll see."

The air blowing through the vent gradually warmed. Allie cupped her cold hands in front of it. Eric turned the fan on higher, and she lifted her feet toward the lower vent to warm them too.

Allie had told him all about her opportunity to keep Sally Jo's Varie Cose records on her computer the minute he walked through the door this evening. He'd been as excited as she. They'd discussed the sale of her inventory last night. So that just left one thing to talk about.

Allie gulped. The silence in the cab gathered around her like the darkness. God had become such a constant presence in her life in the past few days, more and more real with each minute that passed. She knew how Eric felt about anything to do with religion. But this thing she'd found had nothing to do with religion. It was far more personal than that.

"Eric, something happened to me Saturday night, and I need to tell you about it."

He took his eyes off the road for a moment to glance at her. "I'm listening."

Hesitantly, Allie began telling him about her mounting fears over the past few weeks, her feelings of insecurity over her weight, her irritation with his absorption with televised sports games. As she talked her confidence grew. By the time she got to the encounter in the kitchen at the sleepover, the words rushed out of her like water from a rain gutter.

"It sounds crazy, Eric, but I *felt* God there. I know he was telling me that he loves me, that I'm precious to him. That feeling hasn't gone away. I've felt him ever since. Even in the seconds before my car ran into that cow, I knew he was right there, watching out for Joanie and me."

She leaned across the seat, straining against the shoulder strap, and placed a hand on his leg. "The other night I stayed up late praying. About my job. About us. That's why I decided to close my business, because I felt like the Lord was telling me that it was okay, I could rely on him to take care of me. On him," she paused, then went on in a small voice, "and on you."

His glance slid sideways to lock with hers. "You didn't know that before?"

She held his gaze as she shook her head. "Not really, not deeply. I finally figured out why. It was Daddy."

He turned the steering wheel and down-shifted. "Your father? You mean because he was unfaithful to your mother?"

"Not just to Mom. To me and Joan and Tori too. I realized I've been watching for warning signs that you were going to leave me like Daddy left me. He used to come home from work and plant himself in front of the television set and stay there for hours."

Understanding dawned in Eric's face. "You thought I was becoming like him."

"Exactly. And when I saw Molly flirting with you . . ."

She faced forward, unwilling to look him in the eye.

The car rolled to a stop on the side of a dark road. Eric turned off the engine and cut the lights, then popped off his seat belt and slid toward her.

"Do you see where we are?" He released her seat belt.

Allie looked through the windows. They were parked on a cul-de-sac with huge houses around them. She didn't recognize the neighborhood.

"I'll give you a hint." He slipped an arm around her shoulders and pulled her close. "I brought you here one night after a date between our junior and senior years at college."

Allie gasped. "Eric! Are we in Cumberland Hills?" She was glad the darkness hid her blush. They'd gone parking here, but that was when these houses were still under construction.

"We are."

He pressed her head to his chest and slowly caressed her hair until the tension left her body and she relaxed against him. She heard his heart beating a slow, even pulse against her ear.

"I don't mind telling you that I said a prayer or two myself yesterday. On the way to the hospital." His hand stroked her head. "I haven't prayed since I was a kid, but after I stormed out of the house the other night, I ended up at the church. I had a conversation with Reverend Jacobsen."

"You talked to the minister?" She tried to sit up and look at him, but he held her tight. His chin moved against her head as he nodded.

"He talked about God the way Joan did tonight. The way Ken does. Like you did just now. I realized for years I've let one jerk sour me against religion in general, and especially against God. I'd forgotten what my grandmother taught me a long time ago, that God is personal. He's not a building, or even a group of people. He's real. And he's not just about showing up for church on Sunday morning." She felt his throat move as he swallowed. "He's about love."

A sense of wonder crept over Allie. She never in a million years thought she would hear her antireligious husband speak of God's love.

Thank you, thank you. Eric might not be ready to join the mission team or anything, but he was making progress. God must be working overtime on her problems.

Eric pushed her back with a gentle hand until they were facing each other. His eyes were black pools of passion that bore into hers. When he spoke, his breath felt warm against her lips.

"You don't have to worry about Molly or any other woman, ever. You are the only one for me."

Her stomach gave a delicious flip-flop. "Even though I'm not as skinny as I used to be?"

He slowly leaned forward until his lips rested against hers with a featherlight touch. "You are so incredibly beautiful you take my breath away."

Allie surrendered to a kiss that she felt all the way down to her toes.

28

Allie saw a strange car parked in their driveway behind Betty's when they turned the corner onto their street. "Whose car is that?"

Eric shook his head. "I've never seen it before."

She grasped the shoulder strap in a tight grip. Betty didn't know anyone in town. What if something was wrong? Eric guided the truck to the curb in front of the house, and Allie was out the door before the engine died. She dashed across the yard, barely noticing the cold that seeped from the grass through her shoes, aware that Eric was right behind her.

They burst through the front door, and then stopped.

A gray-haired man was seated on the sofa beside Betty, Joanie in his arms. It took Allie's brain a few seconds to process what she was seeing before she recognized him.

"Don!" she exclaimed, at the same moment Eric said, "Dad!"

"Hey, there they are." Don's voice boomed. He turned to Betty and awkwardly extended the baby toward her. "You'd better take her. Been too long since I held one that size. I'll drop her if I try to walk with her."

The transfer made, Don came around the coffee table and wrapped them both in a strong-armed hug. "Good to see you."

"It's good to see you too, Dad." Eric clapped his father on the back. "Bit of a surprise, though. I didn't know you were coming."

Don pulled back to give them both a bushy eyebrow shrug. "Neither did I, till yesterday. But it seems my wife had other plans. She rented me a car and told me to get my hind end down here so I could drive her back home in her car."

Allie looked at Betty, who wore a smug smile. Well, well, well. Looks like her mother-in-law had finally developed some communication skills.

"We've made some other plans too." Don returned to the couch while Allie and Eric each sat in a chair. Don placed an arm across the back, and Allie noticed how Betty shifted slightly so her head rested against his arm. "I hope you two can stand us hanging around more often."

Allie's gaze flew to Don's face. For a second she entertained the horrible thought that Don was suggesting they *both* move in.

"I'll be retiring when this job ends next summer. We're going to do a bit of traveling, see the world. And we're going to put the old house up for sale, look for one down here." He cupped Betty's shoulder. "Your mother has taken a liking to Danville."

Eric's smile made Allie's heart light. "That's great news, Dad! We'd love having you and Mom close."

Allie locked gazes with her mother-in-law and they exchanged a private smile. Her eyes held a spark of something Allie hadn't seen there before. To Allie's amazement, Betty looked happy.

On Sunday morning Allie walked proudly beside her husband down the sidewalk from the parking lot to the front entrance of the church, carrying her baby. Sunlight sparkled on grass wet with melted frost. When she'd stepped out on the front porch this morning to pick up the paper, Allie had seen her breath. Frigid weather had officially arrived to stay.

They blended into a line of people filing

toward the church. Allie noticed the tight set of Eric's jaw and slipped a hand into his. Though he had not been to church on Sunday morning in over fifteen years, he didn't even blink an eye yesterday when she mentioned attending as a family.

The moment they stepped through the double-glass doors, Joanie was snatched out of her hands.

"There you are, you little darling! Come see your favorite aunt." Tori tried to whisk the baby away, but Joan blocked her.

"Favorite aunt? In your dreams." The stern look she leveled on Tori melted when her gaze lowered to Joanie. "Oh, look at her fuzzy white coat and her little hat and her mittens! Isn't she the most adorable child you've ever seen?" Her diamond sparkled as she rubbed Joanie's coat.

People were starting to stare. Besides making a spectacle of themselves, Allie saw that they were blocking the entrance. She shepherded her sisters to one side. On the other side of the foyer, she noticed Ryan Adams covertly watching Tori across the heads of the people who filed into the sanctuary. That one deserved keeping an eye on.

Joan glanced through the glass doors behind them. "Eric, did your parents go back to Detroit?"

He nodded. "They left yesterday. Dad said he didn't bring any clothes suitable for church. Besides, I think this week has been the first time he's taken any time off in years. He was getting antsy to 'get back to the grindstone,' as he put it."

Tori still clutched the baby. "A shame they couldn't stay for Sunday dinner. I haven't seen your dad since the wedding."

Allie grinned. "In a few more months you'll be seeing plenty of them both. They're planning to move here to be near their granddaughter."

"I don't blame them a bit for that." Tori dropped a quick kiss on Joanie's forehead.

The organ began the prelude, the deep tones vibrating through the open sanctuary doors. Joan edged away. "Gram and Ken are saving our places. I'll see you in there after you get Joanie settled in the nursery."

"I'll go too." As Tori transferred the baby into Eric's arms, she looked at him through narrowed eyelids. "I'm kind of surprised to see you here this morning. I thought you didn't like hanging out with religious fanatics."

Allie saw Eric's gaze slide over to Ryan, who was obviously waiting to follow Tori into the sanctuary. Eric really enjoyed playing basketball with him and the other guys

Thursday night.

He shrugged a shoulder. "Let's just say I'm prepared to revise my opinion."

When Tori had disappeared, Allie tucked her hand into the crook of Eric's arm. They headed for the nursery, a sense of well-being settling more deeply over Allie with every step. She clung to the arm of the man whose breath she still took away, and leaned on the everlasting arms of the One who cherished her as his precious child.

She was loved. Truly, deeply loved.

ACKNOWLEDGMENTS

Any writer will tell you that no book is created by only one person. It takes the combined knowledge and experience of a lot of people to produce a story rich enough to capture the imaginations and touch the hearts of readers. This book is no exception. The task of thanking everyone who helped me with *Age before Beauty* is almost as daunting as writing the book itself!

My husband is my biggest supporter in every way. Thank you, Ted, for believing in me.

Susie Smith and Beth Marlowe are my sources of inspiration and encouragement in so many areas of life. Thank you both for being awesome sisters. And Susie, thank you for crying in all the right places.

My daughter, Christy Delliskave, is not only one of the best blessings God has given me, she's an incredibly encouraging reader. Thank you, Christy, for loving Allie's story as much as I do.

My stepson, Dennis Smith, set me straight on a couple of important matters related to police procedure, and I'm really grateful. How cool to have a police officer in the family so I can pester him with all the questions I'm too embarrassed to ask a stranger!

Lisa Roller of the Danville/Boyle 911 Center introduced me to the world and language of the dispatcher and gave me awesome insights into her day-to-day experiences. I'm thankful for the time she and her co-workers gave me, and for the inspiration they provided. And I'm also deeply grateful for their dedication to saving lives and helping people in need.

Tambra Rasmussen helped me tremendously by explaining the inner workings of an at-home sales business similar to the one I created in *Age before Beauty*. Her enthusiasm is contagious and couldn't help but spill over into Allie's business. Tambra is a great proofreader, too, and I really appreciate her attention to detail.

Ronda Wells, MD, helped me understand emergency treatment procedures after an accident. I'm grateful for her expertise and for her willingness to respond to my questions quickly. (And for the house call during the ACFW conference.)

Thanks to Cindy Swanson, the professional voice behind the book trailer for *Age before Beauty.* If you haven't seen it, go to my website (www.VirginiaSmith.org) and listen to Cindy's work. She's awesome.

My dear friend Trudy Kirk has a sympathetic ear and the most comfortable kitchen in the world. Thanks, Trudy, for listening to me talk through the plot and for offering advice when I needed it.

Elizabeth Ludwig is not only an incredibly talented writer, she's also a gifted freelance editor. Thanks so much for your help!

Thanks to Barbara Penegor for proofreading the manuscript and making great suggestions. Barbara, if I could afford it, I'd get you a Kate Spade handbag, but you'll have to settle for my gratitude.

I had several excellent critique partners who read the first few chapters of this book and provided insights to make it better. Thanks to Vicki Tiede, Tracy Ruckman, and Richard Leonard. And special thanks to my mother, Amy Barkman, not only for a terrific critique, but for picking up on some local inconsistencies that no one else would have caught. No doubt she saved me from receiving tons of emails from people who want to make sure I know the 911 Center is on *Fourth* Street, not Second Street.

Thanks to my agent, Wendy Lawton, for everything she does on my behalf. She's awesome, and I'm blessed to have her as my partner in this crazy industry.

The people at Revell and Baker Publishing Group are wonderful to work with. Huge thanks to Vicki Crumpton and Barb Barnes for helping me craft this story, and for polishing it until it sparkled. To mention everyone who worked to get this book from my computer to the bookstore shelves, I'd have to reprint the company directory. Since that's not possible, please know that I truly appreciate your efforts and your expertise.

Finally, not a single word of this book — or any book I write, for that matter — is possible without my Lord and Savior. Thank you, thank you! You did it again.

ABOUT THE AUTHOR

Virginia Smith is a writer of humorous novels, a speaker, singer, snow skier, motorcycle enthusiast, and an avid scuba diver. Someday, she insists, she's going to find a way to do all those things at once without killing herself or her long-suffering husband. She launched her career as a novelist with the release of her debut, *Just As I Am* (Kregel), in March 2006, and has been cranking out God-honoring fiction ever since. An energetic speaker, she loves to exemplify God's truth by comparing real-life situations to well-known works of fiction, such as her popular talk, "Biblical Truth in Star Trek." She attributes the popularity of that talk primarily to the Star Trek uniform. Visit her website at www .VirginiaSmith.org.